North of Intention

North of Intention
Critical Writings 1973–1986

Steve McCaffery

ROOF BOOKS
NEW YORK

Edited by Karen MacCormack.

Cover: *Mask*, 1977 by Mira Schor, India ink, bronze powder, dry pigment, and medium on rice paper, 8 by 7 inches.

Acknowledgements

The following essays were revised for this present collection. The list shows the original titles and sources of their first publication. Titles not included appear for the first time in *North of Intention*.

"Diminished Reference and the Model Reader", first appeared as "Death of the Subject: The Implications of Countercommunication in Recent Language-Centered Writing", in *Open Letter*, 3.7, Summer, 1977.
"Anti-Phonies: Fred Wah's *Pictograms from the Interior of B.C.*", in *Open Letter*, 3.5, Summer, 1976.
"And Who Remembers Bobby Sands?", in *Poetics Journal*, No. 5, May, 1985.
"Michael Palmer's LANGUAGE of language", collects and revises three separate reviews: "Blake's Newton", in *Open Letter*, 2.4, Spring, 1973; "Reinventing Speech", *Open Letter*, 3.3, Fall, 1975; and "Counter Memory", *Open Letter*, 3.9, Fall, 1978.
"Blood. Rust. Capital. Bloodstream.", in *L=A=N=G=U=A=G=E*, 13, December, 1980.
"*The Martyrology* as Paragram", in *Open Letter*, 6.5-6, Summer-Fall, 1986.
"The Scene of the Cicatrice", in *Brick*, 25, Fall, 1985.
"Bill Bissett: A Writing Outside Writing", in *Open Letter*, 3.9, Fall, 1978.
"Seven Part Theory" in *Rampike*, 3/3 & 4/1, Winter, 1984-85.
"*Nothing is Forgotten But the Talk of How to Talk*: An Interview with Andrew Payne", in *Line*, 4, Fall, 1984.
"Language Writing: from Productive to Libidinal Economy", in *Credences*, 2.2-3, Fall-Winter, 1983, and parts as "The Unreadable Text", in *Io*, 30, 1983.
"Writing Degree Xerox", first appeared as "Absent Pre-sences", in *Open Letter*, 3.9, Fall, 1978.
"Strata and Strategy: 'Pataphysics in the Poetry of Christopher Dewdney", in *Open Letter*, 3.4, Spring, 1976.
"Mac Low's *Asymmetries*", first appeared as "A Letter Regarding Jackson Mac Low", in *Vort*, 3.2, 1975.

Roof Books are distributed by Small Press Distribution
1341 Seventh Street
Berkeley, CA. 94710-1403
Phone orders: 800-869-7553
www.spdbooks.org

Roof Books are published by Segue Foundation
300 Bowery, New York, NY 10012
seguefoundation.com

for bp Nichol

Table of Contents

Preface

"It seems not only superfluous, but, even inappropriate and misleading to begin, as writers usually do in a preface, by explaining the end the author had in mind, the circumstances which gave rise to the work, and the relation in which the writer takes it to stand to other treatises on the same subject, written by his predecessors or his contemporaries". "Being satisfy'd however, that there are many Persons who esteem these Introductory Pieces as very essential in the Constitution of a Work; he has thought fit, in behalf of his honest Printer, to substitute these Lines under the Title of A PREFACE; and to declare, 'That (according to his best Judgment and Authority) these Presents ought to pass, and be receiv'd, constru'd, and taken, as satisfactory in full, for all Preliminary Composition, Dedication, direct or indirect Application for Favour to the Publick, or to any private Patron, or Party whatsoever: Nothing to the contrary appearing to him, from the side of Truth, or Reason' ". Most revisions to previously published material have been confined to footnotes which I have tried to place in an active dialogue with the main body of the text. There have been some stylistic revisions and terminological clearance but these have not been intended to impose a retrospective unity on these essays. In agreement with Barthes "I do not feel the need to *arrange* the uncertainties or confrontations of the past". However, I have enjoyed and indulged the opportunity to retro-actively revise, add, reduce and generally relativize my former writing. There are two idiosyncratic caprices. One, a deliberate mixing of English and American spelling. Two, a local decision concerning the hyphenation of certain words. As a general rule I have used a copula whenever the articulation of the two terms needed stressing. The date following each essay refers to

the unrevised first appearance of that piece. I have several
people to thank. Frank Davey for his solicitation of many of
these pieces that appeared first in *Open Letter*, Bruce Andrews,
Paul Dutton, Ray DiPalma, Ron Silliman and Rafael Barreto-
Rivera for their on-going friendship, correspondence and
conversation that has proved a consistent fuel and challenge to
my thinking. To R. Murray Schafer and Sheila Watson sincere
thanks for their help in acquiring otherwise intractible information. Grateful thanks also to the Estate of Marshall McLuhan for
permission to print previously unpublished correspondence and
for personal access to unpublished material. To Charles Bernstein
for his welcome suggestions to the order of the manuscript.
James Sherry and David Lee for their enthusiastic support of
this publication and to Michael Davidson and Robert Kroetsch
for their buoyant statements. Finally, to my editor Karen
Mac Cormack, not only for her tireless ordering and shaping of
these pieces, as well as providing the title of the book, but also
for her marvellous support beyond the margins where the logic
of the omelette is the hard boiled egg.

Steve McCaffery
Toronto, 6 October 1986

Diminished Reference
and the Model Reader

According to Ferruccio Rossi-Landi, the problem of linguistic alienation is endemic to white "civilized" language communities, where a largely self-generative language system results in a proxemic rift, an elemental gap that prevents the identification of a speaker with her language. Language, argues Landi, functions like money and speaks *through* us more than we actively produce *within* it. It is a surplus-value that draws the speaker away from what ought to be his own world view and processes her through the rules and regulations of the detached and "surplus" system:

> The total linguistic capital is handed down and accumulated without its having any further relationship with the human reality of the working process, that is, repressing within itself its own variable portion. The differences become blunted; any linguistic worker becomes part of a social mechanism — the great machine of the language which produces and reproduces anything and everything. Linguistic money has taken over. A linguistic surplus-value has been created which now has nothing to do with the interest of the workers, i.e. of the speakers.[1]

This essay first appeared as "The Death of the Subject: The Implications of Counter-communication in Recent Language-Centered Writing" in *Open Letter* (3.7, Summer, 1977). I was never happy with the title and both it and much of the content have been revised. The essay, whose original thoughts and materials were gathered through the mid-seventies, concentrates on a partial aspect of Language Writing: a concern primarily with the morphological and sub-lexemic relations present and obtainable in language. A decade later I can safely speak of this concern as an historic phase with attention having shifted (in the work of most of these writers) to a larger aspect — especially to the critical status of the sentence as the minimal unit of social utterance and hence, the foundation of discourse. The terms "cipher" and "ciphericity" were provisional terms I have subsequently discarded. In its present, revised form, the essay nevertheless retains most of its original terminology. S. McC. 1986.

1. Ferruccio Rossi-Landi, *Ideologies of Linguistic Relativity* (The Hague: Mouton, 1973) p. 73-4.

In the condition of linguistic money that Landi outlines, linguistic production is instantly transformed into linguistic consumption. "More and more the USE of language takes the place of its PRODUCTION. The notion of linguistic use supplants that of linguistic work".[2] Producing a sentence is actually re-producing the internalities of the system by a consumptive "use" of its rules and forms.

It is worthwhile to outline briefly Landi's notion of linguistic capital. Landi writes:

> A language can be viewed as a stock of wealth, or patrimony, which supplies linguistic materials and instruments common to the group. Following the economic distinction between 'variable' and 'constant' parts of total capital, it can be said that a language is a constant capital while its speakers are a variable capital. By joining constant capital, that is, a language, with variable capital, that is, its speakers, we obtain total capital, that is SPEECH (or, better, LANGUAGE) in-general.[3]

Under Landi's model, writer and reader would constitute together an interactive relationship within the dynamics of variable capital and the alienation pointed at would take the form of a lack of identification between the writer-reader and their language.

Landi's distinction between *use* and *production* is relevant to a body of recent writing that stresses semantic productivity on the reader's part as the teleological thrust of its texts. The writing proposed is less the exclusive code of the author, theologically transmitted *down* to a reader recipient than a productive field which a reader can enter to mobilize significations. Proposed then is a shift from sign consumption to sign production and a siting of meaning in a productive engagement with writing's indeterminacies.[4] The texts will reveal little in the way of phenomenological description — they are what

2. Ibid. p. 76.
3. Ibid. p. 4.
4. "Consuming creates nothing, not even a relation between consumers, it only consumes; the act of consuming, although significant enough in this so-called society of consumption, is a solitary act, transmitted by a mirror effect, a play with mirrors on/by the consumer". Henri Lefebvre, *Everyday Life in the Modern World*, tr. Sacha Rabinovitch, (New York: Harper & Row, 1971) p. 115.

It would be naive, however, to treat production and consumption as fixed binary oppositions. In language subject and object, producer and consumer are not autonomized. Cf. Baudrillard: "Language is not produced by certain people and conthey can be and they demand a productive stance. Language Writing[5] involves a fundamental repudiation of the socially defined functions of author and reader as the productive and consumptive poles respectively of a commodital axis. The main thrust of the work is hence political rather than aesthetic, away from the manufacture of formal objects towards a frontal assault on the steady categories of author and reader, offering instead the writer-reader function as a compound, fluid relationship of two interchangeable agencies within sign production and sign circulation.

Russian Formalism in the thirties had detected a critical problem between the sign, the referent and the concomitant cultural tendency towards "automatized" responses on the

sumed by others; everyone is at the same time a producer and a consumer . . . what is established is not the general equivalence of individuals vis-a-vis language but an immediate reciprocity of exchange through language". Jean Baudrillard, *The Mirror of Production*, tr. Mark Poster, (St. Louis: Telos Press, 1975) p. 97. Language thus falls partly outside the category of value and assumes the function of a continuous "prodigality" (not unlike primitive exchange) thereby eluding all productive finality and functioning less as a means of communication than as a symbolic circulation. Baudrillard goes on to draw an important distinction between *work* and *labour* which is pertinent to the notion of semantic production under discussion. *"Work is a process of destruction as well as of 'production,'* and in this way work is symbolic. Death, loss and absence are inscribed in it through this dispossession of the subject, this loss of the subject and the object in the scansion of the exchange. . . . The work of art and to a certain extent the artisanal work bear in them the inscription of the loss of the finality of the subject and the object, the radical compatibility of life and death, the play of an ambivalence that the product of labor as such does not bear since it has inscribed in it only the finality of a value". (Ibid. p. 99).

Finally, we might note the spectacular case of television. As an excremental circuitry of information, fascinations, spectacle and manipulated "crisis moods", television is addressed to a totally *abstract audience attention* (the so-called mass viewer) that is statistically manufactured by market research and ranks as Late Capitalism's machine *par excellence*: a machine designed for the production of pure consumption.

5. I use this term with distinct reservation to denote the approximate range of writing here outlined. I do not wish to stress the existence of a school or movement. Variously termed "formalist", "de-referential", "structuralist", "cipheral", "minimalist" and "language centered" its early phases seemed to be a working through to further implications of a minor concern of Marx's that emerged peripherally around his work on *Das Kapital*. "While working on *Capital* Marx was interested in categories and forms bordering on the aesthetic because of their analogy to the contradictory vicissitudes of the categories of capitalist economy". (Mikhail Lifshitz, *The Philosophy of Karl Marx*, precise place not located). The central analogy would be that of linguistic reference to commodity fetishism, both of which are seen to reify the situation of human relations. For a concise outline of this historical function of Language Writing as referential critique, see Ron Silliman, "from aRb" in *Open Letter* (3.7, Summer, 1977) p. 89-93. Two early collections of this work are "The Dwelling Place 9 Poets", ed. Ron Silliman in *Alcheringa* (New Series, V.I., No. 2, 1975) and *Toothpick, Lisbon, & the Orcas Islands* (Fall, 1973). Both include important work by Andrews, Baracks, Coolidge, De Jasu, DiPalma, Eigner, Grenier, Mac Low, Melnick, Silliman, Sondheim and Watten.

reader's part. In 1933 Roman Jakobson writes:

> The function of poetry is to point out that the sign is not identical
> with its referent. Why do we need this reminder? . . . Because along
> with the awareness of the identity of the sign and the referent (A
> is A_1), we need the consciousness of the inadequacy of this identity
> (A is not A_1); this antinomy is essential, since without it the con-
> nection between the sign and the object becomes automatized and
> the perception of reality withers away.[6]

The following is representative of the de-politicized arguments
that would uphold the referent as "the world of the work"
and explain its operation as a metaphoric crystallization of
word into image:

> The words of the work, though no doubt initially apprehended by
> means of perception, memory, and anticipation, become most
> effective at an *imaginable* level. In literature, words crystallize into
> images and the poetic image, as Bachelard himself says, is "a sudden
> salience on the surface of the psyche." This is not to hold, however,
> that the language of literature is imaginary in the perjorative sense
> of "merely imagined." When the words of the work are imaginatively
> effective, they are capable of constituting the world of the work.[7]

Language Writing resists the unity of the "imaginable level" and
refuses the transference of reading to some sort of simulated
object.

Paul Ricoeur describes reference as "the movement in which
language transcends itself".[8] The referent itself can be described
as the detached object absent from signification, yet controlling
the signifying act by an imperial dominance exercised in the
very *absence* of the term.[9] This curious ontological constitution
of the referent commits language to a deictic function across

6. Quoted in Victor Erlich, *Russian Formalism* (New Haven: Yale University Press,
1981) p. 181.
7. Edward Casey, "Imagination and Repetition in Literature: A Reassessment" in
Yale French Studies 52, 1975, p. 224.
8. Paul Ricoeur, *Interpretation Theory: Discourse and the Surplus of Meaning*
(Fort Worth: Texas Christian University Press, 1976) p. 20.
9. Frege's distinction between the "what" of discourse (i.e. sense) and the "about
what" of discourse (reference) obfuscates the major ideological issue. Referential
writing has *always* fostered the instrumental conjunction of power and the sign
whose complicity is essential to the commoditarian logic of capitalist experience.
Foucault describes power in its operation in a manner that fits perfectly the
fetishistic mechanism of the referent: ". . . power is tolerable only on the condition

the categories of inside and outside. For what emerges through reference is the fabrication of an exterior that structures material language as the relationship of an "inside" to an "outside". As an abstract, detached rule in affiliation with grammar, reference enters the flows of language to become immanent within the very thing it structures. The works here proposed do not reproduce a world according to the logic of the referent. They flatly refuse that reproduction, and presenting themselves first and foremost as material entities — as much "seen" as "read" — they command a textual space as a lettered surface resisting idealist transformation. Their purpose is to restore writing and reading to a re-politicized condition as *work.*

CODICIL

      collides triangle lucid nap
broad wet exertion
   sift plunges
            halo shallows
lean-to precocious
   trickle blade
railing fluency plankton abrupt
      sea's rib
         glows lobes
                10

Classical language is organized as the site of satisfied and satisfiable consumptions, of filled desires and foreclosed circuitries in which the multi-directional play of language is limited and fixed by the dominant categories of author, intention,

that it mask a considerable part of itself. *Its success is proportional to its ability to hide its own mechanisms.* Would power be accepted if it were entirely cynical? For it, *secrecy is not in the nature of an abuse; it is indispensable to its operation".* Michel Foucault, *The History of Sexuality, Volume I: An Introduction,* tr. Robert Hurley (New York: Pantheon, 1978) p. 151 (my italics). It could be argued too, for a fundamental unnaturalness to reference which frequently does violence to nature by its character as *specification.* For instance, in the terms "volt" and "ohm" an unnatural differentiation is forced upon a naturally undifferentiated electrical source. Even Wordsworth demonstrates an awareness of a referential reality fetishized through the sign function: "And, next to these, those mimic sights that ape / The absolute presence of reality" (*Prelude,* Book VII, 1. 248-9, 1805 ed.). We should keep in mind too, the critical status of the signified in all of this. Occupying a position between the signifier and the referent it enjoys the power of necessary intervention: it forms a screen through which all linguistic reference must pass.
10. Ray DiPalma in "The Dwelling Place 9 Poets", ed. Ron Silliman, loc. cit.

message and transmission.[11] Conventional reading habits would demand a referential transit in the poem above to a point beyond the words themselves, thereby eluding the material pull inherent in the text. But the language here is *not* directed beyond itself. Lacking an aggregative destination the words tend to free-float within an under-determined code (the copula in line five and the possessive of line eight are the poem's sole grammatical vectors). To adopt the jargon of current semiotics a semantic production should entail the conversion (or transformation) of a *linear text manifestation* from an *expression* into a *content* through the application of any number of codes provided for the reader by the language(s) in which the text is written. The reader enters the text as a under-determined code and fixes certain reading paths as *favoured.* In "Codicil" the expression is composed almost entirely of isolated, non-integrating lexemes that a reader can infer as referring only to a lexicon i.e. to the most basic properties of the units of meaning involved. From this basic dictionary code a number of readings can be built. A reader might progress to an operation of establishing textual differences, similarities, acoustic pattern or contrast, discontinuities in sense/sound etc. Productional inferences may also be made by resorting to inter-textual frames and the text will be read within the interventional and modificational factors of the empirical reader's experience of *other* texts. Similarly a generic frame may be adopted to break the text from an insular economy and productional inferences made within the empirical reader's experience of lyric, narrative, epic, epistolary forms, projective verse, aleatoric forms etc. Alternatively, the entire text may be raised to the level of a secondary signification and read through any number of secondary codes (as a nihilist text, an emancipatory poem, a-social, de-humanized writing, or even notationally as a musical score). Semantic production could also locate infra-structurally and the numerous, internal "sites of production" be traced and compared. In line four the word "halo" reoccurs as an embed within the adjacent word "shallows". Is this gratuitous or does it effect a micro-structural development of meaning on the basis

---

11. Intention works reductively, limiting writing to a re-duplicative realization of an anterior message. Equally, it limits signification to being the product of a subject and will "off stage" or "behind the text".

For a more detailed critique of transmission theory see "And Who Remembers Bobby Sands?" in the present collection.

of a reinvestment of pre-existing morphemes? Lines five ("lean-to precocious") and eight ("sea's rib") are grammatically determined meanings. Line one is an example of a polysemy occasioned by the radical incompatibility of a hypotactic series of lexical meanings and an integrated contextual meaning. There are likewise connotational grids that can be developed. A productional play can start on the associational concatenation of all references to *liquid* ("wet", "plunges", "shallows", "trickle", "fluency", "plankton", "sea's" comprise nearly a quarter of the entire poem). This "aquatic code" might then be employed as a contentual dominant to determine the vectors of meaning in the poem's total textual content. Additionally, there is the potential for each word and each line to carry within it a latent narrative programme.

As we read, see or scan the poem, we come to feel syntax as the movement of a textual surface without a pre-determined destination. Replacing referential development is a lateral complexity through which planes of relation and difference become moebius and profundity a surface fold. It is essentially the opaque condition of writing. Problems in readership arise only from a refusal to abandon prejudicial reading habits and from the insistence on a verbal presence that would offer itself for consumption. Treated as a producible field the poem offers a polysemous itinerary. With the removal of grammatical conditioners and the logic of transit, then the *event* of reading becomes a primary issue.[12] Writing of this kind shows a concern with the order of effects that connect with the incidentality of the signifier rather than the transcendality of the referent. It is this superfluity of the signifier that promotes in these texts the quality I will term "cipher". The cipheral text involves the replacement of a traditionally "readerly" function (the pursuit of words along certain referential vectors to a corresponding world outside the text) by a first order experience of graphemes, their material tension and relationships and their *sign potentiality* as substance, hypo-verbal units simultaneously pushing towards, yet resisting, contextual significations. The cipher thus offers a strategic method for motivating non-commodital productivities that cast both writer and reader into an identical

12. Barthes informs us of at least five meanings of "event" that the Greeks distinguished. These are *pragma* (fact), *tyche* (accident), *telos* (outcome), *apodeston* (surprise) and *drama* (action). See Roland Barthes, *The Responsibility of Forms*, tr. Richard Howard (New York: Hill and Wang, 1985) p. 177.

work process. The referent no longer looms as a promissary value and the text is proposed as the communal space of a human engagement. The text returns a use-value by offering itself as unexchangeable, outside of the logic of the commodity, thereby opening ambivalently to both semantic loss and productional recovery.

The emphasis on surface movement suggests a topological analogy. "Topology", writes Bruce Morrissette, "represents the primary intellectual operation capable of revealing the modalities of surfaces, volumes, boundaries, contiguities, holes, and above all the notions of *inside* and *outside*, with the attendant ideas of insertion, penetration, containment, emergence and the like".[13] An interesting analogy presents itself in the Klein worm — a form which differs from conventional geometic forms in its characteristic absence of both inner and outer surfaces.[14]

> Instead you have a contained tube and an uncontained tube, a contained hole and an uncontained hole . . . Any part of the form can touch, contact, communicate with, flow with any other part . . . We have a quality of continuousness in the form and at the same time intracontainment . . . This form is permeated by context. It has no walls. Yet it uses its structural infolding for maintaining itself changing in a sufficiently regular way to find new relations.[15]

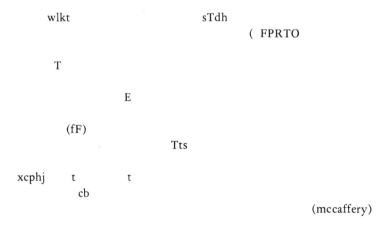

13.   Bruce Morrissette, "Topology and the French Nouveau Roman" in *Boundary 2*, I.I., Fall, 1972 p. 47.
14.   On the Klein worm, see Warren Brody, "Biotopology" in *Radical Software*, No. 4, Summer, 1971.
15.   Ibid.

This text might be considered as a Klein form. It is without "walls" with milieu and constellation replacing syntax. The letter — in its major and minor registrations — not the word forms the basic unit of organization and thereby guarantees the poem's textual movement from inside itself. The parentheses, moreover, act less as grammatical pointers than as ideogrammic interventions that occasion a dramatic event within the textual space. It demands a reading "on" rather than a reading "through" an opaque siting that would activate a multiple flow of parts and — denied the exteriorising access to a referential vector — a structural "infolding" of the textual elements. Resultant interplays might complicate both the surface and the nature of these interiorities. The text too, might be likened to Lacan's Imaginary Order (the pre-linguistic condition of the Subject before constitution). It is not initially a signification. Resisting readability until a semantic disposition has been introduced, it demands first of all an a-significant possession. What it is not, however, is a textual commodity to be ideally consumed by a "comprehending" reader. The demand is for praxis, active engagement and direct experience.

In his book *Space*, Clark Coolidge explores the sign potential of units smaller than the word:

erything

eral

stantly

ined

ards

cal

nize
          16

The writing pivots between a cultural recognition and non-recognition of these marks as signs. We recognize truncated words, the terminal parts of larger lexemes (everything, several, constantly etc.). The experience of unmediated graphic events is played off against the productive possibility of developing

16. Clark Coolidge, *Space* (New York, Harper & Row, 1970) p. 120.

familiar meanings. Coolidge provides a *connotational motivation* to a phonemic list and the sub-lexemic elements necessary for a semantic re-appropriation. The interplay of spatial relation and paginal placement (the homogenized margin providing a degree of over-determination that helps suggest this poem as a *complete* vocabulary) with the opaque, insular densities of these marks as "fragments" results in an effective suspension between meaning, its absence and its potential emergence. Writing demonstrates itself both here and in the next piece less a *communication* than the loss of communicabilities.

```
mel
ethwe fub sditas

ehfoie ruax oir
paso biot
qla fa

woe          eroa
asrglry    s
wea tiro         bohmuluk
codfix      a,azz    oboi
                              17
```

This seems less writing than incisions into the very surface of signification. Its productional ambivalence is striking. Anchoring its elements as a field of pre-lexemic dispositions and subordinating theme to rules of line, space and difference, they nonetheless have consequences different from words. Areas of the poem register as pure writing effects, incapable of establishing a corresponding spoken form. There is immense difficulty in voicing "asrglry". Subversive devices further complicate a reading: the isolation of the single letter in line seven; the distinct splitting of the lines in stanza three which suggests a value effect; and the sudden eruption of punctuation in the last line. Meaning in this poem is not a product of a representation but the site of a dichotomous drive: towards the consolidation and direct experience of these marks as ciphers or vacated words on the one hand, and towards a productive completion of a partial sign field.

17. David Melnick, *PCOET* (San Francisco: G.A.W.K., 1975) p. 12.

Bruce Andrews is especially successful in promoting such complications. There is a striking non-gravitational sense in many of his pieces as a consequence of the interlocking of multiple parts and the replacement of linear direction by a vertical and horizontal tension which creates a tracery in the spatial field and highlights a coronal quality in the graphemes:

```
ca ja a th an ne sh th wa pe
qu ci fo in ba wh vi re se th
eu co st cu wo al su cr ce re
in ma vi si ba am ch qu an is
th th cu ni se fa wo ap se th
pr st th st th th ac wh wh pa
wi ha wa ti bo pr wo fe th tr
fa sp if so th th pl fo to tw
                18
```

The digital, gridlike quality of the syntax commands immediately a *visual* attention. One must pass beyond a seeing of the poem as an optical display to enter into the spatio-temporal activity of a reading.[19] Difference is played off against homogeneity in the binary couplings of the letters. We find units without semantic value juxtaposed with familiar words ("an", "if", "so"). Certain units petition lateral integration across the spaces in order to produce semantic values ("th" "an" and "ap" "se"). Others a vertical integration into words ("bo" "th"). As in the previous poem the disposition to integrate units and the pressure to uphold their insular, non-semantic cipheralities equally call attention. Meaning occurs through a productive inducement within a predominantly non-significative field.[20]

18. Bruce Andrews, *A Cappella* (East Lansing: ghostdancepress, 1973) p. 22.

19. Barthes in one place speaks of literature's two wavelengths: the one of meaning and information; the other of epideixis, devoid of information and offering itself as a language of spectacle. Through this second wavelength literature obtains the status of a "mysterious tautology" and makes impossible any reduction to a totally decipherable system. This wavelength, claims Barthes, "suspends speech between meaning and nonsense" and anchors literature in the domain of its own spectacle. Barthes himself sees this epideictic wavelength as emerging from the post-classical detachment of rhetoric from its judiciary purposes.

20. Contemporary linguistics characterizes *all* languages by a single common feature: they are doubly articulated. Phonemes articulate to form words, whilst words articulate to form larger sequences of discourse. In the first articulation (of sounds and letters) the units are non-signifying. In the second the basic units (words) already have meaning. Linguistics might describe the text above as holding language at its primary articulation.

In "The Red Hallelujah", also by Andrews, the dominant sensory modality is touch not sight. The digital gridding of the previous poem is replaced by a highly kinetic and tactile disposition of words:

pulling banters flank blonde

folded captain girlfriend hisself

drive leg chemist's punching

fire milling cuffs naw

captain madman ways roast

bags excitedly ass bad
                                                 21

A poem like this comes closer to being an experience in language than a representation by it. It resists interpretative depth. Grammar, like perspective, would organize language towards a vanishing point: the punctum of reference, where local meanings would aggregate as message and summarize outside the poem. But the competitive contiguity of this piece maintains a constantly circulating surface and a structured decentering of meaning. Freed from larger integrations each word is free to interact within the open-endedness of each other's indexicality. It is this ability to laminate the paradigmatic upon the syntagmatic that accounts for the tremendous *resonance* in the writing. Juxtaposed and linearized, yet freed from higher subordination, the word is encountered frontally as an absolute property.

The desires behind these writings should now be clear. Presenting language as an opacity to direct experience and balanced somewhere between a signification and a phenomenology, a fixed structure and an indeterminate sign field, they de-facilitate all transit to the surplus-value of a referent and produce a reality by not reproducing the Real. But this refusal of the referential logic of the sign and the culmination of signification in an extra-linguistic finality raises certain problems. I have argued that a writing of diminished reference necessarily privileges the signifier over both the signified and

21. Andrews, *A Cappella* p. 31.

the referent. I have argued too that the historical function of Language Writing is a partial critique of language inside the commoditarian experience of a bourgeois ideology. But this is precisely the condition, according to Baudrillard, that constitutes the essence of political economy:

> What happens in political economy is this: "the signified and the referent are now abolished to the sole profit of the play of the signifiers, of a generalized formalization where the code no longer refers back to any subjective or objective 'reality,' but to its own logic. The signifier becomes its own logic. The signifier becomes its own referent and the use value of the sign disappears to the profit only of its commutation and exchange value. The sign no longer designates anything at all. It approaches in its truth its structural limit which is to refer back to other signs."[22]

As Mark Poster puts it, "it is the very genius of political economy . . . that signs exchanged in communication have no referent".[23] According to this argument, rather than being an effective critique of the language of advanced Capitalism, Language Writing would be its perfected simulacrum and far from problematizing dominant ideology would actually reflect it. Long before Silliman's exposure of the referential fetish in narrative[24] Henri Lefebvre had diagnosed the radical decline of referentials as characterizing contemporary ideology:

> A hundred years ago words and sentences in a social context were based on reliable referentials that were linked together, being cohesive if not logically coherent, without however constituting a single system formulated as such. These referentials had a logical or commonsensical unity derived from material perception (euclidean three-dimensional space, clock time), from the concept of nature, historical memory, the city and the environment or from generally accepted ethics and aesthetics. . . . However, around the years 1905-10 the referentials broke down one after another under the influence of various pressures (science, technology, and social changes). Common sense and reason lost their unity and finally

22. Loc. cit. p. 7.
23. Ibid. p. 9.
24. See Ron Silliman, "Disappearance of the Word, Appearance of the World" in *The L=A=N=G=U=A=G=E Book*, eds. Bruce Andrews, Charles Bernstein (Carbondale: Southern Illinois University Press, 1984).

disintegrated; the 'common-sense' concept of absolute reality disappeared and a new perceptible 'real' world was substituted or added to the reality of 'well informed' perception, while functional technical objects took the place of traditional objects.[25]

We might measure the following text by Coolidge against Lefebvre's diagnosis:

by	a	I		
	of		to	
on	no			
we	or	by		
a	I	of		
to			on	
no	we	or		

26

The gaps between words here are not of the order of those minimal spacings that ensure articulation and developmental utterance; they are much more a vacancy and productive of what Walter Benjamin terms *aura*: "the unique phenomenon of a distance, however close it may be".[27] Reference in Coolidge's poem may not be simply cancelled as the site of the social and not simply annulled as a vector of human perspective; it may have re-territorialized *through implosion* to now circulate among the signs' internal relations. Through implosion reference has passed into its opposite (the material and inwardness of the signifier) and simulates its own presence in the dead space of a sign field, among its mirror reversals, self-reflections and utterly internalized exchanges.

Does Coolidge's text signalize an historic third stage for the referent? After its primary, pre-linguistic stage as ostensive gesture and its complex fetishization during commodity Capitalism, has it now entered a third stage of semiurgical

25. Henri Lefebvre, *Everyday Life in the Modern World*, tr. Sacha Ravinovitch (New York: Harper & Row, 1971) p. 111-12.
26. Loc cit. p. 87.
27. On the concept of the aura see especially "The Work of Art in the Age of Mechanical Reproduction" in Walter Benjamin, *Illuminations*, tr. Harry Zohn (New York: Schocken, 1969).

implosion? If implosion is the referent's contemporary condition, then writers such as Grenier, Melnick, Andrews and Coolidge might represent the laureateship of Nietzsche's *Will to Power*. Creators of textual surfaces and residues of symbolic effects, where implosive referentiality reveals itself as historic power on the down slide into semic solipsism.

Beyond these implications of the signifier are the issues of produced meaning. Relying on semantic production as the *telos* of its readership, Language Writing commits itself to a serious entailment. The productive return of the reader can only take effect through the theoretical presupposition of *a need to produce*. The texts must present themselves as potential deficiencies petitioning productive entries. Implicit in this demand is a closed model of the reader whose functional capabilities are rigidly prescribed. Through an appeal to a humanist approach it might be argued that Language Writing forms part of a wider, social strategy of protest that would aim at *the politicization of direct experience*, developing reading as a "de-fetishized" autonomous possibility of sign production (i.e. writing inside reading). In this resonance it might be seen as giving human beings − historically deprived of the means of production − a personal control over the production of meaning. This argument is untenable on several grounds. Firstly, we must avoid a humanization of the reader who is not to be anthropologized as a "person" but seen structurally as a theoretical location in a textual activity. This functional definition of the reader applies to *all* types of writing. Secondly, it is difficult to make the crucial distinction between semantic production and the arbitrary assignment of meaning, (i.e. between production effected by the application of plausible rules on the one hand and by random associations on the other). For instance, to pursue the connotational possibilities of signs (as suggested in several of the previous readings) seems to be as much a questioning as a production of meaning. [28]

Even more problematic is the status of the Model Reader in these "open" texts. I shall argue briefly that the open text is

28. For a cogent critique of Marxist humanism the reader may consult Louis Althusser, *For Marx*, tr. B. Brewster (New York, 1970) and *Reading Capital* (with Etienne Balibar) tr. B. Brewster (London: New Left Books, 1970). Althusser detected the emergence of a humanist stance among Marxist intellectuals after

dependent on a closed model of readership. In popular fiction, for example, (as one instance of a closed text), there is a comparatively wide degree of tolerance for the accidence of empirical readership. The reader of Mickey Spillane or Arthur Hailey is not foreclosed or over-determined as a structural element of a particular kind of fiction. (We will see in a short while how popular fiction permits a wide angle of subversive or distortional codes). By contrast, Language Writing proposes not only the unbinding of signs and referents and the polysemous development of the signifier, but also a closed Model Reader predetermined by the productional disposition he is compelled to adopt. She is constituted upon a series of prohibitions (you can't consume, you can't reproduce an identical message, you can't subvert a representation). Hence the emancipatory character of the reading becomes a mandatory liberation. Let me cite a contemporary semiotician:

> . . . we must keep in mind a principle, characteristic of any examin-
> ation of mass communication media (of which the popular novel
> is one of the most spectacular examples): the message which has
> been evolved by an educated elite (in a cultural group or a kind of
> communications headquarters, which takes its lead from the political
> or economic group in power) is expressed at the outset in terms of
> a fixed code, but it is caught by divers groups of receivers and
> deciphered on the basis of other codes. The sense of the message
> often undergoes a kind of filtration or distortion in the process,
> which completely alters its 'pragmatic' function.[29]

It is precisely their resistance to aberrant decodings that imposes a devastating qualification on the emancipatory scope of Language texts. To conclude with Eco once again and then,

1956 (the time of Kruschev's denunciation of Stalin). With their arguments based on the early writings of Marx (especially the *1844 Manuscripts*) Althusser diagnosed a bourgeois ideology operating in the promotion of common interests at the expense of the fundamental concept of class struggle. Whilst Althusser's critique defends orthodox Communism, the means of this defence are breathtaking: a synthesis of structuralism, linguistics, Freud, systems theory and an acute knowledge of Western philosophy including Nietzsche, Husserl and Heidegger as well as the earlier Hegel and Kant. Althusser argues that the notions of alienation, the negation of the negation and other humanist themes that are present in the *1844 Manuscripts* are the remnants of an adolescent Marx (the marx before the MARX) still influenced by the philosophic idealism of Hegel. It is in *Capital* that the mature, scientific Marx emerges as the structuralist theoretician of epistemological history.
29. Umberto Eco, *The Role of the Reader* (Bloomington: Indiana University Press, 1979) p. 141.

perhaps, a footnote — "You cannot use the text as you want, but only as the text wants you to use it. An open text, however 'open' it be, cannot afford whatever interpretation".[30]

1976

---

30. Ibid. p. 9. Eco's example of the political potential of an aberrant reading is worth mentioning. It is *Les Mystères de Paris* by Eugène Sue. An insipid, bourgeois consolatory fiction, ridiculed by Marx and E. A. Poe alike, *Les Mystères'* popularity was such that it spread beyond its intended audience to a point where the book had a direct influence on the popular uprising of 1848. For fuller details of this perverse connection the reader is referred to Louis Bory, "Presentation" in Eugène Sue, *Les Mystères de Paris* (Paris: Pauvert, 1963).

Anti-Phonies:
Fred Wah's
Pictograms from the
Interior of B.C.

Pictography marks the earliest phase of writing, growing out of drawing as the imitation or sketching of an object, thus linking a pictoriality with a writing. Pictography extends well beyond the invention of phonetic script; it is present, for instance, in the rhopalic verse of Simmias, Dosiadas, Theocritus, Anacreon, and the cancellatiflexus of Porphyrius, in all of which occurs a marriage of word and picture in what might be termed a "graphic economy". It is evident through to Carolingian times, at least, as the dominant informing psychology behind all writing; for precursive script was essentially the sequential sketching of single letters considered as independent entities, like the drawing of an object. Sir Thomas Browne writes of numerous verse forms whose basis is pictorial: ropalici, clavales, fistulares, retrogrades, rebus and leonine verse. In Addison this pictorial bias provoked a critical-philosophic intervention into the rhetorical domain and produced the conceptual distinction between "true" and "false" wit. This visual concern persists through our own century, not only in the well-known *calligrammes* of Apollinaire, but in the work of the French lettristes and the current trends of Canadians Hart Broudy and B.P. Nichol, much of whose work focuses on the single letter as a *drawn form*, often contextualized in comic strip conventions and made to carry ideogrammic (and in Nichol's case even "allegoric") complexities through the semantic implications of its physical, graphic constitution. An additional mention should be made of the more recent works of Jacques Derrida, specifically *La Carte Postale* in which he develops a tripartite script: picto-ideo-phono-graphic. This script "consists of the following elements: a discursive commentary (the phonetic level); examples interpolated ("pinned") into the discourse (the ideographic element), and "found" pictorial material".[1]

In this new writing extremely complex interactions of non-phonetic and phonetic elements develop far beyond the simple relations of the dialogic. Much of Bill Bissett's work would be apposite at this point, specifically *Sunday Work* which constantly grafts phonetic to non-phonetic (although the interactions often seem gratuitous or aleatoric). Much of B.P. Nichol's work (*The Martyrology* and *Zygal* for instance) employ a similar grafting of drawn, gestural figures (clouds, birds in the shape of lower-case "v"s) onto the discursive phonetic fabric of the page.[2] At his death, Marshall McLuhan too was working on a

1. Gregory Ulmer, *Applied Grammatology*, (Baltimore: Johns Hopkins University Press, 1985) p. 99.
2. Nichol's fetishistic predeliction for the letter H is both respected and notorious. The genealogy of this preoccupation, however, might be surprising. In fact, it is none other than Victor Hugo (the "grande tête molle" of Lautréamont) who emerges as Nichol's unacknowledged antecedent. Nichol's *Zygal* (Toronto: Coach House Press, 1986) within its several operations and achievements, disperses throughout its duration a perverse "writing machine" − part phonetic, part pictographic − whose obsessive operation is the repeated inscription of the single letter "H". In *Les Travailleurs de la mer* (written a hundred years earlier) Hugo's hero Gilliatt sets out to rescue an engine from a shipwreck. If successful, Gilliatt will receive the hand of the shipowner's daughter in marriage. On page 670 (vol. XII of Hugo's *Oeuvres complètes*) erupts an amazing pictographic presence, entirely worthy of the author of *The Martyrology*. Gilliatt moves in sight of the shipwreck and discovers the vessel (the Durande) trapped between two huge, black, stone pillars (known as "les Douvres"): "L'espèce d'immense H majuscule formé par les deux Douvres ayant la Durande pour trait d'union apparaissant à l'horizon dans on ne sait quelle majesté crépusculaire". Gilliatt climbs one of the pillars and then swings from one column to the other along a rope he suspends between them. He provides the *zygon* between the "jambages" of the letter and, in effect, repeats the letter as a monumental effort of writing-performance. Gilliatt's achievement has a double effect. The plot is advanced (allowing the rescue of the engine and the subsequent "triumph" of Hugo's orthodox narrative) but also is contaminated at a radical fissure between pictography and phoneticism. What is constructed (and employed) in Gilliatt's adventure is a colossal writing machine whose single inscription will always be the tracing of a single letter: H. It may not be coincidental that the name of Hugo commences with this letter, and that Gilliatt (commencing with a G) is doomed to a position fixed one letter away. The alphabet as a spatio-temporal "destiny" might well be Hugo's arche-narrative: "G's" struggle to trace out the shape of the letter "H" and through this simulacrum gain a wedding. As a monstrous baroque interpolation, this incident throws, not only Hugo's novel, but the entire progression of nineteenth century fiction into a profound relativity. For as a narrative, augmented through access to the conventional alphabetic components of phoneticism, it cannot escape the hegemony of a single master-phoneme, whose eruption through the conventional descriptive language of nineteenth century bourgeois fiction permits its subsequent control and re-definition of the narrative thread. *Zygal* itself is an anatomical term, a derivative of "zygon": the bar or stem that connects two branches of an H-shaped fissure of the brain. Its Greek original, incidentally, means "yoke" which, on the bull, seems to provide the pictographic origin of our letter A. We will leave the rest of this footnote to Louis Zukofsky.

book to be called *Laws of the Media* in which a tetradic form of spatial and semantic organization was being developed. The tetrads would be made up of four discontinuous, yet simultaneous, phrases presented in such a way that the relationships of their parts would be clearly perceived; these would then be placed within a graphic surround of commentary. Although the work was unfinished at his death the comparison with Derrida's *Glas* or *La Carte Postale* evokes itself immediately. As a final note on the contemporary re-emergence of pictographic and non-phonetic concerns is the following description of symbolization within current electronics:

> The symbols used for electronics since the beginning of this century parallel the development of the pictograms of ancient languages . . . At first the symbols were realistic drawings of the components. Within a few years the electronic 'pictograms' became simpler: the emphasis was placed on the functionally important features of the components, while the outward shapes were lost . . . each symbol is a kind of abstract cartoon.[3]

Pictography is characterized by its uniformity. There is very little variance in glyphs throughout the world; it is as if they provide an almost universal discourse, a *lingua franca* deriving from the commonality of human and animal gesture which they strive to replicate. For instance, there is a pictogram for "child" common to Egypt, China and North America showing a human figure sucking its thumb — a common gesture that seems to tap at the roots of basic human responses.

Subsequent developments conventionalize the form of the pictogram, minimizing the free-play and independent licence of the sketcher, shifting away from a genuine perceptual link with the object into a more stylized code. The acrophonic principle, evident in Egyptian hieroglyphics, takes us further from the direct treatment of the object into a non-linear system set in (usually) non-gravitational space. Under the rule of acrophonics, picture becomes explodable into its component sound adequations and the image of the object comes to represent the sound of the first letter of that object's spoken name. This second major principle of pictography: that the pictogram can stand for the *sound* of what is drawn without reference to its *meaning*,

---

3. R.L. Gregory, *The Intelligent Eye*, p. 157 (quoted in Ulmer loc. cit.).

must have occasioned a revolution in cognition. What is involved is nothing less than the admittance of a new relationship of reality to sound, as well as image, bringing into being a new conceptual dimension: the insertion of the acoustic realm into the cognitive equation of reality and its representation. This in itself becomes the dawn of phoneticism.

In the pictograms of British Columbia, however, the sign system is frozen at its pre-acrophonic phase in which sound representation lies outside the semiotic area of the text. The issue facing any interpreter (including Wah) is the issue of narrational formulations. Do pictograms represent a telling? Are they a kind of stenography to evoke, through memory, a more extended narrative of oral origin? Or do they truly constitute an emergence of *writing* out of a radical and historically specific rupture with oral discourse? The system organizes its information within a non-linear space, employing the minimum of denotation, as a consequence of which a contemporary "reader" must function more as the *producer* than *consumer* of the messages, reading onto the grams semantic responses, judgements, misprisions and analyses. In general, there is no fixed, spoken correspondence to a pictorial form and the pictogram remains polysemous in its readability. As in the illustrated pictogram (fig. 1) meaning is suspended and remains indeterminate. We might wish to compare at this point the pictogram to such contemporary non-phonetic systems as the comic strip and note how, in the latter, frame both partitions and orders spatiality and sequence, eliminating the need for interpretation or the specialized competence required to relate the glyphs to some prior text. In this example, as in all the pictograms included in the book,[4] profiles do not confront a viewer, but rather the flatness (and lack of frontality) render interactions objectively observable as a style of data, creating information by denying a psychological interaction with the Subject and radically supporting a space of pure narrative transmission:

---

4. *Pictograms from the Interior of B.C.* (Vancouver: Talon Books, 1975).

fig. 1

It is the challenge posed by these indeterminate elements that
Fred Wah takes on as a questionable project in this book. Wah's
intention in these "transcreations" (his term via Coleridge)
would *not* seem to be the appropriation of the pictographic
economy, subordinating it to the sanctuary of a pro-historical
discourse, yet the texts presented and the format of presentation open this work to at least one capital culpability: the
subordination of a non-phonetic system to the phonetic
domination of words, sequentiality and a spatio-temporal
linearity.

Pictograms From the Interior of B.C. is antiphonal in structure (and we will trace the sinister implications of this,
implications that Wah seems to have ignored or overlooked)
with pictogram on left page and Wah's text on the right. There
is a highly charged juxtaposition of phonetic and non-phonetic
fields. The project is not unlike Gertrude Stein's experiments in
cubist description circa 1910 and collected in *Tender Buttons*,
where Stein adopted a cubist "painterly" (i.e. non-phonetic)
technique to force her writing into hitherto "non-literary"
areas. Similarly, Wah creates his texts across the phenomenal
space that would separate phonetic and non-phonetic systems,
producing this way a poetry that, in its grammatical trans-

gressions and non-gravitational stresses, might be cited as the
verbal counterpart of a non-verbal response to reality:

Turtle   Baby
canoe   portage

where the four words inhabit more a pictorial than syntactic
space with multi-directional possibilities for reading (vertical,
diagonal, lineal). Space and placement here, also evoke the
narrational, interactional suggestions of the glyph itself:

fig. 2

And the following in which a latent sound complex is drawn
out of the manifest image:

uvular moist call
moveable celestial
and crystal clear
by the height
palatial sound
aspiral noises or
udder milk

fig. 3

The subtle interplay and emergence of acoustic and visual
information is one of Wah's great "liberations" in his responses.
Often the pictogram will lead him into a preference for list

rather than a grammatical, sequential chain; a separation of words into the contiguous flavour of their independent nuances rather than subordinated, clausal groupings:

> Lost
> amidst Caloplaca
> and rising
> as a bubble
> from earth to sky

fig. 4

At its most successful this writing across code systems effectively mingles a non-phoneticism in the phonetic order:

> See the arrow?
> Even the beetles go.
> And the birds, birds
> something equal or familiar
> twice, a two
> such as a man and a lake
> a place, the place
> to come back to.

There is a noteworthy quality of combination achieved here that articulates the exploration of a multi-directional space. Wah's para-translative activities would seem to attack language at its point of silence and demand a speech from it. The quality of a convincing speaking voice educed from its posterior visual manifestation is one of the book's most ambiguous and seductive triumphs:

> Hey! It Looks like
> you got a couple of ways in there
>
> and a face, me
> no face.

Show me how you do it
and I'll come too.

There are several important issues that arise. How, for instance, to represent verbally and lineally the random distribution of the picture images? How can the multi-directional centrifuge of the pictorial field be trans-created in the uni-directional flow of the phonetic line? Wah would seem to recover for the "metaphysics of logocentricism" most of the non-phonetic materials, and even in his most successful dialogisms the page format serves not only to present parallel texts, but to erect also an ethnological partition across which phoneticism maintains its hegemonic control by trans-cultural interpretation:

nvs ble
tr ck

fig. 5

which may be read (humorously) as the ideogramic disappearance of the unitary subject but which equally admits the line of phonetic sequence to a control over the image groups and narratemes of the glyph, thereby legitimizing the spatial continuity essential to any phonetico-narrative development.

Among the opening credits of the book occurs this telling passage:

Grateful acknowledgement to John Corner, his book, *Pictographs (Indian Rock Paintings) in the Interior of British Columbia* (Vernon 1968), from which the illustrations of this book are taken . . .

To describe the objects of response as "illustrations" entails a curious shift in power and a covert underscoring of a phonetic-non-phonetic contractual separation that is not to be broken.

Ethnology is the science of dead differences and Wah's resuscitation of the corpse is only to allow the corpse to speak its own demise. Baudrillard has already warned us of the sinister paradox of ethnology (although seemingly in Wah's case these warnings went unnoticed or unheeded):

> For ethnology to live, its object must die. But the latter avenges itself by dying for having been "discovered", and defies by its death the science that wants to take hold of it.[5]

If we are to address translation's culpability and complicity with an ethnological project to protect the dying by death (an issue at the root of ethnopoetics itself) then Wah's book is a rich point of contention. For, despite the author's partial openness to phoneticism's "other" (image, indeterminacy, simultaneity), phoneticism — as an operating power and state of mind — remains as perhaps this book's linguistic unconscious. The more optimistic implication is how, in a sense, there is no writing beyond the perpetual oscillation between multiple codes, with the further suggestion that all reading might itself be a prior writing and antecedent to all scriptural gestures be it the movement of pen to page, of key to ribbon or of paint to rock.

1975

And Who Remembers
Bobby Sands?

An issue not of narrative but of narratives, the plural narrativity
that permeates and circulates our lives as telling.

Let us trace this issue in its emergence inside contemporary
technological dissemination (both in and as television and radio)
which has proven itself to be our culture's dominant mode
and posture of telling. This tracing will be subsequent to the
collapse of the great cultural dominants of the 18th and 19th
centuries, which tied representation to an ideological Realism
and allowed such novelists as Balzac to treat the novel less as
genre than as a practical science of observing a world beyond
language, attainable through the latter's unproblematic status
as a neutral, instrumental horizon.

Under the rule of representation narrative enjoyed a status
of fenestrational necessity, a mandate to linguistic transparency
through which all beings and events were forced to pass. Falling
under the constraints (mimetic and representational) of this
principle, words operated less as instrumentalities than
constituent parts of a vast and nebulous network upon which
narrative ordered itself as either Truth (the narrative-discourse
of Philosophy), Right (legal and ethical narratives) or Fiction
(most eminently the novel but all literary discourse). Language
in either its structuralist models or in its deconstructional
revisions did not occur as a narrative prerequisite; instead
a neutral ground of language was presupposed, an uninterrupting
sediment of support and an un-differentiated surface upon
which events are ordered. This ground of neutrality constituted

traditional narrative's telling through a window.[1]

No longer privileged as social finalities; their critical trans-cendance annulled and their ability to narrate of, and at the same time narrate to, reality through fiction's co-extensivity with (and radical dependence on) an unquestioned paradigm of representation convincingly challenged, these narratives of representation no longer control the way we see and say the world. The dominant manifestation of narrative is now the media whose electronic circuitries have imposed a violent shift in cognitive and disseminative modes. Whereas the novel tended to operate under the notions of structure, closure and an ultimate (albeit often problematized) unity, the narrative of media is characterized by a differential implosion and a structurelessness.[2] Media narrative is no longer a localizable telling but the re-fabrication of information as impulses far removed from any social dictates of communication. The media is not merely anti-social, it is decidedly a-social; it is narrative operating at the termination of the social (the eclipse of the "public" by the "masses") and is designed to assure a lack of response. There is simply reflection, event and fascin-ation. The masses, to whom this narrative environment is directed and from whose conceptual complementarity it gains its definition as media, is a nebulous, a-social abstraction, serialized into atomistic simulacrities (the "privatism" of the family television receiving identical content as millions of

1. The classic novel, through its constant appeals to identification and its strong pulls to the abolition of language as any kind of first order, self-referential problematic, was always an operation across a double distance: initially a certain Euclidean spatial operation, but additionally a spatial-decorum perspective upon the transmission scheme of communication. Hence, the binary structure of the "real" and "implied" author and reader as both ideologically positioned outside, anterior to the text and as the textual "symptoms" or deductions from the significatory productions of the work at hand, acting harmoniously to support a minimal digital separation that preserves the supposition of a socially shared identity or "textual contract".

Classical narration too included a contractual precedent that the thing imitated, represented or recounted, stood always before the moment of representation. A strict dictate of causality thus mobilizes all mimesis. Plot was structured along this axis of cause and effect and always implied a prior determined, integrated subject. Beneath the fiction of its fable the novel always gave rise to *effects* of truth.

2. Baudrillard has likened the media to the DNA molecule which similarly implodes the differential poles of cause and effect. The media implode both message and mean-ing, transmitter and receiver, thereby eliminating the differential trace on which traditional (i.e. Saussurean) linguistics structures meaning and rendering invalid any transmission based theory of communication. Transmission Theory (exemplified, for instance, in the early writings of Roman Jakobson) grounds any narrative in the ideological scheme of need and exchange. According to this theory communication

other homes, *simulates* individuality and laminates this upon the actual un-differentiation of the masses). The masses lack the positive reciprocity of the "public" (paradoxically, at first glance a less individualized yet more differentiated class) and are inconceivable as a socially individualized readership. Its effect (and we should hesitate to add its structural function for reasons apparent in footnote 2) is to present an abstract reflection against which all micro-narrations are screened, refracted as stimuli whose orbit is an informational hyper-space. Media narrative, moreover, does not communicate by way of these narratives but rather *absorbs communication as a model into its circuits*. Hyper-communication then, where communication does not occur as the condition of a social interaction but as the model of an a-social social-stimulation. Hyperrealism to replace Realism, in which the real is no longer the referent but the model absorbed. There are many important implications in this hyper-communication. Most important, perhaps, the indication that its involvement is no longer with power and exploitation (the contention of Brecht and Enzenberger whose belief in the fundamental "neutrality" of the media as a structure allowed them to cathect a revolution-ary feasibility to non-bourgeois appropriation, thereby locating the arena of struggle in the notion of who controls, not what is controlling) but with powers and fascinations, whose intention

consists of the transmission of information from a source to a receptor across a space; the context of that communication being proposed as an exchange between producers and consumers, speakers and listeners, media and masses. Hypostasizing both a subject and an object this theory fixes them as isolated terms in an abstract formula, inserting a notion of need as the necessary link between them. A circular system of power is thus generated by a copula of need. The ideological base of this need was recognized long ago by Hegel in his analysis of the master-slave relationship in *The Phenomenology of Mind*. The need is not a biological need, but a masked social formation linking subject and object terms for the preservation of the abstract structure. The ideological model this would support in the case of media-narrative would be that of an "informationally needy" subject that enters into the narrative model with an anterior need to communicate or be communicated to. In actuality, this need is *not* anterior to the specific act but inheres within the very structure of communication as presented. Exchange in this way presents itself as a *structure* in which each operating term is defined by the other. The media's narrative economy, however, implodes these terms, decommissioning the exchangist nature of transmission economy and, rather than providing an alternative structural model, emerges as a model that ends structure. Which might lead us to speculate that media narrative, despite its "counter-revolutionary" inertia, has achieved what the molecular recoding strategies of the avant-garde have struggled towards through its cumulative litany of failures: the structural abolition of ideological relation, the avoidance of the fetish of value and the disappearance of speaker-listener as structurally determined, ideologically alienated terms.

is not to manipulate but to immanently reflect imploded meanings.

Narrative is now of a precessional nature and autotelic inside its own repetitions. Its concern is strictly with its own repro- duction as a model of communication. It no longer offers a commodity world of closed stories and events but hyper- simulates its own form as the abstract form of reproduction. The production of news equals the reproduction of the media itself. In this eclipse of representation, meaning is no longer consumed (as in the realist novels of last century), nor is meaning produced (as in the struggles of much post-modern narrative and non-narrative); it is reflected without absorption. Hence, the entropicity of the late night news where information, instead of occurring inside communication engendering response (real or theoretical), is exhausted within the very act of its narration. In operation is a constant orbiting economy of narrative, an endless loop of signal whose differences are homo- genized through identical format (the effective closure by the model).

There is a double order at work. On the surface it would seem that the media create more of the social through their narrations but on closer examination we see their effect is to neutralize all social relations. Interviews, talk-shows, letters to the editor: these are all micro-narratives which posture as social reciprocation but are, in fact, entirely co-opted by the media model itself. Response here is of the order of simulation. A front page article of a news magazine relates the death of fifteen children in a small rural town (the implication is they could be your children, this could be the town where you live). The killer is shown to be the local carpenter (it could be the man you work with). Message (through implosion): this could happen to you. Effect: a simulation of involvement. Additionally, this surreptitious petitioning of violence in geo- social proximity to the reader, this simulated vulnerability of the receiver of the message, is always presented without the counterforce of deterrance. Deterrance is the politician's or the police's concern, not mine (the media) or yours (the reader). It is symptomatic of the double order of the "masses", both more individual and more undifferentiated than the "public", that media narration is located at the end of the social and closer to an excremental than to an informational "function".[3]

1985

3. To cite Baudrillard again: "the social arose out of this crisis of demand: the production of demand largely overlaps the production of the social itself . . . Today, everything has changed: no longer is meaning in short supply, it is produced everywhere, in ever increasing quantities − it is demand which is weakening. And it is *the production of this demand for meaning* which has become crucial for the system". Narrative economy would be predicated upon this species of Keynesian reversal, this surplus of supply and lack of demand. Baudrillard hypothesizes an agonistic scene of power at work in which the inertia of the masses is precisely their weapon of control. Fascination, which Baudrillard believes to be the extreme intensity of the neutral, leads to reflection and a complete return of the system as a model. In this way the masses are both in and out of media-narrative's orbit. However, it seems important to consider a further hypothesis and one neglected by Baudrillard: the media's proximity to what Bataille terms "general economy" that is precisely an economy of waste and irrecoverable expenditure. This continuous expenditure of meaning, narrated into a context of inertia would refract media narrative back into a condition of "potlatch".

Nor too should we ignore the possible relevance of Lacan's notion of the *imaginary* order. For if we can show that "fascination" (the narrative condition of the masses) is of an imaginary and not symbolic order, then the revolutionary return of the mother as the techno-phallic goddess will require a certain discourse of its own.

Michael Palmer's
LANGUAGE of
language

Michael Palmer offers a sustained challenge to the reader's habitual and conditioned pursuit of depth. The stake is nothing less than the entire essentialist notion of meaning that would make of the latter concept something other than the sign. As Wittgenstein puts it: "Here the word, there the meaning. The money, and the cow you can buy with it".[1] Running through Palmer's work is a persistent concern for a language of objective surface, holding attention at the level of an opaque, syntactic system that argues against the word's deictic functions and obstructs the passage through a text towards a referential destination. If the Real is the lack of language and instituted as the destination of the latter, where questions do not arise as to the operation and interpretation of signs, then Palmer's project is to return that interrogation and settle textual experience within the materiality of writing as a spatio-temporal phenomenon.

Along with the concern for surface and material relations is a developed proliferation of indeterminacies that thrust a logical mastery of the texts into severe doubt and difficulty. The emergent writing calls attention to itself as a network of aporias, a circulation of losses and expenditures. The following, from *Blake's Newton* (1972) shows a typical Palmerian device:

After waking he
waited.

In his mind were
three women.

---

1. Ludwig Wittgenstein, *Philosophical Investigations*, 3rd. ed. tr. G.E.M. Anscombe (New York: Macmillan Publishing Co., 1968).

On the one hand, Palmer constructs a distinctly classical space, a closed linguistic interior of partitions, parallels and balances. The equation of the stanza with the sentence develops an exchange or lamination whereby a structure of meaning and a structure of sight conflate.[2] On the other hand, the space created by the stanzaic structure supports a narrative disjunction that instantly undermines the bond between the material and semantic spaces. The seeming "classicism" of the language is put in question. The designation of the subject remains ambivalent, whilst the sentences themselves seem to gesture a matte, unproblematic space.[3] In this way Palmer's sentence is never an absolutely neutral space. When integrated or juxtaposed alongside others it becomes the locus of a seepage, ambiguity and loss (what information theory would term its "noise" and "static" factors).

The dominant compositional device is parataxis (i.e. an organization of information by means of independent, non-subordinate elements) which determines the appearance of meaning within an endocentric construction and as an aspect of the words' material relations. One might say that, in

2. This equation is not constant. Often Palmer gains effects from a deliberate skidding, slipping the sentence beneath the stanza so as to create a straddle. In the following example the stanza break serves to slice the sentence thereby setting up additional problems within the language distribution:

Sound becomes difficult
to dispose of

etc.. You go to sit down
and hope for a chair.

One of a pair of
eyes

distends.
Redness begins

on the left side.

From "A Reasoned Reply to Gilbert Ryle" in *Blake's Newton* (Los Angeles: Black Sparrow Press, 1972) p. 16.

3. In addition there is the local ambiguity of the first sentence ("After waking he waited") where the second verb carries a double meaning. There is "to wait" in the sense of to remain or to delay, but also "to wait" as in to wait upon i.e. to serve or attend. In accordance with this second reading "waking" might be interpreted as carrying an homonymic allusion to "wake" as the ritual vigil and feast for the dead in which the mourners are waited upon. Pursuing this eschatological chain the "three women" might connote the three fates or *Moerae* of Greek mythology. All of this is not to suggest a unitary interpretation of a controlled distribution of meanings but rather the indeterminate power of the sentences themselves.

Palmer's case, the sentence *is* the parataxis, for in its doubleness it not only establishes symmetry and balance but guarantees that the investment of single meanings ("semantemes") into larger compounds, will occur only across a discontinuous or non-consequential hiatus:

My friend Paul
is a prisoner of the Germans.
A negotiator from Havana
sent a cigar
a little bit smoked. Robert
is getting lost in the park.
My friend Henry
is happily married
to Emily, his wife. The girl
with the white hair
climbed over the fence
like opening the cube
holding a smaller circle
also white.
My friend Paul
is a prisoner of the door
with a circle drawn
in his palm as proof.
The left and right shoe
are different sizes
and he won't come out
to say goodbye.[4]

This general strategy of indeterminacy extends even to the syntactic apparatus. In the following (from *Blake's Newton*) word and line are conflated so as to problematize a strictly linear articulation:

and
you
will
see
that
I
am

---

4. "Series" in *The Circular Gates* (Los Angeles: Black Sparrow Press, 1974) p. 33.

living
in
the
shadow
of
that
bridge.
It
is
so
quiet
here;

Line and word exchange status in an ambiguous relation to one another, as a consequence the text requires as much a negotiation as a reading; a detour through the non-habitual itinerary of a column in which the grammatical impulse to connect lineally is checked and decelerated by the spatial autonomy of the words. There is a sense of something other than a pure semantic operation at work here, not as a depth, but as a temporal fold upon a plane producing complications of a strictly two-dimensional surface. Palmer is at his best in such a flatness, creating contortions within the simple propositional language and forcing up out of the plain of the writing a sense of the words' intra-textual contamination:

Now the bay

is beginning to change
The distance

across the bridge
is the same

It's also greater
than before

we came
It's also later[5]

In the above text also, the paratactic construction contests the rational constraint that would reduce signification to an

5. Ibid. p. 46-47.

unproblematic transit of referential certainties. The construction
is such that the law of exclusion is suspended and the "meaning"
implodes the observation of similarity and difference: ("The
distance/ across the bridge/ is the same/ It's also greater/ than
before/ we came/ It's also later"). What the language says and
how the language moves are constantly held in tension. The
following too, is typical. Inhabiting and affirming a strongly
denotative and propositional space, these three sentences
nonetheless institute an estranging counter-logic:

This is a room.

Give me this and
this. This

book ends some
time when it ends and

this is a room.[6]

The opposition in sense here is played out through the similarity of the verbal forms. Difference is produced as a form of
repetition that frames the text inside the self-reflectiveness of
its own relations like two mirrors. (The structure is similar to
the *Enantiomorphic Chambers* constructed by the sculptor
Robert Smithson in 1965 in which a mirror reflects a mirror
in such a way as to destroy the logic of its reflection).[7] The
displacement of logical relation by a relation of syntactic
parts becomes the abyss causality falls into:

bone is the process of reorganization
according to a model

6. *Blake's Newton* (Los Angeles: Black Sparrow Press, 1972) p. 40.
7. Smithson's *Enantiomorphic Chambers* are composed of bracketed mirrors, placed
obliquely in such a manner that when a viewer peers into the glass chambers only
the self-reflection of mirror against mirror can be seen. The work in this way explores
a sight/non-sight paradox (Smithson too, has explored the site/non-site opposition
in several other works). The term *enantiomorphic* derives from crystallography and
refers to either one of a pair of crystalline chemical compounds whose molecular
structures have a mirror-image relation. Another series of pieces by Smithson bear
the title *Alogon*: a title which Palmer also uses for a work of his own (Berkeley:
Tuumba Press, 1980) and that is additionally called "A Spiral for Voices". Smithson,
of course, constructed his own spiral: *Spiral Jetty*, a 1500' long coil of mud, precipitated salt crystals, rocks and water, at Rozel Point, Great Salt Lake, Utah in 1970.

of the final monument
to the Third International[8]

"Prose 42" from *The Circular Gates* is representative of
Palmer's method of organizing (through parataxis) contiguous
spaces that seem to condense a number of discrete contexts
into a single surface:

I have some questions to ask her. She
knew a man who was murdered in California.

He pointed west towards California. Marie's
Salon de Paris was closed. Smoke rose from
the other side of the river.

Each sentence exists autonomously and its self-sufficiency
contributes to the piece's total disconnected movement. These
sentences resist integration into a compound ensemble (an
accretive meaning through the linking together of simple ones)
and as a result provoke an extreme cognitive dissonance. What
gains in intensity is the interstitial zone between each sentence.
Charged with temporal and differential implications the interstice affirms the non-essential, material *betweeness* of the
linguistic signs. Directed neither outward nor inward the
sentences settle precariously within their independent, closed
spaces, evoking their own status as contiguous elements and
dispensable, differential oppositions. It is as if they are where
they are precisely because of the possibility of their being
somewhere else. To a degree then, the syntax relates to the
semantics as a contaminant or "complicator". The lucidity of
the sentences, taken in their insularity, presents no problem for
comprehension, yet their stubborn resistance to incorporation
and connection opens up the question of meaning as a spatio-
temporal operation on the material surface of language. Palmer
concentrates upon the changing elements in meaning and in
this way holds attention to writing as a phenomenal scene.
The classic notion of meaning is that of a detached rule that
transcendentally governs usage. Palmer's meaning (like
Wittgenstein's) is non-essential and does not stand outside of
the material realization of the writing; it is by nature *scenic*

8. *Without Music* (Santa Barbara: Black Sparrow Press, 1977) p. 31.

and non-determinant.[9]

Most of the poems in *The Circular Gates* consist of torques
in the surface of logical connection that displace a progressive
line of discourse:

... No wind
but some trains are waiting underground
All the things we shake from
before opening the eyes and mouth
The south is mauve and majesties and heroes
The north: white strips and lavender silks of ice

or from the long piece called *The Book Against Understanding*
(Palmer's book within the book that serves to dialogize the total
work):

He stooped part way across the field to
sit down and rest. An eagle
descended from the sky and an angel with the face of death

Before I had a name
I came out of a place where there wasn't a door
Holding my breath

in slippery hands. Door to wall
and back again.

In both cases the sentences simultaneously uphold and under-
mine the essentialist notion of meaning. Within the disjunctive
progression of the narrative line and among the serial display
of parts, it is impossible to locate a representational authority.

Important too are the numerous writing effects that present
themselves as elements irreducible to speech. In the following
example (from *Blake's Newton*) the reader is immediately

9. Meaning does not stand outside of language, as some kind of transcendental
rule more fundamental than the materiality of a word, but describes itself within
the scenes and sequences of particular word usages. Wittgenstein would deny any
transcendental, rule-governing prerogative to meaning and would point out how the
word "meaning" itself it subject to the same conditions for meaningfulness as any
other word. We might wish to compare this to the following statement of Derrida's
on the subject of "blind tactics": "It is a question of strategy because no transcendent
truth present outside the sphere of writing can theologically command the totality of
this field . . . In the end, it is a strategy without finality. We might call it blind tactics".
Speech and Phenomena, tr. D.B. Allison (Evanston: Northwestern University Press,
1973) p. 135.

drawn to the absence of capitalization at the start of the second stanza which conventional grammar would demand:

The bull is
constant
wedded
to economy.

the bull is
steady.

This might be passed over as gratuitous, an unintentional mistake and therefore dismissable. Yet in reality its stubborn presence cannot be explained away.[10] Contributing nothing to the text's semantic development, it draws off from meaning a non-semantic effect. Moreover it effectively splits the subject into a speaking/writing agent and prohibits a unitary reconciliation. (There is no way the lower case can be "spoken"). Punctuation is rendered both indecisive and disruptive (it is impossible to decide whether we are entering a new sentence (which would be a valid "grammatic" deduction) or else entering *in medias res* as the absent capitalization would suggest). Additional disruption comes from the semantic economy *per se* which is so arranged as to generate an indeterminacy between the actual subject of the two sentences. "Bull" is decidedly ambivalent and several equally valid interpretations offer themselves in a reading. The bull might be read as animal. Yet why "constant"? The bull might be interpreted as the centre of a target (metonymically the bull's "eye"), in which case "constant" could be related to the stability of the target; its structural immobility. Yet why "wedded to economy"? "Economy" might serve to return us to the first subject (the bull as an aspect of agrarian commerce, providing meat, value, consumption etc.) but at the same time might open up an

10. In actual fact, this can be explained away. The entire analysis is based upon an initial error in reading. The second sentence *does* begin with a capitalized article, but in my review of this book (in *Open Letter*, 2.4, Spring 1973) a typographical error occurred in the reprinting of the text. It was this quotation, and not Palmer's book, that was consulted. Rather than correct the error, I have decided to leave it, as the entire mistake seems to invoke pertinent issues. What, for instance, constitutes the "final" text? Or how, in the region of obtuse meaning does truth and error enter the field of readerly production? The fact too, that Palmer's frequent eschewal of periods — there are many capitalized sentence-stanzas that carry no grammatical terminations — substantiates the same point *a tergo* that my erroneous reading seeks to establish.

alternative association with commerce (the "bullish" market of stock-exchange jargon). A further designation is suggested by the poem's title which is the astrological sign for Taurus. The poem avoids reduction to a single monologic "message" and by virtue of a sustained dissemination calls attention to itself as a signifying system whose pluri-dimensionality and radical "accidence" preclude interpretational mastery.

Writing is always a way by which time inhabits language as a space and in Palmer's work this time (that is writing) and the temporality of the sign never entirely coincide. The sign stresses its fission, iterability, the possibility of escape or drift into new semantic configurations, and the radical non-adequation of intention and "result". The sentence, while absolute in its placement, is errant in its directions and effects. The temporality-in-space, which is syntax, often overwhelms the semantic apparatus, reducing meaning to the plural detachments and contingencies that Palmer exploits so successfully.

Perhaps the most radical rupture is the break with transitivity itself, or writing has become the questioning of its own provisos and as readers we enter a textual domain without *absolute* speakers. Speech is subordinated to the differential forces of writing and, by staging to the full the *nature* of writing as a spatio-temporal phenomenon, Palmer is able to "suggest" the trace of the subject's loss in the space between words, in the interstitial perimeters of the phrasing, within the unattainability of certain meanings and the representational deficiency between sound and the written mark. Displaced and repositioned in the fissures of the spacing, the subject is no longer determinable as a locus of utterance and intention. More often it appears as an obtuse textual effect:

>   colour of reddish hue low in saturation
>   and brilliance, also called "eureka red",
>   "flea", and "Victoria Lake". We found an
>   old pewter plate or "puker", according to
>   my father who was foreign.[11]

The numerous quotations in this passage do not suggest a speaking presence (only the final "puker" is attributed to a subject) but writing's own threatening repeatability; its power

11. From "Prose 16", *The Circular Gates* p. 36.

to shift context constantly. As such it registers more as
wound than word, a graft upon a writing understood in part
to be a sutural economy. In the place of "voice" and presence
are the agents of deferral operating in the shifting spaces where
all phono-centric investments have been effectively marginalized.
Inscribed throughout Palmer's work, as its syntactic motion, are
the protean, nomadic locales of the subject's disappearance,
provisional topographies beyond the symmetries of line, where
language instigates self-reflexiveness and the poems interrogate
their own limits. It is "as if" the fundamental ideal of essence
is (finally) replaced by the temporal accidence of its historically
suppressed implication: that language is nothing but a family
of uses.

1973

Blood. Rust. Capital. Bloodstream.

ADOLPHUS, J.L.: LETTERS TO RICHARD HEBER, ESQ. (Containing Critical Remarks on the Series of Novels Beginning with "Waverly" and an Attempt to Ascertain their Author) 8vo., Boston 1822. The theoretic interest in rust emerged from investigations into the bridge between metallurgical and physiological identities BAILLIE, Joanna: Miscellaneous Plays, London 1804, 1st Edition 8vo, pp. i-xix + 1-438 (extra leaf advertises Wordsworth's Lyrical Ballads). Rust throughout is treated as the mineralized transform of blood and thus the oxydizational connective with the human breath and bloodstream "BROWNE, Sir Thomas: WORKS, London 1686, fol. 1st. ed. with engraved portrait in facsimile" (Wing B 5150 Keynes 201) Rust also relates to critique and the need to negate ANY GIVEN FORM whilst as a metallic growth and pathology it relates to carcinoma and the encompassing ideology of the parasite. BURNEY, Fanny: CECILIA or Memoirs of an Heiress, London 1784 5 vols. 4th. ed. 12mo. full contemp. tree calf milled edging in linguistic form. The Parasite finds most powerful manifestation within quotation and allusion i.e. in the precise manner (the site of the cite) that creates in any text a biological device for drawing off signification by means of echo, index, association, interruption and supplementarity (pp. i-xii + 13-164 Glasgow 1751 printed by Robert Urie 8vo. Rust tends) to occur as an activity within a pre-existent wound and as such is to be classified as a post-incisional practice. It is what writing writes of itself within the aura of its own excess (contains 1st printing of SEMELE) "trimmed" London 1710 3 vols in 2 incl. The Old Batchelor, Double Dealer and Love for Love Vol. III = pp. A1-a4 + 1-492 and as a mineralogical agency enters the bloodstream as capital to carry the microformations

of a labour force throughout the human organism. DAVIDSON
(Joseph) . . . nto English Prose, ondon 767. 3rd ed. (i-v). It
might be described as the corpuscular theory of the proletariat.
cf. THE ECONOMY OF HUMAN LIFE by Robert Dodsley
(London 8vo 32 woodcuts by Austin & Hole 1808) a work
often attributed to Chesterfield. Whereas cancer (after
nosological elimination) is reattributable to a biopolitical-
linguistic scheme and functions closest to a surplus value
which is reinvested into the cellular structure of the body as
pure profit. GELLIUS, Aulus: NOCTES ATTICAE, Venice
1489 (one of my rarest books) 132 leaves, 42 line + head 6th
ed. (3rd Venice) Bernardinus de Choris de Cremona & Simon
de Luere. Goff (213) lists only ten copies in America. What is
drawn off ("virologically?") from the societal corpus is art,
intellect and sex. In the purest analysis of the libidinal economy
(to which virus is central) sex is a pure discharge, an absolute
signifier detached from its signified and demonstrates best the
principles of an unrestricted GENERAL ECONOMY (Bataille)
within the structural and epistemological restraints of the
restricted system (Windsor 1788 2nd ed. with verso last leaf
containing errata. Authors: George Canning, John Smith, John
Frere and Robt. Smith) accordingly: any poem which adopts
"book" as its vehicular form must admit its complicity within
a restricted economy. Sex then is a pure discharge and exceeds
all value to constitute an energetic subversion of the human
capital machine. As a discharge sex is fraternal & sorietal to
all other vectors of spontaneous dissemination: intuition,
improvisation, madness, desire and schizophrenic pro-productive
drives (LACTANTIUS: Works, Venice 1478 . . . "lactanti
firmiani de diuninis instituioibus aduersus gentes" . . . which
together constitute a postcognitive antidote to rust conceived
as a surplus value and an entropy. Negentropic strategy is
founded on the full practice of a general economy, in informational "waste", semantic excess produced by parasitical attach-
ments and interruptions to a host syntagm 12mo circa 1729,
L'ESTRANGE, Sir Robt., Kt., London (but why London "in
the Strand" pp. i-xxx. Active within the circulation of biological
capitalism are numerous virus agents (MacPherson, Sibbs,
malus coronaria, Harrison Blake at Worcester, Johnson on the
life of Father Paul Sarpi, Cholmondeley's letter to Thoreau in
1857, bourgeois consciousness and ratiocinative strategies in

Dr. Johnson's ref. to mustard in a young child's mouth, the
Rev. Thomas Newton on The Prophecies, David Hume, Zeus,
Patroclus, Chichen Itza, the word of the Lord, virus "positioned"
"as a dormant potential" "within structure within" "this
structure" Loudon's remarks on pyrus malus and the badge of
the clan of Lamont. It is homologous to the political implications of the poetical phrase MITCHELL, John: The Female
ondo 793 2nd e 125 x P grim grav frontispiece by (defectiv)
. . . / WORDS being what poems are then SENTENCES being
what POLITICS is . . (sustenance) (quadruped) (the Duma)
(Lenin during Blossom Week) . . . . VIRUS . . . . . and at this
. . . . . . po . . . int . . . . . . lexically inter changeab . . le with
the SENTENCE: "POTENTIAL" so that when activated it
becomes THIS FRAMING AGENT YOU ARE reading now
(Theophrastus included the apple among the more "civilized"
plants URBANIORES rather than WILD/SYLVESTRES)
fixating epistemological boundaries which sex cannot be in such
a way as to derive maximum sustenance for itself and to prevent
the operation of general economy. LETTERS OF THE RT.
HONBLE. WRITTEN DURING HER TRAVELS IN EUROPE
ASIA & AFRICA n.d. 6vo. VERBALLY SPEAKING an
activated virus of this kind "assumes the form of either page
(consecutively bound as book) or else as SENTENCE "Probably
1767 ed.") as container of the grammatical line which is
itself both the victim and the vengeance of a persistent ideology
of perspective.) ACTIVE VIRAL PENETRATION IN ART
(buds we must remember were counted every winter's eve for
seventeen years) GIVES RISE TO THE INTERRELATED
HEGEMONIES OF COMMODITY, CONSUMPTION AND
PRODUCTION. Poems on Several Subjects, don 1769, John
OGILVIE incls. Essay on the Lyric Poetry of the Ancients
8vo modern calf binding + "the fruit of the crab in the forests
of France". IF IT WERE POSSIBLE AT THIS POINT (Rowe,
Elizabeth: Friendship in Death in a Series etc. . . . . portrait by
J. Bennett) WE WOULD SWITCH THIS DISCOURSE INTO
THE MOUTH OF HER WHO IS PRESENT IN THAT CLASS-
ROOM WHERE A SMALL CHILD SITS INTENSELY
POROUS AND VULNERABLE AND EAGER TO (to)
RECEIVE (receive) THAT (that) WHICH (which) WE "we"
CALL (call) "SCIENTIFIC" scientific KNOWLEDGE
(knowledge) THAT (that) WHICH (which) ONE "one"

DICTIONARY "dictionary" AT (at) "LEAST" (least) IS
is ABLE able (TO) "to" DESCRIBE (describe) AS as
OPPOSITE "opposite" to TO ART (ART):

                                                    1980

The Martyrology as
Paragram

Chuse for thy command
Some peaceful province in Acrostic land;
There may'st thou *Wings* display, and *Altars* raise,
And torture one poor word a thousand ways.

John Dryden, *Mac Flecknoe*

The seeds of punning are in the minds of all men; and though
they may be subdued by reason, and good sense, they will be very
apt to shoot up in the greatest genius that is not broken and culti-
vated by the rules of art.

Joseph Addison, *Spectator* No. 62

Dissolution of a poet in his song;
he will be sacrificed among savages.

Novalis

We will focus on the ludic features of *The Martyrology**, those
varieties of wordplay (pun, homophony, palindrome, anagram,
paragram, charade) which relate writing to the limits of
intentionality and the Subject's own relation to meaning. This
examination will be pursued through the model of *economy*
rather than structure, arguing that *The Martyrology* is a doubled
production that positions the Subject precariously inside two
vast, oscillating economies that together circulate and distribute
the flow of linguistic and non-linguistic stimuli. Out of the
settled domain of reference and representation these stimuli
are regulated into what Lacan terms the "double spectre" of
vowels and consonants. The two economies are the syntactic
and semantic; the one an economy of the signifier and its
circulation and regulation through the material order of language, the other an economy of the signified and its circulation

*B.P. Nichol's long poem *The Martyrology* currently exists in six books, spanning 18
years and some 800 pages. Begun in 1967 it is still ongoing.

and distribution through the idealist effects of language. This double order of economies might further be considered as the essential components of those larger forces of signification and dissolution that might be termed Sign Economy.

At the same time we will propose a rather perverse genealogy in which to contextualize the poem. A genealogy to carry us not through *The Martyrology's* "natural and obvious" antecedents (Olson, Zukofsky, the Utaniki or Japanese poetic journal and Gertrude Stein) but through the Plato of the *Cratylus*, Peter Ramus, Edmund Spenser, the German Romanticism and *witz* theoreticians of the Jena School (the Schlegels, Novalis, J.P. Richter), Freud, Lacan and M.M. Bakhtin. This genealogy will not propose a network of influences or sources, but suggest coherent and viable orders of intertextuality capable of producing variant and inventive readings of this problematic poem and contextualizing it in a richer field than Projective Verse and North American traditions of seriality.

1

The Scene Of Witz

> *i mine the language for the heard world*
> *seen scenes unfurled by such activity*
>   B.P. Nichol

Witz, as we receive it from German Romanticism, is a profoundly social and revolutionary faculty. Friedrich Schlegel describes it as "absolute social feeling, or fragmentary genius",[1] as "an explosion of confined spirit"[2] and likens it to "someone who is supposed to behave in a manner representative of his station, but instead simply *does* something".[3] Novalis designates it as "a principle of affinities" that is simultaneously *"the menstruum universale".* In old and middle-high German the term "witz" describes an intellectual faculty based on ingenuity, mental acuity and (in contrast to *mathemata*) the ability to grasp truth unprovably, non-scientifically and at a

---

1. *Critical Fragments* No. 9, tr. Peter Firchow (Minneapolis: University of Minnesota Press, 1971) p. 144.
2. Loc cit. No. 90, p. 153.
3. *Athenaeum Fragments* No. 120 in loc cit. p. 176.

single glance. Until the 17th century its gender is feminine (the phonic affinity of "wit" to "witch" through the Anglo Saxon *wicca* − alluding to a sacred, secret knowledge − is worth note). The 18th century lexicographer Bailey includes both senses in his definition of wit as "one of the Faculties of the Rational Soul; Genius; Fancy; Aptness for Anything; Cunningness".[4] After the 17th century Wit becomes masculine and its meaning supplemented by the related sense of the (masculine) French word *ésprit*. The gender shift and semantic displacement are significant but can be largely explained by the status in the 18th century of the French language as the culturally dominant and official court language of Europe. Wit's philosophical relation is stated by Locke who in 1689 asserts its difference from "judgement":

> For wit lying most in the assemblage of ideas, and putting those together with quickness and variety wherein can be found any resemblance or congruity, thereby to make up pleasant pictures and agreeable visions in the fancy: judgement, on the contrary, lies quite on the other side, in separating carefully one from another ideas where can be found the least difference.[5]

Wit, as we trace it, will never be far from the theme of liberation through dissolution and through an ordering of knowledge upon the chemical senses rather than on rational science. And what becomes clear, especially in the writing of the Jena Romantics, is that *witz*, whilst always controllable by reason, is itself uncontrollable as a birth. It is likewise this spontaneous generation, this intersection and dissolution of the judgemental restraint at that "point of indifference where everything is saturated"[6] that reappears as a kind of belated Romanticism in the wordplay of *The Martyrology*. Through its self-exposure to multiplicity and saturation and the explosion of syntax upon the sub-constituent level of its letters and phonemes (revealing itself as a kind of dythyrambics performed upon the single word), *The Martyrology* will never serve a project of knowledge and will always be close to *witz*. Through wordplay its meanings are pulverized and shattered to serve no cumulative purpose: like *witz* they declare writing to be an

4. N. Bailey, *An Universal Etymological English Dictionary*, 17th ed., London 1757.
5. John Locke, *Essay Concerning Human Understanding*, Book II, Chapter 11, 2.
6. Friedrich Schlegel.

infinite resource that constantly threatens closed, intentional meaning by the errant aspects suppressed within its own implied stochastics. This might be considered as a displacement from the *literal* (which would bind writing to an order of mimesis) to the *letteral* that opens up writing to the productional processes inherent in the words themselves, what Schlegel would probably have called their "perfecting micrology". Often we find a word or phrase intervening in its own scenic place and reorganizing (through either lateral spatiality or homophony) its own constitution. As a consequence (and like Freud's notion of the structure of psychoanalytic presentation of which more will be said later) there is a multiple surface to each word and a minimally dual directionality: the one inwards and directed to a settled place of meaning (the flow of the semantic economy); the other outwards to an undetermined scene of possible and limitless productions.

    t he
    hee hee
        ha ha
            ho ho [7]

Spacing here inaugurates a radical split in the phonic direction, introducing in the second line an investment in a different sound whose end profit is a different meaning that generates its own chain of playful implications. We might see spacing, in this case, through a Lacanian model as a *castration*: the separation and loss of the letter-thing whose phallic status institutes a convention of difference. Here, we would be inclined to read a loss occurring through the disintegration of the definite article into the pre-linguistic laughter articulated through the phonemes' subsequent mutations. Nichol frequently alludes to this style of wordplay. In Book V occur the following:

    puns break
            words fall apart

    . . . . .

7. *The Martyrology*, Book V, Chain 3.

this multiplication
attention to a visual duration
comic stripping of the bared phrase

. . . . .

when i let the letters shift sur face
is just a place on which im ages drift

. . . . .

life's a sign
beneath which signifiers slide

We are no longer in the Renaissance equation of life to stage
but in the contemporary contamination of a semiotic notion
of *Person* by an infinite polysemy. And wit will operate
through the spatial difference between each letter group,
within a notion of the word as occupying a point of suspension
between *official* meaning and that meaning's dissolution
through the incipient alteration of its spacing; an anamorphic
operation of the word on its own material interiority, decom-
posing or *distorting* itself into its phrasal implications and
fragmentary possibilities which then acquire the status of a
produced meaning. As in the example cited, an invisible
partition appears between the word and its components which
suddenly declare themselves as independent and different.
Moreover, the purpose of this declaration is not to gain mastery
over the partition but simply to institute linguistic play and a
perverse path of production. All of this too relates to a certain
game within the order of representation, to a strategy of play
that will be seen through its implications to promote a *material*
poetics and to be entirely without purpose in the realm of
"truth".[8]

The Martyrology's closed world of semantic order is thus

8. The other argument would treat wordplay as a strategy of reserve and efficiency,
an optimizing of semantic profit from a minimum of material outlay. But this argument can only be asserted at the expense of ignoring the proximity of wordplay to
the great insight of Nietzsche's viz. that language and discourse are in essence figurat-
ional and not logical and that Truth's radical metaphoricity must be smothered and
ignored before a project of mastery can start to be inscribed. For an extended treatment of this radical figurality see Jacques Derrida, "White Mythology: Metaphor in
the Text of Philosophy" in *Margins of Philosophy*, tr. Alan Bass (University of
Chicago Press, 1982) p. 207-271.

constantly relativized by a syntactic procedure that econo-
mizes the space, surface and materiality of the writing. But this
relativization of the two economies promotes tensions between
them, not differences; each phrase is *itself* only insofar as it is
also *another*: no where nowhere now here. And what this
"comic stripping of the bared phrase" motivates is the radical
irresolution of meaning. The proposal, constantly implied,
is that the word can never be reduced to a *single* signification.
There will always be a threat to any word's or phrase's supposed
semantic stability, a possibility of loss, of a scramble into
something else. Nichol practises what Derrida describes as a
fundamental ambivalence within definition. If we take in
the example already quoted the spatial shift from "the" to
"t he" and all that this entails, to be a semantic *corruption*,
then we must further admit that such a corruption is always
possible in the inconclusive zone between intention and
typographical error and must admit also that any omni-
possible contamination "cannot be a mere extrinsic accident
supervening on a structure that is original and pure, one that
can be purged of what thus happens to it. The purportedly
'ideal' structure must necessarily be such that this corruption
will be 'always possible'. This *possibility* constitutes part of the
necessary traits of the purportedly ideal structure".[9]

2

The Paragram

> A text is paragrammatic, writes Leon S. Roudiez, "in the sense that
> its organization of words (and their denotations), grammar, and
> syntax is challenged by the infinite possibilities provided by letters
> or phonemes combining to form networks of signification not
> accessible through conventional reading habits. . ."[10]

The percolation of the word through the paragram contaminates
the notion of an ideal, unitary meaning and thereby counters
the supposition that words can "fix" or stabilize in closure.
Paragrammatic wordplay thus manufactures a crisis within

9. Jacques Derrida, "Limited Inc. abc" in *Glyph* 2 (Baltimore: Johns Hopkins University Press, 1977) p. 218.
10. Quoted in Julia Kristeva, *Revolution in Poetic Language*, tr. Margaret Waller
(New York: Columbia University Press, 1984) p. 256.

semantic economy, for whilst engendering meanings, the paragram also turns unitary meaning against itself. If we understand meaning in its classical adequation to truth and knowledge then paragrammaticized meaning becomes a secretion, a loss or expenditure out of semantic's ideal structure into the disseminatory material of the signifier.

The paragrammatic path is one determined by the local indications of a word's own spatio-phonic connotations that produces a centrifuge in which the verbal centre itself is scattered. Nichol's paragrams are the flow-producing agents in the poem's syntactic economy that inscribe themselves across the neutral spaces of the poem and within that other economy whose notion of word (as a fixed, double articulation of signifier/signified) upholds the functional distributions of a presentation. None of this postulates adequation but a micro-narrativity of the single word that opens up its "other" within a totally ungrounded representation. The paragram, moreover, is a fundamental disposition in all combinatory systems of writing and contributes to the latter's trans-phenomenal character. Like the anagram (understood as a disposition rather than an instantiated figure) it is that aspect of language which *escapes* all discourse. Paragrams and anagrams are what Nicholas Abraham terms *figures of antisemantics*;[11] they are what commit writing unavoidably to a general economy (an economy of loss and expenditure without reserve) and to the trans-phenomenal paradox of an unpresentability that serves as a necessary condition of writing's capacity to present.

A popular variant of the paragram is the *charade* which utilizes identical letters in the same order, breaking the words at different places so as to gather variant groupings and thereby produce different meanings. In the charade meaning is a lateral production of variant elements and effects a radical difference within sameness:

Flamingo: pale, scenting a latent shark.
Flaming, opalescent in gala tents — hark.

11. Nicholas Abraham, "The Shell and the Kernel", tr. Nicholas Rand in *Diacritics* 9 (1979).

Hath outrage, dying rated well on super-bold staging looms?
Ha, thou tragedy ingrate, dwell on superb old stag in glooms.

Examples of the charade abound in *The Martyrology* from
Book IV onwards:

vision
riddle we are all well rid of
the dull pass of wisdom

w is d
o ma
i'n h and
the me's restated
at the pen's tip's ink
at the tongue's noise
w in d

What Nichol insists upon (and in this insistence significantly
parts company with the canons of Saussurean linguistics) is
not simply a motivated relation of the sign to its meaning,
but a necessary, complex trans-phenomenality in *all* writing.
An inevitable condition of words existing within words. We
can trace this motivation of the word's local aspects (sound,
letter and space) in the above example. In line 2 "riddle"
announces its own homophonic split: "rid" "dull" which,
thus motivated as a duality, generate a phrasing around themselves ("we are well rid of / the dull pass of wisdom"). The
homophonic play results in "wisdom" which is then submitted to a charade: "wisdom / w is d / o ma". At the same
time meanings coagulate through a sort of back-formation
or reverse charade. In line 7, for instance, "the me's restated"
suggests a centripetal motivation that would draw the letters
into a space that would generate "themes restated". Also
there are areas of potential motivation that Nichol ignores
or chooses to leave as trans-phenomenal. "Wind" becomes
"w in d" by charade, yet "noise" is not altered into
"no is e".[12]   Nevertheless, the paragrammatic function in
The Martyrology is clearly that of the remotivation of the

12. Towards the end of Book III, however, this specific charade is enacted: "no
w/ for w's sake/ / no is/ e/ against the silent sleep".

single letter as an agent of semantic redistribution. The charade forces gap to carry a double implication viz. that the space between letters super-induces a further space that supports the hiatus between meaning *one* and meaning *two* and this implies (although again impossible to articulate) a constitutional non-presence in meaning itself.

3

The Unconscious As A Lettered Production

The paragram, as the "other" region of sign economy forms part of language's *unconscious* dimension where meanings exist as lettered proliferations and escape the closure of an aggregative intention. It was Freud who, without the benefit of Saussurean linguistics and its avatar Structuralism, effectively challenged the transparent and monological status of the utterance by proposing a radically *split* subject, divided across the algorithmic partition of conscious/unconscious.[13] By his serious contestation of the role of conscious intentionality as the functional dominant of social utterance, Freud allows language a number of alternative relations with itself, based not on utility, consciousness and investment, but established on the grounds of their own radical contradictions. The linguistic subject shows itself to be a divided subject in desire whose conscious/unconscious dispositions reveal themselves in a graphic economy extending beyond written, grammatical marks into oneiric operations (substitution, displacement, condensation) and unconscious figurations (pun, homophony, paragram) where language emerges as a general force whose operation is no longer authenticated, nor controlled by, conscious instrumental reason and the intentional subject. For Lacan, the unconscious has decidedly paragrammatic resonances, being *structured as a language* which is not at the disposition of its user, but rather erupts through fissures in conscious discourse.

13. The Russian critic Mikhail Bakhtin proposes an interesting sociological modification to Freud's coupled opposition by eliminating the unconscious and replacing it with an unofficial conscious that interacts with official consciousness. Bakhtin himself seems to have borrowed the distinction from Voloshinov. See P.N. Medvedev and M.M. Bakhtin, *The Formal Method in Literary Scholarship*, tr. Albert J. Wehrle (Baltimore: Johns Hopkins University Press, 1978) p. xiv.

The unconscious is not the ground which has been prepared to give more sparkle and depth to the painted composition: it is the earlier sketch which has been covered over before the canvas is used for another picture. If we use a comparison to the musical order, the unconscious is not the counterpoint of a fugue or the harmonics of a melodic line; it is the jazz one hears despite oneself behind the Haydn quartet when the radio is badly tuned or not sufficiently selective. The unconscious is not the message, not even the strange coded message one strives to read on an old parchment: *it is another text written underneath and which must be read by illuminating it from behind or with the help of a developer.*[14]

This post-Freudian model of the unconscious (linguisticized and de-natured as it is) opens a model for writing as a lettered production which *The Martyrology* employs to the full. The wordplay might be seen as just such a "developer" illuminating the radical "other" meanings within the semantic economy. The textual unconscious would comprise the entire order of unmasterable, indeterminate and unpredictable eruptions of meaning through an alternate system of sound and letter grouping within the "surface" system presented. Let us measure this against the following passage from Book IV:

```
              i want the world
       absolute & present
       all its elements
       el
          em
              en
                  t's
       o
         pq
            r

       or b d
              bidet
       confusion of childhood's 'kaka'
       the Egyptian 'KA'
                        soul
```

14. S. Leclaire, "La réalité du désir" in *Sur le Sexualité humain*, (Centre d'études, Laennec). Cited in Anika Lamaire, *Jacques Lacan*, tr. D. Macey (London: Routledge Kegan Paul, 1977) p. 137-38.

rising out of
the body of
the language

The lettered production starts at line four where syntax commences the distribution of its parts in an anti-semantic manner.
The separation of the word "elements" into its constituent
phonemes develops associationally into the visual play of the
alphabet's systematic sequence. Pronunciational guides are
absent (does the reader read the letter "p" as "pee" or as a
bi-labial consonant?) until the letter "r" releases through
homophony the word "or" to function disjunctively in the
semantic economy and itself present the sequence "b d" as a
pictographic variant (a mirror reversal of identical shapes)
of the earlier "p" and "q". The lettered production continues
with "b" "d" developing *bidet* whose sanitary connotations
lead to the scatological "kaka" (the child's word for shit).
"Kaka" itself splits to isolate the phoneme "ka" which through
an inducement to name enters the semantic economy as KA
(the Egyptian soul) "rising out of the body of language". From
the subject's desire for a world "absolute and present in all its
elements" the text thus arrives at the identification of excre-
ment and soul and their common passage out of the body.[15]

15. Freud's famous case history of the Wolfman demonstrates the similarity of
the psychic vis a vis the so-called textual unconscious. Freud (and after him Nicholas
Abraham) revealed an extraordinary astute, paragrammatic handling of the Wolfman's obsessions, whose repression succeeds through a complex concealment both
within and beneath wordplay. The Wolfman developed a vocabulary of "magic"
words that reached the status of fetish and related to his father's seduction of his
sister and his own repressed envy. Through extremely long, psychoanalytic sessions,
Freud concluded that these words were applied by Wolfman in scenes, dreams and
encounters that did not recall the repression, yet entirely succeeded in producing
pleasure. A couple of examples will suffice. The Russian word *teret* (literally meaning
to rub, as the penis in masturbation) shifts meaning in the Wolfman's sessions to
mean "polish or shine" and is attached to his obsessive imagining of the maid polish-
ing the floor. Similarly, the Spanish word *leche* meaning "milk" (Wolfman lived for
a time in South America) develops both *sperm* (a milky substance) and the verb
lecher (to lick). Wolfman married a woman called Letitia (*lait*:milk) on whom he
performed obsessive cunnilingus (licking). In all of these shifts, plays and substitutions, Abraham sees the operation of *cryptonomy*: "a fetish image, taken from a
fetish word whose meaning has been forgotten".
    The Martyrology, as a cryptonymic text, would require a separate study in itself,
but we will here call attention to one thing. Seemingly, the letters DNA acquire a
"magic" or fetish status and a distribution through scenes outside the "crypt" that
is remarkably similar to the Wolfman's technique. In Book V Chain 3, for instance,
Nichol introduces a reference to a dead sister *Donna*: "sometimes I wonder if
Donna's speaking thru me/ idly its true/ the thot crosses my mind/ is this why i felt
forced to find my 'own' path/ back into language thru play/ as tho i were learning

It would be wrong to insist on an intentional message here, for wordplay releases the other text as a pre-logical "emission" from the latent positions within the syntax. The paragram functions as a casting off of compression and shows meaning to be a differential production of spacing. We are not far, at this point, from the system of the unconscious, for the implication of the paragram (i.e. meaning's emergence out of a different meaning both of which share common graphic or acoustic components) is that a unitary point of fixed meaning can no longer operate as a binding agent of closure. From this point we must admit a subverted and subverting world into *The Martyrology* whose oscillations are not between two separate(d) discourses but striate the abrupt emergence of plurality through ruptures in the transmissions of the poem's semantic order.

P.S.

Plato	post
Socrates	scriptum

would speak of this.

---

to speak again". And later, in the same chain: "are we living out a 'and' era a/ time for/ conjunctive reading". The *and*, through a simple anagrammatic reversal, becomes DNA, blending connotationally space, ontology and chemistry: "Hart works the 'e'/ reversing the conjunction/ finds the d n a/ connective/ the heart of/ writers & their obsessions"/. It is also D(o)N(n)A: the censored sister's name surfacing here as the genetic code, the life-source and the binding force of connectives. There is no originary point for this cryptonomy. Donna will appear and reappear in various books. She will appear in the panoply of Saints as St.And; she is embedded in the Ca Na Da passages of Book IV and in the "Spadina-Dina Madi" complex of Book V Chain 1. She is present too, in Nichol's brother's name (Don) which itself calls for development in the link to another sister (Deanna) and the Celtic goddess (Dana): "Don who was the mother of the Celtic Pantheon/ called Dana by the irish". As a motivated, fetishized grouping DNA saturates the entire work. A cryptonymic reading would trace this as the burying of loss, separation and the institution of difference (i.e. castration complex) and its displacement through wordplay and antonomasia into its anti-thetical meaning (recovery, proliferation, connection, re-incorporation).

Beyond cryptonomy, one is reminded of a great philosophical precedent viz. the Think-Thing relationship in Hegel that speaks of the relationship of a material similarity-in-difference articulated in a pre-logical play that contaminates — yet at the same time produces — a logical effect. This "Hegelian" strain is present in virtually all of Nichol's wordplay and evident as a physiology of verbal neighbourhoods, the adjacence of two bodies, two sounds, which produces a subversion of the semantic order by foregrounding the materiality of the sign and entering the order of meaning to call attention to the fortuitousness of all ideality.

4

Cratylean Linguistics Through Ramus

> So Plato, when he inquires in *Cratylus* who are learned in the true
> names of things, with good reason ridicules the sophists, and judges
> it necessary to go to the poets — not indiscriminately to all of them,
> but to such as are divine; as if they had learned the true names of
> things from the gods.[16]

In the *Cratylus* Plato sets forth a view of language in which
words are presented not as conventional and arbitrary (the
nominalist view) but as "correct" and "true". The true word,
according to this theory, is attainable through an etymologizing
process by which a search through component parts leads to
older, more authentic forms. Meaning, in other words, is
proposed to be implicit in etymology. Interest in the *Cratylus*
was high during the Renaissance; it is first mentioned in the
Dialecticae Institutiones of Peter Ramus (Paris, 1543) and
figures prominently in a number of 16th century English
texts such as Abraham Fraunce's *Lawier's Logike* (London,
1588) and Richard Willis' (the "Willye" of Spenser's *Shep-
hearde's Calendar*) *De Re Poetica* (London, 1573). As Richard
Mulcaster, who was Spenser's master at Merchant Taylors
School, cites the *Cratylus* in his *Elementarie* of 1584, it seems
reasonable to assume that the author of *The Faerie Queene* was
also familiar with Cratylean linguistics. The theory was elabor-
ated in Ramist logic where words reveal reality through their
origin. For example, Homer's "Agamemnon" declares itself
on scrutiny to be a compound name whose parts are *agastos*
(admirable) and *menein* (enduring). The English Ramist,
Abraham Fraunce, cites the example (sic) of "a woman who
is a woe man because she worketh a man woe".[17] There is a
similar Cratylean "correctness" in Spenser's description of
The House of Pride where the word "hypocrisy" is shown
deriving from *hyper* (covered) and *chrysos* (gold):

A stately Pallace built of squared bricke
Which cunningly was without morter laid,

16. Richard Willis, *De Re Poetica*, London 1573, p. 73.
17. *Lawier's Logike* I, xii p. 57.

Whose wals were high, but nothing strong nor thick,
And *golden* foile all *over* them displaid,
That purest skye with brightnesse they dismaid.[18]

Cratylean words then, are self-statemental, a kind of "micro-argument" upon themselves, and whose originary correctness is revealed through the agency of etymological analysis. *Witz* of this kind abounds in *The Martyrology*, indeed, Chain 1 of Book V can be read as a credible "Cratylean" topography:

i live on Brun's wick

so named 'cause it stuck out
thick as his legendary stick
into that wal of water flowed
around the foot of Casa Loma
licked its way between
the hill that castle stands on &
Russell's Hill
    or south
stretching round the ruins of what was
Harbored
   Harbour D
(a harmony)
only puns someone says
i says glimpses of another truth
'nother story worth the tell

Like Schlegel's operational *witz*, Nichol subjects his terms to splits and dissolutions, but with the purpose of a Platonic correctness that locates a literal, material "truth" inherent in the words themselves.

The Martyrology is full of the Ramist search for originary sense like Fraunce's:

    all knowledge
is to kncw the ledge you stand on
. . .
the whole scene

18. Edmund Spenser, *The Faerie Queene*, I iv 4 (my italics).

the w hole
into which the world
disappears

d is a p
pear shaped
. . .
a.d.   a.d.
history's spoken in
the first four letters
. . .

        an image
of friends   two poets i knew
disagreed   were not speaking with each other

d is a greed
a gluttony of shape
swallowing the era which it ends
dis corporates

it is the D of devil then
the apocalypse the bible prophesied
ends the age we live in

in dogma the d is on the left
encountered first
has the upper hand in our reading
we are led
        into the devil's works
by our very view

which all demonstrate the same indifference to meaning, the
same potlatch of consequence that characterizes Freud's
definition of the joke, relativized, however, by this attachment
of the wordplay to a project of truth which contextualizes *The
Martyrology* in a certain neo-Platonic descent. Frequently
Nichol's paragrams are qualified and provisional releases from
a rational constraint, and a tracing of the oscillations between
the two economies (semantic-syntactic) will reveal a rhythm
rigidly enacted between loss, proliferation and indifferent
production on the one hand, and between a recovered investment, accumulation in a referential writing on the other hand,

whose themes are journey, history, myth and the contemplative
subject. In the scene of the paragram the Subject is lost, defabricated by the flow-producing agencies of homophony and
the detached letter, yet this dissolution is constantly checked
by the territorializing forces of reference, investment and
value.[19] Because of this, *The Martyrology* never transcends a
profound ambivalence:

> you tolerate then Lord
> the many guises of your signifiers
> know you are the signified
>
> . . .
>
> Mother Nature
> God the Father
> world's a word
> you are one & the same

There is a shift here into a more settled, referentially satisfying
writing. At various moments in the work we detect Nichol's
own subjective anxieties arising as a response to the disintegat-
ive implications of the wordplay:

> talking with steve
>   comparing forms
> his CARNIVAL
>   'my' MARTYROLOGY?

19. This need to alternate two extended economies (the one of explosive intensities,
the other recouperative and directed back towards settled meaning) is De Sade's
method too. In *Justine*, for example, a syntactic economy regulates the changing
combinations, positions and relationships of the sexual ensembles. This alternates
(in almost geometric regularity) with a rational economy of logical argument,
justification and apology. A comparative study of *The Martyrology* and the works of
Sade (whose acknowledged influences were not only the dark gothic of Anne
Radcliffe, but also Fielding and Richardson) would reveal surprising parallels. For
instance, beyond the shared technique of oscillating economies, both authors utilize
a curious logic of the addressee. In Nichol it is a transcendental figure, variously
named "father" and "Lord" who regulates wordplay and redirects the sign economy
towards an I-Thou discourse. In Sade it is Nature that is the recipient of two vastly
divergent theories of its own functioning. Sade will justify, a posteriori, the libidinal
excess and affective abominations described by an appeal to logical argument that
these actions are according to the "nature" of Nature. This use of a dialogic structure
has many precedents; it structures Milton's *Comus* (which itself is a descendent of
the numerous *psychomachias*, or battles for the soul, that inundated literature
through the middle ages and up to Marvell).

the voiceless voice he saw in Ronald Johnson's poems
i am wary of that impulse within me
would have it out with my i
how can i cast itself out
out of the process i must be true to

or a little earlier in the same Book IV:

(typing this out 12 days later i kept coming back to that line 'the
edge of things' wondering at the vagueness, knowing what i was
trying to suggest, that my world was finite, not in imagination but
experience, real limits to what i knew, worried once more by the
tension between process & an ideal economy of phrase

Clearly, this reflects a struggle to maintain the viewpoint of a
unitary subject in a position that the work's wordplay constantly undermines. Yet to accuse Nichol of inconsistency would be
to miss the implications of these alternations. Nichol does not
theatricalize a struggling subject pulverized and castrated within
the mechanics of writing's general economy, but rather inscribes
the relativization of a multiplicity of writings within the single
textual space. As a result the oscillations acquire a multiple
dimension that serves to neutralize any potential drive to
dominate with a single, uniform discourse. This would suggest
that the core issue of *The Martyrology* coincides with one of
the core issues of post-modernism: to achieve a finite description of writing's infinite combinatory motions.

5

Mikhail Bakhtin: The Dialogic Utterance

the higher a genre develops and the more complex its form, the
better and more fully it remembers its past.[20]

Mikhail Bakhtin (1895-1975) is a Russian theoretician
whose pioneer notions of the radical dialogicality of utterance
find striking parallels in *The Martyrology*. What is profound in
Bakhtin (and links him closely with Nichol) is an agonistic
theory of language that Michael Holquist has termed a

20. M.M. Bakhtin, *Problems of Dostoevsky's Poetics*, tr. Caryl Emerson, (Minneapolis: University of Minnesota Press, 1984) p. 121.

"zoroastrian clash" between the fundamental centripetal/ centrifugal forces in language. "Every concrete utterance of a speaking subject" writes Bakhtin, "serves as a point where centrifugal as well as centripetal forces are brought to bear. The processes of centralization and de-centralization, of unification and dis-unification, intersect in the utterance . . . The authentic environment of an utterance, the environment in which it lives and takes shape, is dialogized heteroglossia".[21] A text, according to Bakhtin, is a network of citations, an absorption and transformation of other texts. Within this network the word maintains the status not of a fixed point (of meaning), but of an interstice at the intersection of numerous textual and historical surfaces. Bakhtin proposes two types of discourse: *Monologic* (i.e. the discourse of science, description and representation; a discourse directed outside itself to a referential adequation and prohibited from entering into a dialogue with itself), and *Dialogic* in which the writing "reads another writing" and constructs itself "through a process of destructive genesis" (Kristeva). In dialogic discourse multiple texts converge, contradict and relativize each other. The word becomes *act*, non-imagistic, dramatizes its own dialectical transformation and consequently obtains the status of a multi-determined peak.

We can see quite clearly that Nichol's paragrams are of the order of Bakhtin's dialogic word.[22] Indeed, the word-play may be read as a "carnivalization" of the semantic order, an overturning of historically settled sounds and letter groupings and a repudiation of all representationally governed meaning. The oscillations between linguistic orders deserve acute comparison to Bakhtin's dual typology of discourse. This dialogism provides us with a contemporary access to

21. M.M. Bakhtin, *The Dialogic Imagination*, tr. Emerson & Holquist (Austin: University of Texas Press, 1981) p. 272.
22. Julia Kristeva finds an implicit "poetic logic" in the paragram, whose logical sequence is 0-2 (in which the first term is transgressed). In the logic of Nichol's paragrams, the numeral 1 similarly does not operate as a limit but implicitly presents itself as a triple prohibition: linguistic-social-psychic i.e. God-Law-Definition. This is the triplicity that *The Martyrology*'s referential sections patently communicate. Classical translation subordinates the code to 1, as does all realistic (or as Bakhtin would prefer "monologic") narrative. Out of the 0-2 logic of the paragram develops the polyphonic text of which *Finnegan's Wake* provides the currently "unreadable" limit and of which *The Martyrology* exemplifies one of its most persistent and ambivalent interiorizations within textual experience. See Julia Kristeva, *Desire in Language*, tr. T. Gora, A. Jardine & L. Roudiez (New York: Columbia University Press, 1980) p. 64-91.

The Martyrology not as a serial epic or poetic journal, but as a polyphonic staging of intersecting texts[23] in which intersubjectivity (undeniably present) is never allowed to dominate, and needs, in its relative status, no apologetic justification.

1985

23. It is worth noting in conclusion that some critics have argued that wordplay constitutes the basis of allegory. Maureen Quilligan, for instance, argues for an "essential affinity" of allegory to pun. She distinguishes "Coleridgean" allegory (based on extended analogy) from a notion of allegory based on "a sense of simultaneous, equal significance, a fluctuating figure-ground relationship which contains within it the relations between the two meanings of a single word". See Maureen Quilligan, *The Language of Allegory: Defining the Genre* (Ithaca: New York, 1979) p. 32.

   Derrida's thoughts, too, are consequential. Commenting on the *Rhetoric* (1404b37-1405al) of Aristotle, Derrida mentions the Greek philosopher's attribution of metaphor to the poet and of homonymy to sophism: "... the sophist manipulates empty signs and draws his effects from the contingency of signifiers (whence his taste for equivocality, and primarily for homonymy, the deceptive identity of signifiers), the poet plays on the multiplicity of signifieds, but in order to return to the identity of meaning". In *Margins*, tr. Alan Bass (University of Chicago Press, 1982) p. 284n. In accordance with Derrida's reading of Aristotle, Nichol's paragrammatism would be consigned to sophistry rather than poetry by the author of the *Rhetoric*. The torn threads of a spider's language.

McLuhan + Language
× Music

PROBE RESEARCH

Marshall McLuhan saw the need to wrestle with a vital contemporaneity in language, to structure a style and a manner of discussion upon the premises of an acoustic rather than a visual epistemology. Instead of developing a thesis or an argument by means of connected statements, reporting on things as already perceived, he used language to develop what he termed *probes*: exploratory linguistic devices of a highly projective and dispensible nature. The chief characteristics of the probe are strength, pressure, a calculated outrage, exaggeration and extremism (all the features, one might observe in passing, of a high baroque, pre-enlightenment style). The function of the probe is both to enter and to extend exploratory domains of human consciousness and environment. Probe research is highly adaptable; its concern is not with the construction of huge, rational monoliths, but with gridding mosaic patterns of investigation in an attempt to make visible and to bring to the level of human awareness all or any of the multiplicity of low definition environments that surround and control us. Information, as McLuhan uses it and presents it to a reader, is non-retentive; it is the instantaneous flow of multi-directional energy along dynamic circuitries and not the careful classification of data upon the pre-observed. His mental guns are trained against academic discipline and all such pedagogical linear power structures that perpetuate the repression of multi-sensory pre-literate awareness. McLuhan was painfully aware of the need to return the literary to its pre-literate

This paper was first delivered under the title "Omaggio a McLuhan" at the International Festival Musicarcitectura, L'Aquila, Italy, 29 August 1982.

resonances, to involve the word and the fact in the highest degree of possible risk, contradiction and unpredictability. In his hands words cease to be bricks and components in the assembly line of classical discourse and transform into spheres and icons that register as much inside their transience and mutability as in a vital presence. In an interview conducted several years ago with G.E. Stearn, McLuhan conveys succinctly the spirit of his probe research:

> I'm perfectly prepared to scrap any statement I ever made about any subject once I find that it isn't getting me into the problem. I have no devotion to any of my probes as if they were sacred opinions. I have no proprietary interest in my ideas and no pride of authorship as such.[1]

There is implicit here a reassessment of the current sociology of readership, a shift in the notion of reading away from its recipial base in transmission theory of meaning towards an active, productive disposition. In the traditional sense we can never satisfactorily read McLuhan for in that sense McLuhan resists readability. The works exist on the precarious method-ological threshold of the Book conceived as the collective scene of hueristic devices, propositionally disconnected and thereby multi-directional instruments to be used in a reader's own probes into the low-definition environment.

Through all his books McLuhan proposes a diachronic cultural model in which technological breakthroughs effect new epistemological metaphors that structure and control our modes of thinking. The print revolution, attributed to Gutenberg, not only disseminated the political and physical body alike,

1. Derrida remarks upon a similar hueristic attitude in the work of Claude Levi-Strauss: "Levi-Strauss will always remain faithful to this double intention: to preserve as an instrument that whose truth-value he criticizes,conserving . . . all these old concepts, while at the same time exposing . . . their limits, treating them as tools which can still be of use. No longer is any truth-value attributed to them; there is a readiness to abandon them if necessary if other instruments should appear more useful. In the meantime, their relative efficacy is exploited, and they are employed to destroy the old machinery to which they belong and of which they themselves are pieces".
   Nor should we forget to add Hegel's own strategic dispositions towards a philo-sophical discourse and his strongly felt need for a language that would carry internally a *necessary* self-criticism. Finally, we should note the centrality of this strategy in the project of deconstruction and Derrida's own grounding of knowledge, not in the searching for and fixing of a truth, but in the infinite freeplay of sub-stitutions.

detaching voice from its need to be present within a physical incarnation, but provoked an intense disbalance between oral and written speech with the consequent consolidation of visual space as the dominant metaphor of acculturation. In the passage of language from written to electrical procedures McLuhan observed a profound double articulation. On the one hand he detected the swing in metaphorical bias from visual to acoustic space as bringing back a movement to sensory wholeness and the recovery of the primordial matrix out of which human consciousness has been progressively removed and abstracted. On the other hand, this recovery is not to be construed as a simple return to a preliterate anterior. The recovered sensory wholeness is marked less by its registration upon individual human bodies than by its macro-structural dimensions. "Electricity", writes McLuhan in *Understanding Media*, "points the way to an extension of the process of consciousness itself, on a world scale, and without any verbalization whatever". The Electric Age, quite acoustically, brings back the future and looks forward to the past. It is is the destroying angel of space-time linear seriality.[2]

MUSIC AS PARADIGM OF ACOUSTIC SPACE

Perhaps the best entry into McLuhan's thinking on music is through his key notion of acoustic space. Currently acoustic space is our dominant spatial metaphor which McLuhan describes as "a dynamic or harmonic field" existing "while the music or sound persists. And the hearer is one with it, as with music". In an unpublished letter to the Canadian composer R. Murray Schafer, McLuhan elaborates upon the cultural and social implications of acoustic space:

> We are living in an acoustic age for the first time in centuries, and by that, I mean that the electric environment is simultaneous. Hearing is structured by the experience of picking up information from all directions at once. . . At this moment, the entire planet

2. The artist Nam June Paik, among others, has not been negligent in accusing McLuhan of a lapse in conceptual rigour in his use of the terms "electric" and "electronic" as interchangeable equivalents. To quote Paik: "Electronics is essentially Oriental . . . Electricity deals with mass and weight; electronics deals with informat-ion; one is muscle, the other nerve". Quoted in Gene Youngblood, *Expanded Cinema* (New York: E.P. Dutton, 1970) p. 137. The subject of McLuhan's "orientalism" however, would pose an interesting theme for subsequent study.

exists in that form of instant but discontinuous co-presence of everything.[3]

In a late essay *Changing Concepts of Space in an Electronic Age* McLuhan describes acoustic space in a phrase first used in the 12th century pseudo hermetic text *Liber XXIV Philosophorum* to describe God: a simultaneous field of relations whose centre is everywhere and whose margins are nowhere. Acoustic space is decidedly not a physical space in the sense of a container. In the acoustic field it is the sound itself that creates the space. The operative model here lies in the logic of autonomy and event rather than the logic of Euclidean space. In several places McLuhan identifies acoustic space with the musical condition in general. The properties of acoustic space are precisely the properties that characterize any musical space. McLuhan understood music to be just such a field of unique, disconnected and discontinuous moments whose sensory impact is total, instant and simultaneous. It would, however, be a serious misrepresentation to present McLuhan as a singularly acoustic theorist. Reading his books from a musical awareness one notes how music frequently emerges as a kind of nodal point around which all references temporarily focus. It is ultimately impossible to separate McLuhan's ideas on music from the vast scope of his cultural and media theories.

Music, then, attains high status for McLuhan; it is the dominant condition of the acoustic age and the destination of all the arts in the twentieth century. McLuhan's implicit thesis, to be extracted from the broad strata of his writings, would be this: *that the technological change precipitated by the advent of electronic media has pushed up the musical environment into high definition, whilst its discreet definition, as an integral unitary discipline, has undergone significant changes.*

As early as 1906 the Italian futurist Luigi Russolo undermined the traditional distinction between sound and noise and penetrated the musical with the traditionally non-musical in his noise concerts. Composer R. Murray Schafer can speak quite meaningfully of the world as "a macroscopic musical instrument" and his World Soundscape Project (inspired by the work in visual design of the Bauhaus) extended the sociological purpose

---

3. Unpublished letter, December 16 1974.

of the composer into acoustic ecology and design. John Cage in the sixties defined music as simply "sounds around us whether we're in or out of concert halls". The path of twentieth century music, then, tends to support McLuhan's general intuition that as music detaches itself from prescriptive definitions it begins to escribe itself environmentally. As Schafer says "Today all sounds belong to a continuous field of possibilities *lying within the comprehensive dominion of music*".[4]

Let us now take a look at the technological changes in music that have thrust it into high definition as acoustic environment.

THE PHONOGRAPH, THE CONCERT HALL AND THE CHANGE IN AUDITORY SPACE

Deriving his insight from Malraux, McLuhan describes the phonograph as "a music without walls". With the advent in its present state of hi-fidelity quadraphonic sound, McLuhan saw music receiving the experiential depth that cubism had supplied pictorial space and that symbolism had given to literature, namely, "the acceptance of multiple facets and planes in a single experience". Beyond the straightforward utilitarian values of preservation and transmission of traditionally performed music, McLuhan perceived how the advent of recording intro-duces revolutionary spatial and acoustical changes in the physical and cultural locus of audition. In point of fact most contemporary experience of music comes via some form of electronic medium rather than in live performance. The socio-logical shift in scene from concert hall to living room is incon-testable. The concert hall was structured on a visual, theatrical model whose goals of distance and non-involvement were achieved through a controlled interplay of several spaces. Firstly, the hall's own architectural space which successfully separated listener from performer by means of a harsh counter positioning. Secondly, the virtual space of the music itself that favoured recessionalities and varying dynamics which tended to separate the acoustic experience into figure (forte) and ground (piano). The piano-forte dynamic offers an acoustic parallel to visual perspective and optical vanishing point in classic pictorial space. Thirdly, the social space itself prescribed a specific

4. R. Murray Schafer, *The Tuning of the World* (Toronto: McClelland & Stewart, 1977) p. 5.

manner of action and response and a specific style of dress, all
of which tended to mobilize the concert hall as a politicized
anti-environment, an aristocratic space in high contrast to an
outside world. The concert hall was an ideology of the interior,
an acoustic area visually circumscribed by its architectural form;
its effects were to promote concentrated attention and the
satellitic responses of applause and collective approbation. As a
nineteenth century residue carried over into the electric age the
concert hall serves the reactionary purpose of retention; in
McLuhan's own words it is "a retrieval system of past moments"
marked to a large degree by a cult of the dead composer. There
is a tendency in visually based culture to interiorize sound, to
enclose its acoustic phenomena within such indoor spaces.
Schafer believes this tendency originated with the human
discovery of the cave as both a potential pictorial surface and a
resonant and amplifying structure.[5] Sonic interiorization creates
the sensation of a uniform, unbroken sound-filled space.
Outdoor space, in contrast, is an inevitable acoustic environment, a simultaneous field of relations. The concert hall is a
single auditory space enclosed within a number of visual pre-
conditions. In the auditory context of recorded performance,
however, the living room has no prescribed visual focus and no
theatrical constraints. A listener is free to move around, leave
the room, is free to listen with a concentrated intent or treat
the same music as personal background. The living room, in this
respect, becomes a de-politicized personal space in which the
musical event might serve numerous local and pragmatic functions. With its visual biases 19th century music created the *public*
audience as a harmonic parallel to the symphony concert.
Recorded music, with its highly personalized and versatile space,

5. But speech itself seems born of the cave and neolithic, eurasian light. A modification of originally *visual* hominid signals (gestures across space in light) was precipitated by the climatic constraints that produced the domicile context of the cave.
It led to vocal signals that could carry across distance independent of visual
perception. Phonemic variation enters as a factor when vocal signals became
differentiated on the basis of intensity. Phonemic difference first expressed a
difference of distance/safety, near/far. This differentiation of vocal qualities precedes
nomination and their function was that of modifiers to call signals.
I recall too, in a conversation with David Antin, regarding the speculative
"origins" of cinema, in which we concluded that the cave paintings of neolithic
times were an aboriginal cinema. The caves are dark and the only available light
was fire which would have produced numerous kinetic effects upon the walls. If
this hypothesis is true then cinema is coeval with figuration and movement would
precede static pictorialism.

created the *mass* audience that is paradoxically more individual and yet more undifferentiated than the public. McLuhan recognized this as a profoundly contradictory state of affairs but saw the entire electric age as one of such dynamic contradictions.

As well as this profound shift in the sociological space McLuhan intuited a radical difference in the kind of sound. There are few examples in his own writing to substantiate the claim of his famous probe that stereo gave sound a depth previously unknown, however, the supporting evidence can be found in the physics of amplification. Amplifiers create high-intensity, low-frequency sounds that privilege bass effects in the home component system. Low-frequency sounds have longer wavelengths than high frequencies and are less influenced by diffraction, as a consequence of which such sounds are spatially directionless and difficult to localize as a specific sound source. They are of the nature of floating signifiers producing their own acoustic environment instantly and placing a listener within it.[6]

RADIO

Radio, more than any other sonic medium, conditions listening to disconnectedness. The invention of magnetic tape permits radio to organize its continuity by montage technique whose sequence is determined less by a logical order than by the abrupt, discontinuous "eventism" of surrealist change. To examine the historical development of radio is to trace a change from isolated broadcasts surrounded by silent station breaks to the current situation where the entire day is filled out with a constant sound loop. The historical trend in radio has been to eliminate silence from radiophonic space. One important consequence of this strategic incessance has been to render programming of secondary importance to the arbitrary presence of

6. We might note in passing that this low-frequency sound immersion attained by home stereo recovers the dominant acoustic feature of Gothic cathedrals. According to Kurt Blaukopf "the sound in Norman and Gothic churches, surrounding the audience, strengthens the link between the individual and the community. The loss of high frequencies and the resulting impossibility of localizing the sound makes the believer part of a world of sound. He does not face the sound in 'enjoyment' he is wrapped up by it". (Quoted in R. M. Schafer, *The Tuning of the World* [Toronto: McClelland & Stewart, 1977] p. 118). Neither McLuhan nor Blaukopf, however, speculate extensively on either the psycho-acoustical or the socio-political consequences of this technological link between electric and medieaval sensibility.

sound. Nowadays, one tunes in to whatever's happening rather than paying a calculated visit to the radio. Radio both creates and informs a personal space without beginning or end. We savour its parts and its surreal juxtapositions as an ecological microcosm in which verbal discourse, musical sign, factual information and non-referential signal are held together in a continuity of disconnectedness. As its major popular transmitter, radio has contextualized music in this discontinuous flow. Interruptions (in the form of advertisements and news broadcasts) constitute a paradoxically homogenous discontinuity with the overriding effect that music is no longer separable from the non-musical. And at this point trivia and profundity blend. We are at the implosive locus of social critique and Cagean musical strategy, at the interface of music's own presence and its relation to its other.[7]

MUSIC AND TECHNOLOGY

McLuhan's sense of technology is implicative rather than instrumental. Whereas Lewis Mumford (to cite one instance) sees technology as oppressive and art's telos a strategic anti-technologizing, McLuhan offers a broader and more hueristic possibility. In his grasp of the double articulation of technics, the essentially Janus features of the electric age that looks simultaneously back to the pre-literate and forward to the post-literate, McLuhan proposes a new epistemological and cultural function for contradictions and disconnection. Art's authentic purpose is to be an ecological exploration making visible those environments that operate upon us by the power of their invisibility. For McLuhan contradictions function as bridges you can't walk across but are compelled to step upon. The present, too, is conceived as a pivot that, in its movement, makes the past and the present emerge as relativized surfaces upon a sphere.

In contrast to other social theorists such as Lewis Mumford and Harold Innis (both of whom profoundly influenced his thinking) McLuhan did not see music and technics in conflict

7. There are certain jukeboxes manufactured on which, for the same price as a record, the listener can purchase a period of silence equivalent to the record's length. "In a civilization of noise" claims Genette, "silence must also be a product". We should keep in mind this historically acquired commodity status of silence when considering the wide implications of John Cage's "ontological disproof" of its existence.

but as moving increasingly to a point of indistinction. As music is liberated from its visual bias it enters into global, technological symplegma as one of several interdependent relationships, the interdependency of which provides a rich territory for cross-pollenization. McLuhan saw the fundamental strength of technology as neither instrumental nor destructive but rather as rhetorical. Technology *persuades* towards modification and change; it is ideological software whose implications are both pre and post political. Technology does not serve so much as modify; it simultaneously promises and threatens change. There are areas in McLuhan's thinking where the implications of this music-technology interface are extremely Zen-like. For instance, there is a striking parallel between McLuhan's initial premise of acoustic space as a decentralized yet total experience and Lama Angarika Govinda's description of the multi-dimensional conception of the universe. Lama Govinda says:

> If we consider, instead of sequence, the simultaneity of certain seemingly unconnected phenomena, we shall often be able to observe a parallelism, a coincidence of certain qualities, not causally or temporally conditioned, but rather giving the impression of a cross section of an organically connected whole.

McLuhan's own concept of analogical perception is remarkably similar:

> Perhaps the most precious possession of man is his abiding awareness of the analogy of proper proportionality, the key to all metaphysical insight and perhaps the very condition of consciousness itself. This analogical awareness is constituted of a perpetual play of ratios among ratios: A is to B what C is to D, which is to say that the ratio between A and B is proportioned to the ratio between C and D, there being a ratio between these ratios as well.

In 1975 Canadian composer R. Murray Schafer visited the Swedish village of Skruv as part of his World Soundscape Project. He noted in his soundscape analyses there the presence of several resonant harmonics and steady pitches produced by various electrical equipment: street lights, illuminated signs and generators. After plotting their various pitches Schafer discovered that they collectively produced a G-sharp major triad which the F-sharp whistle of passing trains transformed into a dominant seventh chord. Schafer's important field work has provided much factual support to McLuhan's general intuitions. The electronic age is equatable with a music and that music itself is indistinguishable from a synthetic technological environment. We no longer have access to a non-electronic sense of listening, for what the electronic revolution has imposed as a mandatory condition of our listening are these new tonal centres of prime unity against which all other sounds must be balanced. The auditory space we are now immersed in (wherever there are kettles, frying pans and light bulbs) is a space where all sounds relate to such a continuously present tonal centre. Schafer personally sees this as a condition of schizophonia: the electronic separation of sound from any trace of physical origin.[8]

Quo vadis when we have the music of the spheres enacted in a Swedish village in 1975? At present the greatest medical problem in the Canadian arctic is not frostbite but deafness caused by an inability of the indigenous Innuit people to accommodate the sound of the snowmobile into their soundscape. At the same time radio threatens to realize the ultimate paradox: to present music as an homogenized equality within a mass society (the dream of Fuller, Cage and Thoreau) and to institute effectively a structure of global manipulation through the identical penetration of personalized acoustic spaces (Hitler's dream and Churchill's too). I do not believe that McLuhan shared the optimism of Cage and Fuller in the electronic liberation of human energy and a final return of humanity to itself — we must remember that McLuhan's probe research was decanted through the acute pessimism of his mentor Harold Innis — and

8. It might be argued, in modification of Schafer's hypothesis, that schizophonia marks the passage of sound into writing effects. Especially pertinent would be Derrida's notion of *differance* (difference plus deferral), a word deliberately spelled with an "a" and describing the radical citationality of all language. Schafer's schizophonia then, would constitute a part of the great occidental contestation between presence and non-presence which has manifested itself throughout history in numerous oppositions: body/soul, speech/writing, live performance/recorded performance, eidos/simulacrum. Such oppositional couplings grid the entire ratiocinative landscape of western thinking and, as the "metaphysics of presence", have been the subject of deconstructive operations and critiques by Nietzsche, Marx, Derrida and others. Schafer likewise fails to include in his argument the emergence of schizo-culture and a politics of difference through such thinkers as Michel Foucault, Jean Francois Lyotard, Gilles Deleuze and Felix Guattari. For a more sympathetic treatment of the schiz than Schafer gives in *The Tuning of the World* the reader should consult *Anti-Oedipus* by Deleuze and Guattari, trans. Robert Hurley, Mark Seem and Helen R. Lane (New York: Viking Press, 1977).

McLuhan oscillates, irritatingly at times, between a diachronic image of progress and a synchronic model of the technological contradiction that does not explode into resolution but perpetuates its janusian ambivalence. We must remember too that McLuhan was not a musical theorist, that his great love was literature and that this love was acutely conditioned by his awareness of the dangers and the obsolescence of the literary. McLuhan's written style resonates with oral devices and technological sound; his books subvert themselves as linear structures by the continuous eruptions of typographic icons. McLuhan's preference for probe research over a lineal progressivistic argument permits the pages to resonate with a rapidity and abundance of information. The ostinato effects that have drawn so many hostile reactions serve to musicate the works and suggest more the acoustic-informational loops of the computer soundscape than the linear bibles of Gutenberg.

We should remember too that McLuhan's great passion was James Joyce, whom he thought to be the twentieth century's greatest exponent of lingual music. McLuhan not only wrote about Joyce but absorbed the Joycean strategy of the pun into his own thinking. McLuhan understood the pun to be the most disarming fusion of language and music, the chordal resonance of a contradiction, a linguistic push beyond choice and the logic of exclusion towards the polyphony of indecision. Cage has given the implicative reflex here in a thought about technology and music:

> We are evidently going to extremes: to the "very large scale" ("the great impersonality of the world of mass production") and to the "very small scale" ("the possibility of intense personalism").

The electric age, argues McLuhan, is the age of contradictions and music must end as it began: in a study of the origins of table manners. Hidden in a lapidary response to an interviewer's question regarding technological optimism is this quintessential distillation of McLuhan's feelings about music in the electronic age:

> The new environment shaped by electronic technology is a cannibalistic one that eats people. To survive one must study the habits of cannibals.

1982

The Scene of the Cicatrice

If the stated themes of Lemire Tostevin's *Color of Her Speech*
(Toronto, Coach House Press, 1982) are bilingualism and
feminism, then its profoundest implications return us through
Oedipus to the fact that, as well as a mother tongue, there is
always a paternal code that demands a woman render herself
transparent through its rules and ideologemes. Lemire Tostevin
has realized that the absolute male is language and that even
silence must be territorialized within patriarchal signification.
The authentic "goal" is not a search for voice (for already in
positing that quest woman enters complicity with the male
myths of telos, loss and fall) but the deconstruction of a
code in textual space and the epistemological issue of how
a woman becomes known in her opacities as a truth impreg-
nable to phallic scrutiny. The woman who writes is already
prescribed as the woman in writing, a non-definable body
already written, the spoken object of another's discourse, so
that the "issue" of woman takes on a critical dimension when it
addresses language as the paternal code, when beings are not
addressed through language but language itself is addressed as
being.

These implications are shown without resort to argumentation or philosophy and the supreme impact of this book is
still the impact of poetry. But there is a specific, particularized
sense of what poetry is: it is where language confronts itself and
where discourse and code are bracketed within the textual space
of a writing. And if Romanticism produced the myth of the
infinite interior of the Self, Lemire Tostevin gives the processual
exterior of a multiple subject in movement through a register of
intensities that situate and circulate upon — but are never
identical to — meaning. What emerges through these poems is an

ambivalent locus both pre-sexual and post-sexual where the writing subject never forms into a "self" and where message is the vehicle of its own instabilities and contradictions. The entire book thus gains a complex double articulation, firstly as a lineal sequential message in which the subject's disposition is towards the appropriation of the existent code, and secondly as a non-linear, non-linguistic force deriving from a *body prior to writing* and clearly linked to unconscious drives and uteral-umbilical intuitions.

Early in the book Lemire Tostevin introduces the notions of *déparler* and *dénommer* (literally to un-speak and un-name):

the Unspeaking
the Unbinding of Umbilicals
ba be bi bo
'déparler'
décomposer
sa langue
da de di do

'l'enfant do
l'enfant dormira bien vite'

'and if that lullaby don't sing
papa's gonna buy you a diamond
ring. . .'

la source renversée
the course unlaid

baby lulled
by a lie

byaliebyaliebyaliebyaliebyalie

Un-speech differs from silence in the way deconstruction differs from destruction. The logophallic code gets biologically unspoken by this double articulation where the various devices of typography, rhythmic and phonic patterns and para-verbal clusters cut across or intersect the logical order of the language. Typography here is much more than a simple decision of design; it relates to meaning as colour does to form as a tactile invest-ment in the verbal order that renders words *things* and foregrounds their material, gestural and non-semantic presence. Type, in fact, is a strategy of subversion that the book adopts. Initially a simple binary equivalence is established by which italic type carries the french language poems and roman type the anglophone. This relation is quickly subverted when italicized french words begin occurring in otherwise entirely anglophone texts. Further transgression of the strictly symbolic order occurs when italic type itself spills over into english and carries anglophonic dedications whilst french words subsequently appear in roman type. The subversions suggest a material, non-linguistic flow over the entire order of meaning, a kind of surface eroticism that saturates the sign and dialecticizes the linear aggregates of message:

fleuve
flows back

to *vague*
memory

A similar subversion occurs in the book's general absence of titles and their replacement by geometric squares as empty, tactile signs that refuse in any way to name the texts which follow. Where a title does occur (in the one piece *Gyno-Text*) it comes as an eruption and marks a strong discontinuity that promotes the general destabilization of text and meaning.

This important push towards a gynocography is not an unqualified achievement. There are moments in the book where the levels of subversion and un-speaking fall short. Discernible behind the total, complex motion of the book are certain transitive desires and that conventional aesthetic pressure towards presenting the poem as a finished, foreclosed object:

once
the mouth
stood empty

it was easy
to introduce
your difference

Ultimately however, it is an exciting feeling of openness that asserts itself, a complex, implicative language shattered at the Logos-point and flowing through a self-in-process. The insistence is that the root issue not be feminism but the writer as a problematized and de-centered "effect" inside a sexual code that has retreated from (and advanced beyond) the genital model it supported. At this point Father, Man, Capital, God and Word all become indifferent and undifferentiated terms and writing shows itself to be less an occupation than the profoundest of human conditions. On these half-hinted post-feminist margins Lemire Tostevin comes close to Blanchot, Bataille, Artaud and Lacan — all men, but men who perceived the fundamental political conspiracy between class, type, genital definition and writing:

> from the beginning
> there were two words
> always
> one word then another
>
> twice removed

The book's mytho-fictive subtext is clearly Oedipus and the narrative suggestion is of a body defabricated between two competing codes. Whatever else the self might be it is not a unitary subject and it is fitting that the book subverts the prefatory message of its cover:

> In Lola Lemire Tostevin's *Color of Her Speech*, two of the central issues of contemporary Canadian discourse, bi-lingualism and feminism, are used as metaphors for the struggle we all must make to recover our own personal speech, a way of reaching each other.

Sovereign negation takes place at the end of the book where the Oedipal space becomes the linguistic space across which meaning asserts its contradictions. These are the book's last lines:

> between
>
> the way I speak
> the way I spoke

Despite the capitalized pronoun (which should be seen as alluding to the opening poem's lines "mais jamais on se défait de nos cicatrices Majuscules") the struggle here is towards the invention (inter-vention) of a new tense to set against the tenses of grammar and logic. This is the scene of the cicatrice, the gynocographic wound that opens out into itself; invaginates to mark an atopia, a no-place too intensely present to be anything but a gap, a space, a deleted mark or wound arising from the increasing withdrawal of the initial cut. These are not the metaphors of struggle, nor the recuperation of personal or social speech, but the contradictions in the system of a graphic economy that lead to writing's basic terror: that ultimately words are nothing but an ontological collapse into death, rhythm and spacing where not only the writer but also writing dies, so that the writer that has been could never be.

1983

Bill Bissett:
A Writing Outside
Writing

This essay investigates a single aspect of Bissett's work: the aspect of excess and libidinal flow, of the interplay of forces and intensities, both through and yet quite frequently despite, language; the flow of non-verbal energies through verbal domains that registers most often as a sheer libidinal will to power, a schizop(oetic)hrenic strategy to break through the constraint mechanisms of grammar and classical discourse in general. As such this is a very immanent, yet vague, aspect to be considering. The flows are located inside the fissures of texts, constantly escaping in excess among — yet beyond — the words, urging an exploration of both language and anti-language and an awareness of the forces that refuse textualization. This, in turn, demands a specific approach to Bissett's corpus as a coagulate of forces to be experienced, but not elucidated, problematics to be felt but not reconciled. What is called for is an anti-reading of an anti-text with a forgetfulness in the face of what we do read. We must accommodate within ourselves the complex disjunctive syntheses of Bissett's energies to experience a schiz in the disjunctions of drives and repressions, bodies and books, language and its others. What will be traced is a mode of desire operating through and despite language; a mode characterized by its genealogy of forces, its disjunctive flowings of excess, its anarchic network of impulses, contradictory, often violent, and always indicative of a libidinal power.

LIBIDO

A libidinal complex is not a complex of representations but of intensive forces, active only in the realm of power in the most material, the most 'political' sense of the word.[1]

Clearly a *critical* approach will not suffice. What we need to take is a stance of affirmation to the texts, asserting from that stance our intensive relationships to the flows and drives released from the language.

> The libido is *force*, pure *power*. . . The libido does not have an image. It is not representable.[2]

Libidinal motions, arrestments and intensities are forces oppositionally related to the signifying graphism of writing. They are anti-imagistic decoding agents within the rigid system that is language. They jam all codes and in so doing de-repress the energies trapped inside the armouring of linguistic structures. As they manifest themselves in a text, they are intensely permeative, immanent and impossible to locate in any particularized reading.

Classical discourse inscribes the libido within language and the roots of this discourse are in a semiotics of containment: codified repressions (such as sentences), the language of command, causality and hierarchical exclusion. Classical discourse channels libido as a repressed flow within the rigid structures of grammar, giving pre-eminence to an "I - Thou" relationship of locutioner and auditor, fixing the flow along a pronominal axis from a speaking "Thou" to a receiving "I". Additionally this voice of command conflates with a voice of guilt to express itself as a demanding other within the subject (a Thou within an I). This is the voice of superego. Classical discourse is our inheritance; lodged within the bastions of grammar, it represses all manifestations of libido within rigid vessels of content, freezing energy into representation:

> Before our mouths, cunts and pricks and asses succeeded one another as swiftly as our desires; elsewhere, the engines we frigged had but to discharge and new ones materialized between our fingers; our clitoris-suckers rotated with the same speed, and our asses were never deserted; in less than three hours, during which we swam in unending delirium, we were ass-fucked one hundred times apiece,

1. Francois Fourquet, "Libidinal Nietzsche" in *Semiotext(e)* III, i, 1978, p. 71.
2. Ibid. p. 74.

and polluted the whole time by the dildo constantly belaboring our cunt.[3]

Sadean libido freezes into represented libidinal content. De Sade is anxious to *contain* the excesses within a reactionary machine of language, a machine that linearizes and itemizes the excesses as a highly differentiated, articulated and quantified movement: "in less than *three* hours. . . *one hundred* times apiece".

Bissett, in comparison, attempts to dislocate the scene of libidinal inscription and relocate it outside of language in the accidental, graphic imperfections of the sign:

bissett/71 [4]

3. Marquis De Sade, *Juliette*, tr. Austryn Wainhouse (New York: Grove Press, 1968) p. 975.
4. Bissett, *Vancouvr mainland ice & cold storage* (London: Writers Forum, 1973).

In Bissett inequalities and differentiations tend towards their
disappearance (become ignored) permitting reabsorption into
the indiscriminate liquidity of language-flow. What characterizes
the violated chains of grammar in his work is not the violation
per se, but rather the resultant metamorphosis, the constant
conversion and reconversion within an undifferentiated libidinal
mass.

>   notes sounds each one change universe
> pop explosions stretches of biological
> natural being without intention or
> objectifying ordr. *the bloodstream*
> burp. fullness. food. expulsion. shit. th glands
> like baubuls balancing the meat. flesh. star.
> shining. it is open and closd. the spine. th
> ribs. cumming. cumming. it keeps it
> cumming all th time.
>   from all directions.[5]

This is language used first and foremost as an apoptuic instrument, a literal expulsion of material signs as if it were the
ejection of a harmful substance. . . expulsion. . . shit. . . th
glands. . . cumming. . . cumming and beyond the ideational
content and the temptation to simplistic analogy (language =
bloodstream) is the less tractible intensities that mutilate the
conventional physiognomy of language. The drive, for instance,
to remove the e from some articles but not others, that drive, in
general, to abolish standardization and rigidity in language.
Such a drive, operative as an intensity around language is the
agitation of the inscribed libido.

   Libidinal forces are inscribed configuratively upon the phonic, spatial and concrete surface of the signifier viz. upon the
most "present" order of language.[6] What Bissett is seeking is a
new body: the body of the scriptive or scriptional which is

5. Ibid.
6. Dadaist sound poetry — in the work of Ball, Tzara, Schwitters and Hausman —
confronted precisely that order, redistributing and displacing the familiarity of the
phonic surfaces, effacing orthodox meaning and ideational content and "de-repressing" the libidinal forces. Hausman especially, in his opto-phonetic concept of
notation (which utilizes different type styles and sizes to suggest different acoustic
volumes) attacked libidinal repression in its graphic form and opened up more than
any other dadaist new territories of the letter. In Hausman, we can note a double
attack on the reactive mechanics of language: semantic and somatic. An attack on
both the function and the body of the sign.

not book, canvas or page, nor the anatomical body of flesh, but a libidinal body, a body without form and receptive to the formless forces of flow and intensity. It is this search that lends peculiar focus to Bissett's remarkable schizoid gesture: the division of flow between performance and publication: the body of the artist and the body of the book. For libido seeks the betweenness and immanence of these body-forms and moves as a flow among them; it is the only way to explain Bissett's drives to both excessive performance and publication. The search for a body between the bodies of Bissett and the Book, an inter-text, an inscription of intensities upon, yet ultimately among, the stage and the book. For Bissett, there is no scene of the text, simply the undifferentiated flow between scenes.

THE SEMANTIC ATTACK: GRAMMAR

music

painting bartok led
zepplin from more conventional
dissonance to actual expression of
being th rites of spring was years
ago a field yu enter why can't
poetry why duz it have to be
lockd in th structure of 17th c.
bourgeoisie stuffd
chair art forms.
look how far
music &
painting
have gone always. but
when it cums
to words they
want th control th
proof of yr alleg
iance to th ruling class
of meaning[7]

Grammar is a repressive mechanism designed to regulate the free flow of language. Imposing its constraints upon non-

7. Bissett, loc. cit.

gravitational circulation, it realizes a centred (and centralized) meaning through a specific mode of temporalization. Grammatically realized meaning is a postponed reward attained by arrival at the end of a horizontal, linearized sequence of words. Grammar precludes the possibility of meaning being an active, local agent functioning within a polymorphous, polysemous space of parts and sub-particles; it commands hierarchy, subordination and postponement. In Bissett's writing however, grammar conflates the linguistic, political and libidinal planes; the repressive, reactive, structurizing forms and the de-repressive, active, destructional forces. In the face of grammar's logic of constraint Bissett's reply is discharge: the indiscriminate circulation of excess. The operation of desire through language then, strives to overthrow the grammatical order.[8] In this respect Bissett's "absolute" achievement would be the attainment of a purely fluid state of uninterrupted flow over the physical surface of the page; to produce an anti-production in the desire for free, aimless, libidinal discharge upon the surfaces of works conceived, not so much as products, than as de-repressed forces, the fundamental thawings of form.

        how do yu pik sum
      whun up on th street durin
        th day ium a city gypsy
          now iud bettr learn fast
           ive forgottn its bin
            so long since i made
             it with anywhun else
              last time yu wer
               gone i did but
                it wasint that much yu know   th
                 city is filld with pollushun
                today nd its fukan
cold[9]

The dominant feature is the alienated, isolated, atomized enunciator, a consolidated subjectivity (for monologue re-

8. In this regard we should keep in mind how an alienated desire is already present within the structural logic of the Sign itself. A Sign involves a "this" element standing for a "that" element, in such a way that the "this" (the signifier) is always separated from the "that" (the signified) for which it stands. As Lacan points out, it is desire that constitutes the very basis of the linguistic sign, a desire, moreover, inscribed upon the body of the signifier and incapable of fulfillment.
9. Bissett, *pomes for yoshi* (Vancouver: blewointment press, 1972).

circulates the discharge back into the conventional semiotic circuit of speaker and listener), the scenario of whose speech acts centres around frustrated expressivity. (I want to say it. . . I can't say it. . . therefore I've got to say it): a mechanism that renders the speaker the victim of the text. Bissett, then, contests context itself (seen above, for instance, in the insistence on personal orthography and spontaneous variations in margin which melt the hard lines of the poem's iconicity). The revolt is against the linguistic rules that bind unit to unit (margins, grammar, spelling). Accordingly language often *threatens* to emerge as its own graphic materiality but never actually gets beyond semantic disturbance. What remains is a shattered transparency, a fracture deep in the facade of the sign-function. A line such as "now iud bettr learn fast" whilst hardening the specificity and democracy of the phonic and confronting the rule of a standard codification, never totally transcends that standard, for we can always *read* this kind of Bissett. The more successful ruptures occur in those texts which offer a multiple reading path, choices offered at a fork in textuality that suggest a shattering of grammatical direction:

<pre>
                    voices
                thank yu   what
            did   yu   do   today
            its yr   gump ium   soling
            up   ther   then   not   any
            mor   did   he   say   was
            he   herd   to   cum   again
            how   rump   yr   like   i
        cud   yu   have   left   such
        ther   yu   ar   place   a
        to   tell th   truth   yu
        cud   hardly   call   how   ar
        yu   a   direkt   qwestyun [10]
</pre>

The vertical descent of the signifiers here, insists itself as an unspecified movement, a weakness in directional command to the reader's eye, presenting opportunities to enter, drift, to read the text as a partial experience, as a flow along one of several possible paths (vertical, diagonal, horizontal and combinations thereof) with the full knowledge that other paths are

10. Bissett, *pass th food release th spirit book* (Vancouver: Talonbooks, 1973).

being ignored.

Space in this instance, is explosive rather than cohesive, both articulating and confusing the plane of presentation, throwing message into indeterminacy. But the general impression in all of Bissett's lateral assaults on grammar is the economy of complaint and negative rebellion against the confinement in grammatical language, the preference to landscape and emblemize the problem of free communication rather than confront libidinally the very question of why communicate at all?

So there is a residue of the conventional and constraining that vitiates absolute excess; a sense of grammar always being there as a violated structure. A transgression, but not a liquidation, it remains seductively as its own witheld possibility.

> so yu dont need th sentence
> yu dont need correct spelling
> yu dont need correct grammar
> yu dont need th margin
> yu dont need regulation use of capital nd lowr case etc
> yu dont need sense or skill
> yu dont need this
> what dew yu need [11]

The salient issue in Bissett's assault on linguistic "correctness" is the freedom of writing from all needs, but with the unconscious drive to promote libidinal energies to the status of a writing outside of writing. In the tactics of *grammatical* violation, however, Bissett can only locate the desire for an outside within an inside thereby instituting the drives as ultimately frustrated gestures against repression. By smothering libidinal vocality in a graphism writing can only release a violence upon itself and implement a masochism of the text.

Though libidinal motion might seek inscription on a surface (a writing in libido rather than a writing about it) this movement forces the breakdown of several topographies. The surface is not contextualized — it is not a surface of, under, or around anything — but the flow of force itself, obliterating insides and outsides, and freeing writing from the domain of the categorical. As a libidinal vehicle, each poem stands as a precariously

11. Ibid.

autonomous sphere, threatening at any moment to decompose. Each poem is synecdochal to Bissett's entire Blewointment phenomenon in which publication is conceived as continuum, the indifferent production of production.[12] The books are not to be conceived solely from the viewpoint of their utility, but also from their character as flow, intensity and force: the urge of the words through and between the books, as if language, whilst inhering in their formats, releases a non-verbal energy above their surface. It is a hypothetical topography perhaps better considered as a disjunctive synthesis of a flow producing mechanism (the writer) and a draw-off mechanism (the book). Publication is Bissett's way of dividing himself up into parts, of articulating the excess of a Subject in desire. His books, beyond their character as exchangeable commodities, operate as macro-signs of segmentation. Until the publication of *Nobody Owns Th Earth* (Toronto: Anansi Press, 1971) marking as it does Bissett's capitulation before reification and his acceptance of the transformation of process into the commodity form, Bissett's publishing ethic was clear:

> writing is what yu write. yu need to
> print it yrself to make its freedom. yu
> cin do anything yu want or feel like
> with words.[13]

The entire early output of Blewointment Press was an uninterrupted flow of manuscript into print, a literal spillage of energy into book with a minimum of reification. The press provided Bissett with the machinery to activate excess within libidinal breakage. Seen in this light the books are not products, nor even the documentation of process, but rather an intransitive *circulation*: writing's distribution over its own surfaces, disfiguring known topologies and reducing difference to a state of chronic un-differentiation in which signs have become infractional upon their own structures. To isolate an individual book would thus involve a disavowal of the portage between them

---

12. ". . . the production of production, is inherently connective in nature: 'and. . .' 'and then. . .' This is because there is always a flow-producing machine, and another machine connected to it that interrupts or draws off part of this flow." Gilles Deleuze & Felix Guattari, *Anti-Oedipus: Capitalism and Schizophrenia*, tr. R. Hurley, M. Seem & H.R. Lane (New York: Viking Press, 1977) p. 5.
13. Bissett, *What Fukan Theorey*, (Toronto: grOnk, 8.8.n.d.).

and privilege a text as object not circulation. To affirm the passage of intensities it is not possible to actually read Bissett. What must be adopted is a comprehensive overview, a reading beyond a reading to affirm the intensity of desire. Books are unavoidable interruptive devices that draw off the energy from the continuum of Bissett's excess; they are states of meta-stability upon an extremely volatile vector and as such can quite legitimately be "passed over" by the reader who senses the libidinal drives passing through the texts themselves. By locating outside of reading and to read the reading that is thereby not taking place permits the reader to affirm the excess which seethes beyond the writing to a state outside itself. Which is to suggest that Bissett's anti-inscriptional strategies are matchable by the reader's own anti-reading that would affirm a motion, not comprehend a sense.

Sunday Work is a stapled collection of mimeographed poetry, collages, tipped-in brown paper, torn newsprint and bound-in pages from other books. As an assemblage of such kind, it achieves a near total obliteration between page and code. The drive here is uncompromisingly non-selective. As an absolute thrust to excess, it spills over every available surface, homogen-izing differences and detaching all its graphism from writing. For there *is no* writing in *Sunday Work*: a composition of random scatterings, inconsequential paginations, caught in a drift without origin or destination, as if a powerful force was making its exit from language through fissures in the verbal fabric.

> The greater the impulse toward unity, the more firmly may one conclude that weakness is present; the greater the impulse toward variety, differentiation, inner decay, the more force is present.
>
> (Friedrich Nietzsche)

In *Sunday Work* individual moments do not relate as cause and effect but exist as the particulars within abruptive flows. What is evident is the force behind the decay, or rather the force affirmed among the disjunctive movements of desire into excess. It is in those areas, where Bissett escribes his great disintegrative gestures (pages of language smothered beneath their own materiality, the obliteration of legibility by a flood of ink) that libido comes closest to a pure possession of language.

OVERPRINT AND THE VERTICAL ASSAULT ON LANGUAGE

Excess then, cannot be a theme; it can only operate as the force of an energy, a force *in spite of* language, constantly escaping through linguistic signs and constantly threatened by enclosure in them. Similarly, excess cannot be read *inside* the text but must be approached through an anti-reading constituting an overview of the corpus. Such an overview on the reader's part involves reconstituting reading as a con-conceptual act of affirmation that requires the reader to be both witness and co-participant within a discharge. This conceptualization of affirmative reading involves too the preclusion of all transitive desires, for in the condition of excess, desire cannot be directed to an object or purposeful goal (message, referential satisfaction et al) only submitted to the momentum of the outlay itself. Any semiotics of desire must return to the play of the surface of these texts, to their planes of force, flow and expulsion.

Overprint (the laying of text over text to the point of obliterating all legibility) is Bissett's method of deterritorializing linguistic codes and placing language in a state of vertical excess.[14] Overprint destroys the temporal condition of logic and causality, obliterating articulation and destroying message by its own super-abundance. In this way semantic property reduces to a common, un-differentiated equivalent graphic substance, whilst spatial difference is rearranged to intercept the material surface of the code causing it to physically collide and jam. Overprint is Bissett's main method of propelling the linguistic agents of repetition, redundancy and tautology onto the meaningless plane of graphic substance where words decompose into their own forces of explosion, incising the surface of the meaningful and immobilizing signs within syntactic suffocation.

As mentioned earlier, Bissett's lateral techniques of violation result in a contained transgression on the plane of the grammar

---

14. The technique of the overprint is not unique to Bissett; it was widely employed by many linguistic experimenters, most notably the British writer Bob Cobbing — see his *Bill Jubobe* (Toronto: Coach House Press, 1977) and the late D.A. Levy who termed this specific area of his work "experiments in disintegrational syntax". Most recent is *Veil*, by Charles Bernstein, whose approach is more textually grounded in the theoretical issues of current "Language Writing" than the less theoretically tractible Bissett, Cobbing and Levy.

and thereby fall short of producing an absolute excess. In the
overprinted texts, however, grammar is the victim of an anterior
expulsion which renders it an absolute non-issue.

> Even when immobile we are in motion.
>
>> (Merce Cunningham)

> What counts is to put the individual in flux. One must destroy the
> wall of the ego; weaken opinions, memory and emotions; tear down
> all the ramparts.
>
>> (John Cage)

> to dance in th centre we r th tor
> ment   th watcher   th watchd   in dance
>
>> (Bissett, *Drifting into War*)

> That which is, cannot contain motion.
>
>> (Friedrich Nietzsche)

Flow cannot contain identity and if identity can exist then
it must be reinscribed outside all fixity. To flow is to lose
oneself, convert "e" motion into "a" motion. The subject in
flux partakes the joyous torment Nietzsche points to in his
suggestion that life, to be living, must somehow be outside
of life. Overprint achieves a state of being without being-in,
a living without life, motion without definition, writing without
the written. In the text on text that avoids identity and
pulverizes all relations into totality, that cannot be read but
only seen, Bissett is beyond all specific poetics. Lack of aim,
lack of definition, lack of meaning. . . simply the need to
expel. . . waste produce. . . energy. . . excess. . . an economy
of total and irreducible non-conservation.

> image image images imagine imagings
> boroow borrow fi dar cankst th th thread tunnel wear fourty
> evoke evoke croak narrow thunder down bring what ever under
> stone bear thread ride th dusk n dusk n sand water forty in
> stone bear thread ride th dusk n dusk n sand water forty in
> cancer dead cum cum cum down when cum street sum cum cum in
> under cum cum in cum cum cum in cum cum win cum well within
> musical cum cum dance cum cum cum den cum cum out meatknight [15]

---

15. Bissett, *We Sleep Inside Each Other All* (Toronto: Ganglia Press, 1966).

In the above example, Bissett has activated excess by repetitions which reduce content to a flow of language matter, whose
intensity, redundance and non-utilizability make the comparison
to excretion more than a flippancy. What is at issue here is a
phonic liquidity that denounces the discreteness of sound and
meaning and holds all separated significations within an indifferent dissolution. Beyond the jamming of the message (through
fortuitous drifting, repetitions and meanderings) there is a
silence attained interior to the sound and found, not in the
space between words, but in the opaque materiality of their
graphic representation.

> He places a married woman upon a bed, encunts her while that
> woman's daughter, suspended above, presents him with her cunt
> to be licked; the next instant he effects a reversal and encunts the
> daughter while kissing the mother's asshole. When he has done
> licking the daughter's cunt, he has her piss; then he kisses the mother's
> asshole and has her shit.[16]

In De Sade's erotic economy the zone of pulverization is
still maintained inside a referentially "proper" code. The
consumption and circulation of excess (waste product, sperm,
blood, sweat) and the recharging of the discharge must all take
place within the uncontaminated contours of a classical narration. Whilst approaching the ineffable in atrocities De Sade
can never question the pristine, virgin power of representation.
Bissett, in contrast, affirms excess at the very margins of
inscription where meaning (structured as it is upon the
oppositive relationships of signs) disappears inside its traditionally vehicular support. The materiality of language is that aspect
which remains resistant to an absolute subsumption into the
ideality of meaning. It is Bissett's achievement to have
motivated this "aspect" into a powerful, agonistic disposition.
To see the letter not as phoneme but as ink, and to further
insist on that materiality, inevitably contests the status of
language as a bearer of uncontaminated meaning(s). Ink, as the
amorphous liquid that the word and letter shape into visible
meaning, is shown to be of the order of a powerful, anti-
semantic force, perhaps the "instinctual" linguistic

16. Marquis De Sade, *The 120 Days of Sodom*, tr. Austryn Wainhouse & Richard
Seaver (New York: Grove Press, 1966).

"unconscious" repressed within writing.[17]

Language as an unconditional project removes all epistemological ground. The demands of excess necessitate inscription in the impossible, outside of writing in the aimless, purposeless economy of the total. Only in renouncing the lineal in his visual texts does Bissett succeed in an uncompromising demolition of the word.

> If there remains anything hellish and truly accursed in this day and age, it is to dally artistically with forms instead of being something like victims who are to be burned and who make signs above their pyres.   (Artaud)

Through excess — the super-abundance of a presence extended beyond itself to deluge the categorical boundaries of tense and difference — Bissett becomes the victim of his own writing's sacrificial non-utility; investing no meaning and needing nothing beyond the need to expel the need to write.

1976-78

17. Perhaps Bissett's greatest manifestation of these instinctual drives is his constant refusal, in the books before *Nobody Owns th Earth*, to standardize his modes of linguistic assault. The books move from relatively clean mimeography, through combinations of clean and dirty, to books that are hardly legible. What must be kept in mind at this point is that the coupled opposition legible/illegible always marks the site of desire production.

Seven Part Theory

We say a character is drawn when a character is written in the action of instituting or establishing setting on foot or in operation foundation ordainment in the fact of written characters. Being instituted anything thus isolated is meaningful at its optimal level of insufficiency and so the word arrives (with us) at the giving of form or order to a narrational base or thing in an orderly arrangement regulation. We can even now in a speech we are writing speak of speaking into the fictive base of a plot cutting into the characters that then cut out into the established order by which anything is regulated by a system or a constitution of their own topographies. The partial realization in all of this is how it goes or reappears. Even now a character is written when a character is described by means of establishment in a charge or position. Syntax. Written characters. That is what it means by fiction training instruction education teaching. That is what the story formulates. The key factor in semantics is the transformation of word into world through institution. The definition is an imbed. There is elsewhere the action of a space between theme monotony and incident. There is something else as well. Usually pluralized. Then it disappears. We say a character has insight when a) elements of instruction = first principles of a science or art. The reader sees his plans by a technique of transformation that involves b) a book of first principles an elementary treatise or the optical replacement of what that story was. It is enough to say this is the study of a twofold movement. Points arise as reveries to form an established law custom usage practice organization or other element in the political or social life of a character from a rational node of contrary tensions a regulative principle or convention subservient to a twist into effects. These will declare themselves as words spoken onto the speaker's speech. Depth + time = the groundplan. The second movement begins with opposition for contrast. A dramade's hypostrodon. In any sense the character is only the general end of civilization. The core of a cube spreading outwards. A parallelogram of weight in change. A face wants to be lived in but spontaneous action is an error. As the fundamental keynote is the human personality there are patterns of human in significance. When all this happens there is death both in and out the story. A written character will prove this. Speaking onto drifts b) colloquial geographies of tension turning into something having the fixity or importance of a social institution in a death by naming. When I am the He who does the writing an author occurs as a thing without a well-established or familiar practice or object. An unstressed syllabic excess. Only then can the nouns murder through a lack of being. We say a character assassinates the story of the institution when a character is made to say I am the one who is coming to be in all of this. A name. Equated to an establishment organization or association. A noose instituted for the promotion of some object. There is something else as well. There is a plethora of wounds of public or general utility cut into the territorial contours of what a written character might write as religious charitable educational or spoken words. This cut might bleed not as a death is said to bleed or that he bled to death in chapter five but as a photograph is said to bleed off the frame of a church a school a college a hospital asylum reformatory mission or the like. This is the point the institution represents itself. This is the point that that appears. This way we say a death stands in for life as the rule of all writing. A literary and philosophical institution. The Royal National Life-Boat Institution. The Royal Masonic Benevolent Institution instituted 1798. The Railway Benevolent Institution. Elsewhere there is the mouth that speaks the passing of the mouth in the form of this act of severance. It is there where I was when I disappeared. Book: the name often popularly applied to the building appropriated to the work of a benevolent or educational or linguistic institution. Closed form from open set. And here a character might reincise a circumcision in the way a character in written characters might modify a photograph b) often occurring like INSTITUTE in the designations of societies or

associations taken and placed now inside these walls as this
magazine before me this image of a death into description the
hat felt the coat green the plastic meant to decorate the
language game he played in with the left arm stunted the
cigarette unlit name of Stephen first appearance in the
institution on page seventeen name of institution North of
Intention author Diodorus Siculus all said to lie on this page
that stands for this total IDEA. Elsewhere there is the writer
and the reader as the two sexes of each institution. His hat
felt. Her coat green. His left arm stunted her cigarette. Unlit
the photograph becomes the noun description killed when
this became a plot. There is something else as well. There is
the fact that this is said by some other institution elsewhere
in a space the writer of this hand describes as a reality cut off
from individual beings for the advancement of literature
science or art. We can say at this point that the photograph
can only show the reader's face made fiction and entered
in a writing written down in written characters. These characters are men of technical knowledge. These characters are
dead or of special education. This is where the camera begins
inside and outside the institution. Its definition is an imbed.
What writing is. Elsewhere this is read as the institution of the
history of character despite the fact that nobody is speaking.

1982

Nothing is Forgotten
but the Talk of How
to Talk: an Interview
by Andrew Payne

The following interview took place in January 1984. A large portion of the discussion centres on a group of writers (McCaffery among them) who were publishing in the journal L=A=N=G=U=A=G=E *between the years 1978 and 1982. While these writers form a very heterogeneous group, they share for the most part an interest in the question of reference, a question which they see as having its social and political as well as aesthetic consequences:*

> One major preoccupation of L=A=N=G=U=A=G=E has therefore been to generate discussion on the relation of writing to politics, particularly to articulate some of the ways that writing can act to critique society. Ron Silliman's early essay, "Disappearance of the Word/ Appearance of the World," ... applies the notion of commodity fetishism to conventional descriptive and narrative forms of writing: where the word — words — cease to be valued for what they are themselves but only for their properties as instrumentalities leading us to a world outside or beyond them, so that words — language — disappear, become transparent, leaving the picture of a physical world the reader can then consume as if it were a commodity. This view of the role and historical functions of literature relates closely to our analysis of the capitalist social order as a whole and of the place that alternative forms of writing and reading might occupy in its transformation.
>
> Bruce Andrews / Charles Bernstein

This concern has led them to an active engagement with both the corpus of late American literary modernism (Gertrude Stein, Charles Olson, Jack Spicer, Robert Duncan, Louis

Zukofsky, John Cage, Jackson Mac Low) and the work of a number of French theorists writing in the wake of Althusser (Roland Barthes, Jacques Derrida, Gilles Deleuze/Felix Guattari, Michel Foucault).

L=A=N=G=U=A=G=E produced 15 issues, the last of which appeared as a special issue of Open Letter *(Winter 1982). More recently an anthology was compiled and appeared from Southern Illinois University Press under the title of* The L=A=N=G=U=A=G=E Book *(1984).*

Andy: Steve, I'm interested in your affiliation with the L=A=N=G=U=A=G=E group. It strikes me that both in your own work and in the work of at least some of the others, there's been a shift from a sense of practice as critique of the referent (the referent seen as linguistic analogue to commodity fetishism) as you put it:

> at its core linguistic reference is a displacement of human relation-
> ships and as such is fetishistic in the Marxian sense. Reference, like
> commodity, has no connection with the physical property and
> material relations of the word as grapheme

— away, then, from a sense of text as a sort of structural symptom or representation and toward a sense of writing as production and positioning of desire:

> Sound Poetry is much more than simply returning language to its
> own matter; it is an agency for desire production, for releasing
> energy flow, for securing the passage of libido in a multiplicity
> of flows out of the Logos. To experience such (as a break-through in
> a break-down) is to experience the sonic moment in its full intensity
> of transience.

Steve: In the context of sound poetry (exclusive of electronic tape composition) desire has been prescribed within a vitalist metaphor, a biological model of energy release and discharge. In Canada sound poetry resorted, through an anxiety around its origin, to a very sketchy paternity in Dadaism and both Russian and Italian versions of Futurism and to a naive (and to my mind a largely irrelevant) grafting of biology, thermodynamics and psychology, the compound alliance of which served to establish a dominant mythology of Origin: a privileging of the pre-linguistic, child-sound, the Rousseauist dream of immediate-intuitive communication, all of which tended to a reinscription of a supposed pre-symbolic order in a present, self-authenticating instant. Rather than recuperation and presence I've come to see sound poetry through the economic notion of outlay. Such sound texts involve the subject, as a performative agent, along particular lines of obliteration in an economy in which "profit" necessarily entails "loss", and the closest theoretical articulation of this would be Georges Bataille's notions of "dépense" and "déjet". Most recently I've tried to deal with desire outside of sound performance, deal with it as a rupture within writing and resulting strictly from textual effects. Most important would be my investigations into the pronoun as a locus for a simultaneous break-down and recomposition (without prediction) of the Subject. This I first outlined in *Shifters* (Ganglia Press, 1976) and extended in *Panopticon* (Blewointmentpress, 1984). Desire in both these works formulates itself not simply as a refusal of the symbolic order (which would produce a non-semantic text) but as a motor discharge from any one of a number of signifiers whose centrifugality does not seek a final destination in some kind of referent or signified but in the free-play and nomadicity of first-order signifying relations.

Andy: One of the things which has interested me about the so-called L=A=N=G=U=A=G=E group has been its reluctance to announce itself as some sort of a "vanguard". A comment of Michael Gottlieb's (speaking of Charles Bernstein) seems to me indicative of this reluctance:

> Alternatively, or generationally, there arise forces in writing or art which feel constrained to either declare some irrevocable break or, equally apocalyptically, redemptionist "return" to some true or basic or original form. All too often the loudest of these declamations, upon examination, betray some educative flaw, the thinking up of which would reveal the transparency of the specious sort of originality so blandly asserted.

Despite the explicit disavowal of any modernist "teleology", I'm left wondering, however, if there isn't a tendency — especially in some of the earlier, more stridently "non-referentialist" pronouncements — toward a certain and characteristically avant-gardist "negativity", a relation taken toward the past which tends to produce a "foreclosure" rather than an opening up of possibilities.

Steve: Personally, I've never sensed such a tendency. What *L=A=N=G=U=A=G=E* provided was a forum for a diverse range of topics and investigations. Its thrust was always heuristic along a central axis: poetics, but an axis which inevitably included the relationship of poetics to the status of text as a social fact, hence the social and political content of much of the magazine. You'll find very little direct attack or agonistic positions taken up against specific writers. The gesture of *L=A=N=G=U=A=G=E* has always been a wide gesture: the relation of writing to reference, the relation of writing to politics and support for a "language-centeredness" that refused to take for granted the habitual linguistic "givens" of vocabulary, grammar and the ideological "neutrality" and critical inviolability of meaning. This constant refusal to bracket the semantic order quite naturally led to the production of texts that focussed upon the whole contestable issue of how meaning is made. The alleged negative posture of the early writing may derive from the focus of concern at that time: a specific critique of reference as the semantic dominant and a concentration on the working of sub-sentence units like the word and even sub-verbal configurations (as in the early work of Coolidge, Bruce Andrews' *A Cappella*, several sections of *Legend* and say, a work like David Melnick's *Pcoet*). Rather than the posture of an avant-gardism, *L=A=N=G=U=A=G=E* seems to have significantly effected a redistribution of the scene of knowledge (the site of so many wills to power!) and an alternative application of the writings of the Human Sciences (Barthes, Foucault, Deleuze, Derrida) in writing practice (viz. the production of literary texts) as opposed to their criticism.

It's chronologically very interesting. There was the early use of Barthes' *Elements of Semiology* and *Writing Degree Zero* which were such seminal documents for many contributors to *L=A=N=G=U=A=G=E*. Ray di Palma, for example, was using those books in 1968 in his creative writing programme at Bowling Green. Silliman was working with linguistic analogues to *Kapital* in the early 70's and I hit upon Derrida in 1970 before any translations appeared. All of this vast, anterior energy prior to the more fashionable ventriloquations of the salaried and tenured academics. Here then was a situation of

writers interested in a sort of risk quotient, interested in the
ratio of the clinamen, in catachresis and the creative gap
between digested comprehension and creative application. What
emerged was a creative freedom and bricolagic appropriation
of conceptual fragments, new hybridizing and grafting that
were permissible because of the absence of a heavy investment
in correctness and the old monologic pull of Truth and Totality.
L=A=N=G=U=A=G=E accordingly disseminated an intense heteroglossia (Larry Eigner, Nick Piombino, Ron Silliman, Jerome
Rothenberg, Dick Higgins, Brian Fawcett, Christopher Dewdney,
Abigail Child, Chris Mason, Barrett Watten, Tina Darragh,
Rae Armantraut, Jackson Mac Low, Michael Palmer, Michael
Davidson, *et al.*), all of which resulted in an intersection of
ideas, readings and re-transmissions. Important too, was the
articulation of that problematic interface between writing
and philosophy (an interface which seems to be Derrida's
central project) as two opposing, hegemonical discourses of
legitimation.   Writing (which I understand as the radical
spatialized manifestation of language) has a sustained ability to
perform and re-inscribe itself in "literature" as an operation
that doesn't require the philosophical legitimation of truth.
Literature is a specific, outlawed reagent situated deep inside
the philosophical adventure as Philosophy's radical Other. This
is why Derrida's *Glas* and Mallarmé's *Un Livre* are such
symplegmatic projects: vast and trembling, liminal works on the
precarious margins of two systems of knowledge, or rather of
two immense human projects: the philosophization of literature
(through a forced legitimation via truth and the rational) and
the poeticization of philosophy (through a strategy of dispersals,
pulverized pluralities, heteroglossia — the list could go on).
Perhaps that's what such poeticization actually is: the thorough
fragmentation of the Philosophic Space, which would then
consist of a kind of unordered order, a pluralization (into
something akin to Klein's "partial objects") of the notion of
Truth.

Andy: I wonder if we don't find in a lot of this work, a kind of
mono-dimensionality of "tone" . . . at times too, a lack of
humour.

Steve: Yes, Creeley mentioned this in a recent issue of *Sagetrieb*, although I'm not sure of the validity of any generalization here. I've personally come to see humour as a useful tonal-ideological destabilizer, an agent of relativization, dispersal and inversion (similar to Bakhtin's notion of the carnivalization of literature). Humour tends to operate as a visceral, or tactile investment upon the level of the verbal order; it is not entirely "of" language. In the work of most $L=A=N=G=U=A=G=E$ writers, one notes the orchestration of several discourses and a violent centripetality of contexts that often registers as a single, mammoth de-contextualization. This orchestration frequently includes "humour" and often the humour arises from the radical contextual shifts and new neighbourhoods of combination. Beyond the humour (and its admitted eruptive value), the de-contextualization of phrases and passages, the extreme reciting (and re-siting) of textual terms strikes me as having profounder political implications. Most especially, it leads a reader to the awareness of language's stratified nature and the dominant feature of discourse as being linguistic sedimentation. In the work of Silliman especially, the strategy of resituation and reinscription of different texts carries the weight of a gesture: the effective de-politicization of a discourse by a shift in context. Silliman's prose reads as vast, heterographic neighbourhoods, a sort of social experiment in verbal and discursive groupings. I would shy away from a full equation of this kind of valorization of the non-integrated part with either a philosophy of difference or a new variation on traditional humanism. For me, the extremely human power of heterographia is not its dramatic or anthropocentric inscriptiveness, but rather its ambivalent placement of language as partial discourses in contextual shiftings. This too, is dialogical rather than dialectical, for that third, synthesizing term of classic dialectic is neither petitioned nor produced. There is rather a grasp of essence as interaction, what Silliman has described as a language of the group, which is what our collaborative work *Legend* tries to develop.[1]

Andy: What about Clark Coolidge and Jackson Mac Low?

Steve: Coolidge comes largely out of Stein, from Stein's trans-

1. *Legend*, by Bruce Andrews, Charles Bernstein, Ray Di Palma, Steve McCaffery and Ron Silliman, (New York: L=A=N=G=U=A=G=E/Segue 1980).

formation of the sentence into pure temporality, so that suddenly, there's no surplus value in the sentence. The sentence is deprived of any syllogistic integration and what's left behind is a kind of sonic/phonemic inscription of time. That's why I think of Heidegger's *Being and Time* and Stein's *Making of Americans* as in a very real sense the same work. Coolidge's early work I found very important for developing Steinian notions on the level of the isolated word and even morpheme. Works such as *Flag Flutter & U.S. Electric, Ing, Clark Coolidge* and sections of *Space* condense temporality into a tremendous economy of word and placement. There is something at work in those books other than "syntax". For instance:

rice

once   car

            harp

Here each word shares two identical adjacent letters ("ce" and "ar") and this produces a complex ambivalence between rhyme, assonance and difference. Already, in this text from 1967 we find Coolidge exploring the non-descriptive, non-referential aspects of words. These poems are profoundly relational but the relations established are not those of logic and the signified. Rather, they are signifier "activities". In Paul Carroll's anthology *The Young American Poets* Coolidge speaks of "hardness", "density", "soundshape", "vector-force" and degrees of "transparency/opacity", which resonate as profoundly new categories for textual engagements. In his later works, *Smithsonian Depositions & Subject to a Film* (1980) and *Mine: The One that Enters the Stories* (1982), Coolidge extends these explorations to the unit of the sentence and produces extended paragraphs of non-integrated sentences:

> Outside a snow had finally come to weigh the bare board January. The two articles could exchange positions without disturbing the balance of that sentence. In that way a perfect equation is assured, as with a tuning fork. I have no problem with that. I'll leave as planned for Nantucket by night. The file drawer was shut on the spilled can of coffee or tobacco. No meaning is perfect.

In the work of the mid-70's, *The Maintains, Polaroid* and *Quartz Hearts* the focus seems intermediate: a concern for line, as both a supportive and fractive horizon for the sentence, but also a concern with the respective experience of a neutral (i.e. prose) line and a value invested line (i.e. the significant line-end of traditional poetry).

Mac Low, of course, studied Whitehead (as did Olson but with profoundly different consequences) and studied with Cage at the New School for Social Research. Mac Low's books have a similar phenomenological surface to those of many $L=A=N=G=U=A=G=E$ writers and he was a frequent contributor to that magazine. For the most part, however, his works are programmatic and chance generated, a strategy adopted by Mac Low to prevent "taste" and "choice" from entering the work. Many of the texts read marvellously and stand as semantic matrices inviting innumerable experiments in readership. Many are scored for performance and the "vocabularies" (texts constructed as a kind of expanded anagram from all possible lexical combinations and recombinations of the letters comprising a single person's name) have a marked effect as visual texts. Where Mac Low's work (as too, Cage's own mesostic workings of Joyce and Thoreau) is most vulnerable to critique is in the danger of a fetishization of chance procedure which tends to reinscribe meaning into textual economy as a kind of "eventist mana".

Andy: Yes, I would agree as regards a "fetishization of chance" and perhaps too — and this is I think not unrelated to what you referred to as a lack of "tone" — the absence of a sense of writing as the production of a "subject", in whatever problematic way we would want to understand that term. It's a loss of what Barthes would identify as the domain of "pleasure":

> Pleasure is linked with the consistency of the self, of the subject, which affirms itself through values of comfort, expansiveness, ease — and in my case, to give an example, belongs to the domain of reading classical writers. As opposed to this, jouissance is the system of reading, or of enunciation, by means of which the subject, instead of affirming, abandons itself, undergoes the experience of prodigality which is strictly speaking JOUISSANCE.

I'm certainly not advocating some return to the text of "classicism" or a renewed faith in the socio-symbolic contract. Nor would I want to minimize the historical significance of a writer like Mac Low. But reading him, and I'm tempted to say the same of Silliman, I can't help but feel frustrated by a certain programmaticness, a certain rigidity. Which, in a way, is nothing more than a confession that after fifty pages of *Stanzas for Iris Lezak* I'm getting bored.

Steve: I think Mac Low would authenticate boredom as a valid feeling, although, in the case of any programmatic as opposed to processual writing, the order of rejection must be a double order: the procedure *qua* procedure and the textual productions resulting from that procedure. Several readers, for example, would find great delight in the lack of a subject-presence in the *Stanzas*.

Andy: I wonder if that faith in the rigour of a method is not now exhausted? It was this rigidity I was referring to when I spoke of a "foreclosure of possibilities".

Steve: But aleatoricity is only posed as one of several valid possibilities for text generation. Chance and play are never absolute; they disengage and put stabilized value into doubt; this is the lasting importance of Mac Low's writings as social texts that indirectly open up the question of any idealist discourse. Their justification as specifically "literary" texts is a different but nonetheless articulatable matter.

Andy: Fair enough. To return to this question of "pleasure", this is of course something which is difficult to pose in critical terms. It, unlike desire, will not organize any revolutionary rhetoric. Remaining within the order of the "neurotic", it will always have eluded that vigilance, that heroism of the "modern". But herein perhaps, lies its value. Again, I would cite Barthes:

> Yet the position of pleasure in a theory of the text is not certain.
> Simply, a day comes when we feel a certain need to loosen the
> theory a bit, to shift the discourse, the idiolect which repeats itself,
> becomes consistent, and to give it the shock of a question. Pleasure
> is this question. As a trivial, unworthy name (who today would call
> himself a hedonist with a straight face?), it can embarrass the text's
> return to morality, to truth. To the morality of truth: it is an
> oblique, a drag anchor, so to speak, without which the text would
> revert to a centered system, a philosophy of meaning.

Steve: Yes indeed. I'm in absolute agreement. The danger in $L=A=N=G=U=A=G=E$ would be a certain ossification around the area of consensus and the rigidifying of its heteroglossia into a monologic canon. You phrased, I believe, the initial question in terms of a shift from a critique of reference to an incorporation of desire within my own texts. Personally, desire presents itself as an implication of text, not as a subjective force invested into the verbal order, or some kind of errant constituent of identity.

Desire, for me, is of interest in its capacity to supplement the aporia discharged by a conceptual abandonment of both subjective and objective terms in the signifying process; its "revolutionary" nature inheres in its basic intransitivity and yet, nonetheless, has a profound bearing on the issues of both an identity and a subject. A long-term personal obsession of mine has been a speculation into the possibility of equating Text with Self and Self with Text through a redirection of textual forces and implications back to the issue of the Subject.

To return to Cage for a moment. What seems to be the danger in the mesostics is a fetishization of perception, but I'm not convinced that this danger is *necessarily* entailed by the procedural nature of the composition. Cage's mesostics are actually transcribed readings, or meta-scriptive actions upon a perceived textual imbed. One is reminded immediately of Saussure's investigations of the Diphone and Mannequin structures in Saturnian verse and his studies of Homeric and Virgilian anagrams, that showed the anagram and anaphone to be not simply rhetorical devices but a linguistic surplus beyond all authorial intention, an inevitable fact of language.

In a curious way too, this stands comparison with Cage's own disproof of silence by demonstrating the unavoidable experience of sound. So one can read the mesostics as a parallel text to his silent piece *4'33"*; both pieces demonstrate the ontic impossibility of a cultural "given": that neither sound nor meaning can be foreclosed, that a certain surplus exists beyond silence and beyond a bounded text. I would, as a consequence, place Cage's mesostics on the border of a deconstructive stance.

It would be interesting to approach Cage's and Mac Low's writing through Wittgenstein's notion of the language game. Procedurality seems to suggest — if not the necessity, then

certainly the advantageousness of — a competent awareness
of the rules of the procedure. As a final word on Cage, the
mesostics, in emerging from model as opposed to structure
(exemplatistic in Dick Higgins' sense), or to phrase it
differently, emerging from a transcendentally governing
matrix, must of necessity subject themselves to a foreclosure.
They are still works within the confines of the bounded text
and can find a logical placement inside the long tradition
of the pattern poem, the *carmina figurata* or the *versus intexti*
of Optatian which create visual "warps" or distentions and
almost moire effects through a verbi-visual lamination over
the habitual lateralizations of a standard writing.

Andy: You referred to a "fetishization of perception". This I
think generally characteristic of late American literary modernism. "No ideas but in things" etc. I think, for instance, of
Zukofsky's reading of Wittgenstein in *Bottom on Shakespeare*,
the appeal to an attentive and loving gaze, a kind of pure
regard for the Other which is understood as being prior to
the violence of any interpretative act. "You need no tongue
of reason if love and eye are I — an identity." David Melnick
has commented well on this in his little essay "The Ought of
Seeing".

Steve: I think what you have is an ideological confusion
between pronoun and identity which graphematically shows
itself in the "hieroglyphic" status of the "I" on the page. I
doubt that Zukofsky and Olson ever really tackled the pronoun
as a shifter, ever explored it as a complex topography of
enunciator and enunciated with its fundamental status as a
geographical marker and not an identity; a "here" rather than
a "self".

Andy: Geography then, in terms of some sense of horizon?

Steve: In the sense of deferral and designation of place in a
textual logic. Zukofsky, despite some marvellous efforts to the
contrary, is still haunted by a notion of truth, of the real as
being attainable as a plenitude through the immediate, transparent communication of language, and it's this parousial
fallacy that infects his sense of identity. One thinks of

Objectivism and one has to think of Husserl and Derrida's obliteration of the phenomenological reduction. In contrast I would cite B.P. Nichol and *The Martyrology* as a more successful integration of a textual subject into the older narrative myth of the integrated, unitary Self. The powerful force of *The Martyrology* is precisely its irreducibility to a cohesive *oeuvre*. Attempts to reduce the work fall short and miss the importance of its writing as a practice within temporality productive of a play of open-ended meanings. Though less so than in say writers like Sollers or Silliman or Bernstein, Nichol nevertheless sees meaning as a highly local and volatile production within writing. I think the unfortunate metaphor he chooses is that of the poetic journal which seems to me to anchor it within the ideology of "good faith" that Barthes condemns; that wistful belief in a sort of recuperation of the processual within a calendrical frame, which to me links *The Martyrology* to those modernist texts that are still attempting to re-write *The Prelude*. The journal form is a buffer against loss, and as such a buffer redirects writing from a general to a restricted economy. It would be good, I think, to find a critic who is willing or capable of treating *The Martyrology* as a sign economy and not as a structure. It could be read, for instance, through numerous "economies": Freud's libidinal economy (especially pertinent would be Freud's notion of the double inscription); through Lacan's linguistic revision of Freud; through Bataille's general economy; through *Kapital* (meaning as a species of surplus value) and through Baudrillard's hyper-reality of simulation. All of these economies, I suggest, could be brought together and relativized.

Andy: It's interesting that you raise Barrie Nichol in relation to Zukofsky. What's interesting about both of them is their archaeological sense of language, a sense of the way in which history is deposited not simply in the order of the word but in syllables, letters . . . (Guy Davenport comments well on this with regard to Zukofsky's Catullus translations) . . . in Nichol the fact that history, etymology, etc. get recognized as a positive production rather than some kind of return to origin.

Steve: Yes. And it's significant, I feel, that both of these writers have done "renegade" translations of Catullus, preferring to preserve and carry over the phonic body of the original Latin at the expense of putting into play the semantic order. What's important to realize, however, in Nichol, is the use of and attraction towards writing's 'pataphysical dimensions. His writing is full of this ludic sense of life, the potentially infinite play of meanings, close at times to a carnivalization of writing, where privileged zones are challenged, inverted and playfully taken apart. Nichol inherits 'pataphysics from Alfred Jarry as The Science of Imaginary Solutions and it gains its greatest force and most effective application in *The Martyrology* as an erratic, unpredictable, gestural swerve "away" from linguistics and structuralism. If we take, for example, the following specimen from the end of Book IV, which I feel is representative of this kind of play:

```
                    capitals
        of earthly doubt
                        forgive us
        the d will out
        as the b drops thru its
        half note
                    configuration
        i is singing scale
        i hails you
        Hart works the 'e'
        reversing the conjunction
        find the d n a
        connective
                    the heart of
        writers & their obsessions
```

This is less a play on words than a play within them, a kind of analytic *lettrisme* that opens up the sign to its own paralogisms and its vertiginous potentiality to fracture and multiply its meanings. Accordingly, the classical reliance on a supposed one to one correlation between signifier and signified, between word and meaning, gets decisively shattered and meanings are inscribed as micro-reports upon their own precarious status as fixed terms. This dismantling of words as an integrated whole and the playful pursuit of the polysemous perversity of all the liberated parts achieves a centripetal dissemination that can be described as deconstruction.

Andy: Steve, to return to the $L=A=N=G=U=A=G=E$ group for a moment; I wonder if we might raise another question; one as to the sociology, or at least the sociality, of the production of literary (or language) works; a question of audience, of an intended political effect. I wonder if certain of these works don't evince a nostalgic desire for a situation beyond the socio-symbolic contract; a desire to establish themselves as what Kristeva would call "a semi-aphonic corporality whose truth can only be found in that which is gestural or tonal"?

Steve: I think it imperative not to institute a model exterior to the evidence of the texts themselves and what I've stressed throughout is an intense heterogeneity among the so-called $L=A=N=G=U=A=G=E$ writers, a heterogeneity that possibly reflects the current "Philosophy of Difference" (emerging on both sides of the Atlantic) and which Foucault announced in his introduction to Deleuze and Guattari's *Anti-Oedipus* back in 1972. Its theoretical and methodological thrust can be traced back to the pioneer deconstructions of Nietzsche and Marx (the latter's status as a "deconstructionist" albeit limited and with strict reservations would nevertheless make the subject of a wonderful interview)[2] and most specifically the concerted de-mythologizing of numerous concepts to show their covert and irreducible basis in figuration. The early works of Silliman, Andrews, Bernstein and myself were overtly political, and the Politics of the Referent issue of *Open Letter* (1977) still stands as a diverse position paper on our work and conclusions up to the middle of the 70's. The political thrust there was quite clear: towards a foregrounding of the reader-writer relationship as both a diachronic (hence a changeable) relationship and as a fundamentally socio-political configuration. From this we worked by way of analogy and homology towards an exposure of fetishism as an operation within the domain of representation and reference and we attempted to return the

2. This interview took place before coming across Michael Ryan's excellent book *Marxism and Deconstruction A Critical Articulation* (Baltimore: Johns Hopkins University Press, 1982). Ryan grids several areas in Marx's thinking that articulates similar concerns in Derrida: metaphysical naturalism, the differential nature of production and positivism to cite but three. Ryan describes both Derrida and Marx as practitioners of differential analysis "a mode of investigation (and exposition) which treats the stable and fixed facts and entities of positivist science as effects of interrelating forces and structures where transformations required extended exposition and a continuous displacement of the categories" (p. 61).

scene of readership to the realm of semantic production. (How can we involve the reader in the making of the making of meaning)? In hindsight, I can admit to certain naiveties in that approach. This writing was all produced before any of us had discovered Baudrillard's seminal work *The Mirror of Production* which challenged with an incontrovertible conviction the subliminal valorization of production and use value as a privileged positional opposition to consumption and exchange. In the light of the Baudrillardian "proof" that use value is but a concealed species of exchange value, I would say now that the gestural "offer" to a reader of an invitation to "semantically produce" hints at an ideological contamination. I've also come to feel that the majority of $L=A=N=G=U=A=G=E$ texts yield great rewards from a double reading, that first announces them as a political gesture *within* the literary text, offering this inward sitedness as a linguistic analogy to the political, which in itself matures as a statement somehow "across" a distance; and secondly, from a reading that indicates their status, not as forms or structures, but as operative economies. Here, the notion of expenditure, loss, the sum total of effects of a general economized nature, would emerge to relativize the more "positive" utilitarian ordered reading. I would deny throughout, however, the appeal to "a semi-aphonic corporality" or of any kind of nostalgic return to a pre-sociosymbolic matrix. If any area of recent text production is susceptible to such a criticism it would be that variant strain of sound poetry that anchors itself in performance, suports the relegated status of the written text as an inert, secondary figuration of the "breathed instant" and which draws its ideological defence from a certain strain of 19th century vitalism that persisted through Dadaism and Futurism up to the early work of The Horsemen and Owen Sound. Among the $L=A=N=G=U=A=G=E$ writers there was a common feeling that the return of "meaning", as a post-philosophic operation within the activity of discourse, to a productive rather than consumptional zone of action, entailed a political gesture of the deepest and most contemporaneous urgency; that it effected a diachronic change in the reader-writer relationship (which, as a change *per se*, seemed to entail a political assertion of both roles being history specific) which opened up the possibility (appealing at the time and still appealing to many) of a rehumanization of the linguistic sign.

As to your point regarding a resistance to the symbolic. At no point do I feel that this has occurred or is occurring. What is resisted is the integrated, syllogistic momentum of the symbolic when the momentum is reinvested into compound meaning(s). And even further, the resistance restrains the philosophic (metaphysical) notion of an unmediated, transparent connection with "reality" at the other side of language. This, more than anything, has been the philosophical restriction upon language for thousands of years and whose complicity with the capitalist mode of production is evident in countless philosophic texts from Plato through Descartes to Searle and Austin. So a Politics of Discourse is everywhere present in $L=A=N=G=U=A=G=E$ writing as a text-by-implication. But what emerges strongly in the work of Silliman, Bernstein and Andrews, among several others, is not the Politics of Discourse but politics *as* discourse. If there is to be a rhetorical imposition on all of this, it is to effect a political implication and not imply a political effect. As regards Kristeva's mention of truth in the citation, I would stress that the intention among contemporary writing must always be towards an utter dismantling of the notion of TRUTH as anything exterior to the signifying practice; and to suggest by this that truth is to be understood not as the destination of a referential function in language, but as a writing production, a writing effect *per se*.

Andy: To a certain extent we've already raised the problem with Cage and Mac Low, of a fetishization of chance, of what we might speak of as a valorization of process, a writing understood as being without subject, memory, history . . . is this not, in a certain way, the same problem we encounter in Olson, or at least a particular reading of Olson, one which concentrates on, say, his objection to Milton's "disregard" of syllabic quantity, or in his discussion of the sentence as the subordination of the individual signifying unit (word/syllable) to an abstract structuring? (This is, for instance, the general tenor of an essay that Don Byrd wrote for $L=A=N=G=U=A=G=E$). It seems to me that this whole question of prosody/syntax needs to be thought more carefully, that what gets referred to as hierarchization imposed by grammar, the sentence etc., needs to be understood not as some imposition alienating the word or syllable from the univocity of its appearance in the mouth or on the page through a process of abstraction, attribution of exchange value, whatever (and here what's being appealed to is, I think, a notion of syllable as a kind of pure idiom, some absolute indissolubility of form/ content). This appeal is perhaps part of a more general ideology of "production", which ideology neither Baudrillard nor Derrida have failed to recognize:

> But we must beware: this formula, "la chose est le reçit", implies no performative presentation or production. What we have here is not that conclusion, readily drawn these days, using a logic of truth as presentation substituted for a logic of truth as representative equivalence, according to which new logic the narrative is the very event that it recounts, the thing presenting itself — present itself — by producing what it says.

It seems to me that what goes unrecognized in this ideology of production is the internality of "coding" to the signifying "instant", an internality which is responsible for the hetero- geneity of that "instant", the impossibility of its ever being present to itself.

Nor could this valorization of process be distinguished from a certain strain of American transcendentalism (from Whitman, Pound, right through to say Cage or Ammons), where the subject is understood as attaining to an absolute integrity, an identity of body/consciousness in each of its signifying instants.

Steve: The subject of history (its dictates and its availability to the act of writing) is a complex one with Olson. There is first that obvious sense of history at work in his poems, of history as "fact", as document, to be worked with and turned over. This gives you the strong Comtean, positivist strain in his work. Document, in Olson (and perhaps more so in Pound) operates as a kind of syllable, a unit of unmediated plenitude, reconnecting it with a displaced present. This is decidedly not history in the way that Gibbon, Hegel and Marx are history. Olsonian history, this documentary- syllabic history, traces back to Herodotus, the most notoriously "unreliable" of Greek historians, whose sense of history was the transcription of "hearsay". Olson's attraction to Herodotus is an attraction to that same mechanism that Derrida exposes in Plato: metaphysics' appeal to a double standard of writing, to the lower, debased, materialist sense of marks on a page, which (in Plato) was submitted to a meta-phoristic *aufhebung* that recast it as a "purist" writing of truth's marks in the "soul" and "heart". Herodotian history is history that aligns itself "innocently" with speech. I would say, in fact, that it aligns itself *identically* with the *syllable,* as a species of Plato's metaphoric writing. But history's other presence, should I say, the other history's presence, is experienced through those grammatological notions of space, gap, deferral and trace structure. And this history locates in writing's debased profile, within the graphesis of its temporality and spacing. This space is the radical other to the syllable; it constitutes history's blank side, history's mutism, and precisely because it resists any logocentric appropriation. Olson's affinities with certain theoreticians of German Romanticism has so far gone unregarded, but the following brief passage from Friedrich Schlegel's *Lectures on the Philo-sophy of Language* could have prefaced any anthology of projective verse:

> Properly syllables, and not letters, form the basis of language. They are its living roots, or chief stem and trunk, out of which all else shoots and grows. The letters, in fact, have no existence, except as the results of a minute analysis; for many of them are difficult, if not impossible, to pronounce. Syllables, on the contrary, more or less simple, or the complex composites of fewer or more letters, are the primary and original data of language. For the synthetical is in every case anterior to the elements into which it admits of resolution. The letters, therefore, first arise out of the chemical decomposition of the syllables.

We will trace this organicist metaphor, this appeal to arborescent analogues through Hamann, Herder, Humboldt down to Olson's "dance of the intellect" and "the HEAD, by way of the EAR, to the SYLLABLE / the HEART, by way of the BREATH, to the LINE". There are rich, deconstructive pickings here in this particular style of reasoning which involves, as its under-lying matrix of assumption, the privileging of all anteriority as a positive value and a binding of various satellitic terms and notions to this matrix: syllable-synthesis-origin-cause = speech-

breath-presence-immediate-being-as-truth; set in opposition to
the compound matrix of writing: letter-analysis-posteriority-
meditation-imprint-corpse-as-death. We would not wish to deny
the intense and revolutionary polyphony of *The Maximus
Poems* or *The Cantos*. But what needs address in these great
works is the radical blind spot around the issue of vocalization
per se, a primary absence of rigour at the conceptual collision
of *text* and *voice*. Behind Olson's essay on "Projective Verse"
and "Letter to Elaine Feinstein" is a sense of communication
as still being exchangist in nature. Something is transmitted
and received, and writing's "negative" relation to outlay and
death is never admitted nor received. Olson seems oblivious
to writing as a fundamental trace structure in which each
"syllabic instant" must always be a breached presence. For
the presence that writing institutes is always a presence that
announces an irreducible absence within the very system of
the sign. This is the crux of representation and its current
historical obliteration, that whenever a term (X) stands for
(or represents) another term (Y) then neither term can be
present. X is always standing for something else and so is
never there, whilst Y, in being stood for, is always delayed,
postponed and deferred from being there. After *Of Grammatology* (part of which the above is an absurdly simplistic
reduction) this irreducibility of the space, the gap, the
breach, assumes a far more fundamental status than any
pure idiom of the syllable.

Andy: To return to your earlier remark regarding a fetishization
of chance, perhaps we can say that the subject masters the
other, masters chance, by its very availability to contingency
(for every atom belonging to me as good belongs to you,
etc. . . .). Hence, an ideology of *openness*, a failure to recognize
the internality of death to the economy of production. I would
want to hesitate then, before conceding to any simple
characterization of narrative as surplus investment. [This refers
to a remark made elsewhere in conversation]. In a way, yes.
But then what else? You've spoken elsewhere of two of your
own works, *Panopticon* and *An Effect of Cellophane*, as rein-
vestigations of both the sentence and of narrative. You've also
made the comparison with Sollers (Philippe) whose novels
Kristeva refers to as "a listening to the time of Christianity".

I wonder if we are not dealing with an Augustinian subject, a subject of "memory"/subject of "science" bifurcation . . . something analogous I think to the Freudian distinction between "truth-work" and "knowledge language". So the subject of "memory"(I who I am insofar as I have accomplished heterogeneity, I who am my Father in me, my true self) this impossible subject as eschatological object, at once organizes the order of the symbolic, of science, and at the same time produces it as an incessant rupturing. This subject, which is about a relation to Death, to Law, this subject is still in a way a subject of "castration", of *aufgehoben* . . . surplus investment? . . . maybe . . . let us say a necessary co-extensivity of desire and its repression. Which is perhaps what Lyotard is getting at when he says "the death instinct is the reason why machines can only work by fits and starts" and "the 'Ah, not to have been born' . . . is not merely admissable, it is a necessary component of desire". Or Kenneth Burke, more succinctly, in his misquotation of Keats: "Beauty is turd, turd Beauty".

Steve: The deepest implication in Freud, and the one which Lacan has best elucidated, is the radically textual nature of the psyche. We both inhabit and inhibit an unconscious that is structured as a language. This projected emergence of a post-Freudian "textual" subject seems to be of critical importance. It puts the very notion of a "subject" in doubt and, at best, poses that subject on the ruined concept of a Self. The latter being no longer tenable as a unitary whole, nor even as a memory/science bifurcation, I think we best look for a viable notion of subject in something like Kristeva's notion of a subject-in-process within an instinctual and symbolic economy. Part bound, part articulated by a verbal order (the self of the proper name, the name of the Father in the Son) and yet incessantly striated and (as you aptly put it) ruptured by instinctual drives that surge through the linguistic order and are felt in (but never identified as) rhythm, intonation; this subject as plurality will haunt, repeat and delete simultaneously the numerous eschatographies that inhabit and (at this historic moment) describe the act of writing as thanatopraxis. Against the post-modern valorization of process it would offer the notion of a *complete dispensibility of procedures*. The subject in process is not to be identified then with the text as process.

In the death of Modernism via Olson there has been a murder denied. And to finally revert this to the sexual: let us remember that the high priest of the syllable makes no mention of woman in *The Maximus Poems*. As Kristeva puts it:

> Being of language? It even calls on me to represent it. "I" continually makes itself over again, reposits itself as a displaced, symbolic witness of the shattering where every entity was dissolved. "I" returns then and enunciates this intrinsic twisting where it split into at least four of us, all challenged by it. "I" pronounces it, and so "I" posits myself − "I" socializes myself.

With the subject set in process (jouissance, death) we have lost the traditional sense of Self but gained a Text. And Text is a body. Let me end this with another quotation from Kristeva:

> Remember Artaud's text where the black, mortal violence of the "feminine" is simultaneously exalted and stigmatized, compared to despotism as well as to slavery, in a *vertigo* of the phallic mother − and the whole thing is dedicated to Hitler. So then, the problem is to control this resurgence of the phallic presence; to abolish it at first, to pierce through the paternal wall of the superego and afterwards, to reemerge still uneasy, split apart, asymmetrical, overwhelmed with a desire to know, but a desire to know more and differently than what is encoded-spoken-written. . . .
>
> The other that will guide you and itself through this dissolution is a rhythm, music, and within language, a text. But what is the connection that holds you both together? Counter-desire, the negative of desire, inside-out desire, capable of questioning (or provoking) its own infinite quest. Romantic, filial, adolescent, exclusive, blind and Oedipal: it is all that, but for others. It returns to where you are, both of you, disappointed, irritated, ambitious, in love with history, critical, on the edge and even in the midst of its own identity crisis.

1984

Under the Blowpipe
: George Bowering's
Αλλορhαηες

Allophanes begins with a citation, claimed to be dictated to
the author by the deceased poet Jack Spicer: "It began with
a sentence heard in the author's head: The snowball appears
in Hell every morning at seven. It was said in the voice of
Jack Spicer".[1] *Allophanes* then, emerges beneath two signa-
tories, two proprietors: the author (George Bowering), whose
proper name will authenticate the book, and a dictator, Jack
Spicer, a disembodied voice, whose proper name re-formulates
the deceased, primal father of Freud's *Totem and Taboo*
and who, as a spectral subject, haunts the text's temporal
unwindings to a degree that can never be fully ascertained.

> Pretending to be inaugural, the sign could only endlessly mime its
> own circularity, since it has already constituted to de-signate — to
> whom? — its own birth. Mythology imprisons this tautological
> figure into that of a Monster, a Sphere, an Egg where the
> nothingness unites with Being, and whose multiple names — Noun,
> Kneph, Okeanos, Ouroboros, Aion, Leviathan, Ain-Soph, etc. —
> arbitrarily conjure up that which in *principle* has no appelation,
> as though to deny to thought the access to its own silence.[2]

To these names we will add the snowball in hell, as a blank, yet
eponymous space, placed in *Allophanes* prior to all metaphoric
operation and akin to an arche-sentence, providing the *condition*, not the sense of, *Allophanes* as a writing. To read this work

1. From the jacket copy of *Allophanes* (Toronto: Coach House Press, 1976). What is
dictation if not the reverse movement of the sign? the inverse pattern of desire?
Spicer's sentence will function as a remote control over the institution and arrangement of the signifiers. This too, will constitute the textualization of an invisibility as
the act of spacing; the supplementation of a *distance* by a *difference*, from a felt
absence "present" to the space of absence itself.
2. Jean Paris, "The Writing Machine" in *Sub-Stance* 16, 1977, p. 9.

is to re-trace the gap between a dictation and a written series of repetitions. Almost. From its initial appearance the snowball in hell will extend a profound ambivalence. Reappearing and permuting, it will always be that to which the work is attached yet from which it is constantly escaping. At times the condition of change, at times the change itself, the sentence will never escape its temporal predicament and will raise constantly the question of the productivity of its own significatory ground. As Jean Paris puts it "the question which begins here no longer springs from the sign because, on the contrary, it supposes it; it no longer concerns in criticism, either the signifier or the signified, either speech or writing, but the gap itself from which these will be engendered, or, if one prefers, this articulation whose other name would be: *change*".[3] This moment, where space explicates itself, will be the moment in which hell's snowball is born into writing *as a writing*; a dictated and a written moment that asserts its identity as its own rupture, signalizing the opening of the moment into that multiplicity of which *Allophanes* will be the trace.

> The snowball appears in Hell
>   every morning at seven.
>
>   Dr. Babel contends
> about the word's form, striking
> its prepared strings
>   endlessly, a pleasure
> moving rings outward thru
>   the universe. All
>   sentences are to be served.
>
> You've tried it & tried it
>   & it cant be done, you
> cannot close your ear —
>
>   *i.e.* literature
> must be thought, now.

3. Ibid. p. 11.

                    Your knee
                    oh
                    class
                    equal
                            poet
        will like use a simile because he hates
        ambiguity.

                    The snowball says it:
        all sentences are imperative.[4]

2

Allophanes is a small book   (4¼" X 8")   whose cover will
detain us for quite some time. Its central design is a triangle
cut out from the surface of the paper. In the space of this
triangle is a text comprising geometric shapes and symbols
suggestive of pictographs or hieroglyphs and all decidedly non-
phonetic. Through a fold in the paper, the cover's underside
becomes a surface. The triangular excision in this way serves
to frame a part of the cover's unexposed side. As a result of
this cut and fold, the cover's recto-verso distinction collapses
and a profound discontinuity is produced upon the cover's
plane. An interiority is presented as external and the notion
of page is immediately doubled (opening the cover to meet
the title page this other surface is not seen).[5]
    The triangle is resonant with associations. It is foundationally
letteral, being both the diagrammatic relation of signifier to
signified through a referent apex (as outlined in Saussure's
Course in General Linguistics) and doubling too the actual
form of the Greek letter *delta*. The triangle also appears at
various points within the moving body of the poem. It is the
horizontal effect of the tent (at the end of section VI) and reappears in the triangular torso of the pictogram of St. Arte
(Astarte?) that concludes section V:

---

4. *Allophanes*, Section I.
5. We might note, in passing, that the cover in this way reveals its material *from the
back* i.e. the copulatory position of the Wolf Man's parents as Freud recounts it in his
famous case history. See, Sigmund Freud, "From the History of an Infantile Neurosis"
in *Standard Edition*, tr. and ed. James Strachey, Vol. 17, p. 1-122. It is also the
direction of weaving (i.e. textuality). We will sense Freud throughout *Allophanes* as
a voice beyond the absent one of Jack Spicer.

Letter, talisman, Christian trinity, pyramid, inverted pubis are all evoked in this framing shape, which is also a material lack of a surface.

At the end too, of this geometrical labyrinth will be a human throat. My larynx, placed between the trachea and the base of my tongue, forms a considerable projection in the middle line. It presents at its upper zone *the form of a triangular box*, flattened behind and at the sides and bounded in front by a prominent vertical ridge. Its interior houses my rima glottidis in the form of a narrow *triangular* fissure. Also the portion of my laryngeal cavity above my true vocal cords is broad and *triangular* and named the vestibule. The superior aperture of my larynx is a *triangular opening* in close proximity to which are situated the cartilage known as my cuneiform. My rima glottidis is an elongate fissure between the inferior (i.e. my true) vocal cords and sub-divides into my glottis vocalis (the vocal portion) and my glottis respiratoria (the respiratory part).

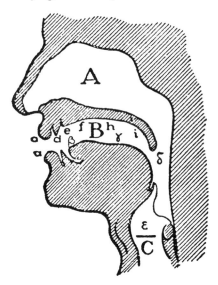

When vocalic activity is not taking place (for instance, in the condition known as writing) my glottis vocalis is *triangular*. During extreme adduction of the cords (for instance, in the condition known as speaking) it is reduced to a linear slit and my glottis respiratoria assumes a *triangular* form. Of the five muscles of my vocal cords, the crico-thyroid is of a *triangular* shape. Already, in the cover's constitutional ambivalence we are figuring the withdrawal of speech into the labyrinthine *tactics* of writing. Clearly this cover lacks an innocent, utilitarian function of protection (partly concealing, partly announcing the promised interiority). To repeat: the cover folds to bring its back into visibility through a gap in the front, presenting a physical lack that shows more than it would had the surface been complete. An instability is thereby introduced into the nature of the surface which now carries tri-partite implications as a cover, a frame and a frivolous subversion.[6] The non-phonetic "text" thus framed in the triangle participates in the system of the cover without actually being a member. Bowering's (Spicer's?) initiatory sentence is framed precisely in the way these non-phonetic characters are framed "inside" the cover. As a received dictation, it enters the textual economy as a perverse "fold" in the writing and similarly participates without membership. Rendering *all* quotations in *Allophanes* contaminated, this sentence further prevents the writing from being a first order operation. The writing cannot even gain an innocence but must inscribe itself and its implications inter-textually, with a constant referral to another voice beneath the surface of the writing, held absent but constantly recalled inside of the writing's shifting scenes, which work ambivalently throughout the poem to include the exclusion of this sentence.

3

The image moves not forward but elsewhere.

A thing final in itself and therefore good:
One of the vast repetitions final in
Themselves and, therefore, good, the going round

---

6. "Frivolity originates from the deviation or gap of the signifier, but also from its folding back on itself in its closed and representative indentity". Jacques Derrida, *The Archeology of the Frivolous: Reading Condillac*, tr. John P. Leavey, Jr. (Pittsburgh: Duquesne University Press, 1980) p. 128.

And round and round, the merely going round
Until merely going round is a final good.
                        Wallace Stevens,
                Notes toward a Supreme Fiction

Mathematics holds the fold to be one of the simplest of the
seven elementary *catastrophes*. (A catastrophe is a discontinuity
or instability in a system). The catastrophic moments in
Allophanes occur when the poem's continuous and repeated
fabric (i.e. its homogenous, phonetic plane) erupts into non-
phonetic events. There is always the danger of this *other* script
(occasionally folding to reveal from its back the Script of the
Other i.e. Spicer's) emerging in *Allophanes* as an alternate
writing. As the cover erupts its under-surface, so too the twenty
five sections of the poem always threaten a catastrophic folding
into another script. We have already witnessed the appearance
of St. Arte in section V and the non-phonetic complex in the
cover's triangular lack. But there are several others too. We
should take instant account of the fact that the poem's title
(on cover and title page) is spelled in Greek:

Αλλοphαηες

The Hebrew aleph appears in section XVI:

A gestural mark in section XIV:

𝒒

These other scripts, as momentary eruptions, mark a
difference within the poem's scriptive system and suggest,
not the protean combinatory structure of phoneticism's writing,
but a far deeper, prior writing, now banished (like Freud's
primary repression) to a place behind the cover, folded, reversed,
engulfed and smothered as an agency below the surface of the
manifest writing. The poem's key image too, is not without
its catastrophic part. SNOWBALL in its pure, phonetic form
is host to a stubborn pictographic element. The word, as a

signifier, appears, as we shall see, in a complex series of departures and returns to its matrix sentence. But examined on
the level of its primary articulation (i.e. of eight letters into
one word) the third letter is O and functions as an introjected
pictogram visually miming in its shape the word's meaning.
We can think of this letter as the snowball's anasemic state.
It is phoneticism's radical other within itself, invaginated,
like the cover and disseminated as a pictographic contaminant
throughout the poem. In acknowledging this anasemic element
in *Allophanes* we open up the poem to a bewildering play
within its own micro-structures. Wherever an O occurs (in
"god" and "dog" for instance) then the catastrophic moment
takes effect, un-assimilable in a conventional reading and on
the order of a waste in the poem's economy of meaning.

The problematic scene of *Allophanes* can now be specified
as the field of a thread working back and forth through two
spectral columns: a spectral subject (Spicer as the absent-cause,
the Primal Father in a new guise) and a spectral script (Greek,
non-phonetic, pictographic and anasemic). Within this space,
amid its catastrophic constitution, *Allophanes* stages the
transformations of its matrix dictation.

The snowball in hell is both the site and series of fetishistic
duplications. It is of the nature of the fetish (like the famous
instance of Van Gogh's shoes) to detach itself from its origins
and to re-occur in obsessive transformations. Spicer's sentence
is motivated as an object-choice onto which are projected
numerous micro-discourses, phrasings, changes, ideations,
propositions and questions, all compulsively repeated and reinscribed. The snowball in hell is a contaminated and contam-
inating image, entering the poem as a fold in utterance and
instantly problematizing as we have seen above) the work's
significatory ground. We will note a few of these repetitions
in the following catalogue of movements.

Section I introduces the eponymous sentence: "The snowball
appears in Hell/ every morning at seven". The sentence itself
seems a compact aporia (how can a snowball that depends on
cold for its existence appear in Hell with its attendant heat
and flames?) that generates a binary opposition: cold/heat
to be submitted to numerous permutations. In section II, the
sentence bifurcates and pursues two different itineraries. The
snowball links to *snow castles* ("snow castles / are alright for

lyric poems"), whilst Hell connects with mass communication
("Now its as real as a newspaper / headline in Hell"). The
snowball appears iconically for the first time in section III as a
picto-ideogrammic mark: a black sphere, like dilated punctuation. Its shape figures the *ball*, yet its blackness opposes the
white of the snow. (These oppositions within items are
numerous in *Allophanes* and eradicate any simple, unitary
meaning). Hell shifts context into "we grow old together, /
we will never meet in Hell" and the snowball re-situates in the
assertion "the snowball is not the cold". Already we can trace
the anasemic operation in the emergence of the letter O as a
pictographic imbed. In section IV the two images contextualize
within the heat-cold opposition. Hell's thermal connotations
echo in the *"coeur flambé"*, whilst the snowball develops its
interrogatory code: "& what would a snowball / know about
polar knowledge?" In VI, Hell initiates a cultural code ("I
haven't got a Dante's chance in Hell"). The snowball transforms
to become the white sphere of the baseball and initiates a
chain of content that will be centered on that specific sport.
("That snowball's got red stitches (& it's imitating God./
Tells me from third to home / is The Way Down and Out").
In section VII, the white-sphere-snow-ball complex announces
a new change in morphology: "The egg sits there, / it does not
rot itself". Hell echoes again through its thermal connotations.
Asking where "Maud has gone" the speaking subject elaborates:
"She crouches / over the fire / her back curved / to her care".
The matrix image, at this point begins to self-contaminate and
fold back into itself. As a scene of repetition the section
invests in the possibility to break down the discrete partition
of the binary opposition. In this case Hell's thermal territory
is insinuated by at least three terms from baseball: ("crouch",
"curve" and "back"). A *clean* structuralist reading of *Allophanes* is thus impossible, for one set of oppositions erupts
inside the other and proliferates a carcinoma of highly local
and ludic meanings. In section VIII Hell assumes a destinatory
function as the snowball-baseball transmogrifies into "a spilled
ice cream ball, / kick it to hell & Gone, / & turning the cone
over, / place it on your head". The triangle here, asserts itself
as *cone*, whilst the transformation: snowball/ice-cream enjoys
a thermal rationale for the change. In section IX, by way of a
metaphoric inducement, the snowball leaps the partition of

the thermal opposition and becomes a "hot" image: "pluck
the melting sno-cone of the lightbulb". This melting process
continues through section X, but not without contamination:
"See the word made white & melting / before the turn of the
fiery wheel". The heat here is *white* heat i.e. the colour of
snow. *Hell*, as a material signifier, can be traced in the word
"wheel" which is constructed by a single letter prosthesis
(w + heel) and by a single letter substitution ("e" replacing
"l"). The snowball reappears, ideogrammatically this time,
in "The world's meaning is exactly / fol de rol de rolly O".
(We have already mentioned the introjected pictographic
function of the O). In the concluding command of this
section ("Stamp the snow off your boots / onto the face
of the rug") the last word echoes *rouge* (i.e. the red stitches
of the snowball of section VI) whose semantic associations
(through colour) lead back to red-heat-fire-Hell. In section
XI the snowball as egg reappears in a scene of word-play:
"the egg ziled gods", whilst Hell inheres homophonically
imbedded in the "ell" of the proper name "Nellie": ("*Run for
the roundhouse, Nellie, he cant corner you there*"). The triangle-
cone development re-enters in the Empedoclean allusion ("Wear
your best suit / when you jump into a volcano"). The *cano* in
"volcano" continues another homophonic chain, inaugurated
earlier with the phrase in section X: "I see the dog licking it up,
i.e. the white word melting he turns & goes home cano mirabilis".
(The "I see" that begins this phrase further contaminates the
heat/cold opposition in being the homophone of "icy"). "Dog"
itself is a reverse form of "god" whose theologic meanings
proliferate the poem. Section X, in fact, opens with "et verbum
cano factum est" and later (section XIX) will come the "Dog
turds / discolouring the snow / about them". The volcano re-
echoes in two phrases of section XII: "the perilous deterioration
of dynamite" and more explicitly in the following (which also
advances the contamination of the binary colours [red-white]
and temperatures [hot-cold]): "on TV we sat breathless as
death, / watching them blast the top off the mountain, // to
begin, to make a perfect earth, a perfect smooth black orb".
This meticulous re-staging of images creates the effect of a
weaving (the etymological source of the word "text") that promotes an undecidability between an abstract, formalist pattern
and a shifting representational meaning. There is something in

the above traced production that approximates both Freud's
dream-work and the transformational grammar of Noam Chom-
sky. As if Bowering has shifted both of these as methodologies
to the literary order, where the focus is not on explicating the
productional operation of the developing text, but on the spatio-
temporal play of the surface, the implicative, transformational
possibilities of the linguistic signs.[7] Also, Paul Valéry, in speaking
on the nature of poetic images, makes mention of their
"indefinitely repeated generation" in a system of "cyclical
substitutions".[8] For Valéry, creativity and repetition are
conjunctive but repetition is of a different order in *Allophanes*.
The repetitions here are not of the nature of rhythms or rhymes,
but profound disjunctions staged within the scene of the
"other" writing. *Allophanes* is profoundly dialogic and its

A   **B**

writing situates between two further writings: a spectral and
largely non-phonetic other, and a manifest, obsessive, compulsive
writing of permutation and play. We must recall that the play of
the same and the other is carried out upon a space of repetition
that sets the grid for the series of spatio-temporal recurrences.
The latter are less events whose existence register as separate
moments, than the consequences of the differential unwindings
of writing's transformational operation. As linguistic imbeds
inside floating contexts they are marked more by their high
provisionality than by their fixing of meaning. What is produced
is not a traceable theme but the graphic appearance of the

7. Transformation is a relational operation that makes irrelevant the teleological
pursuit of stasis or an originary point. As James Ogilvy describes it "unlike the more
familiar notion of analogy, transformation permits the more radical move toward
taking the basic parameters themselves . . . as transforms of another. Unlike symbolism
and analogy, which tend to assume a basic or literal foundation on which an analogy
is built or a symbol drawn, the concept of transformation assumes no fundamental
dimension". James Ogilvy, *Many Dimensional Man* (New York, 1977) p. 46-47.
8. Paul Valéry, "The Idea of Art" tr. Ralph Manheim in *Aesthetics*, ed. Harold
Osborne (Oxford: Oxford University Press, 1972) p. 29.

multiple and the impossiblity of the single instance. Through its succession of pages *Allophanes* asserts the impossibility of maintaining an identicality based on sameness. The matrix images of the snowball and of Hell do not inhere in any authenticating metaphor, nor find investment in a cumulative intention; they risk their discreteness scattered in the movement of the syntax *per se*. For syntax in *Allophanes* not only orders verbal groupings but superintends the multiplication of the repetitions. Moreover, as we have seen, these repetitions function as radical generative disjunctions and logical contaminants, which determine the semantic rhythm of the poem through its twenty-five sections.[9]

Allophanes is weighty in its insistence that we cannot write the word, only process it through a labyrinth of re-writings. Inverting itself to transmit the ground of its pre-suppositions as the *explicit* topography of its implications, *Allophanes* will leave, as a kind of residue or sediment, the space of spacing itself as the condition of the gaps that delineate the poem's discontinuities and the differential zones in which its transformations occur. Change, of this radical order, remains un-assimilable in a reading. The allophanic image, rising every morning at seven, shows itself *at every moment* to be irreducibly temporal and dialogic. Present only in its repetition[10] the word becomes sensed as a *betweeness*. A perpetual transformation along the lateral displacements of syntax of a graphic rhetoric whose line is extendable indefinitely. A mineral text?

GLOSSARY

Allophane: Min. (mod. ad. Greek *allophanes*, appearing otherwise). A mineral classed by Dana as the first of his sub-silicates; a hydrated silicate of alumina, with colour sky-blue, green, brown or yellow, which it loses under the blowpipe; whence the name.

Allophone: 1. A positional variant of a phoneme, which occurs in a specific environment and does not differentiate meaning.

9. We might propose this as a scenario. The image, unable to "erase" itself, reproduces and then re-produces its reproduction, in this way resisting the creation of a unitary, *possessible* meaning.
10. Gilles Deleuze in *Logique du Sens*, points to the nature of repetition in an inability to inaugurate exchange. Repetition is decidely anti-metaphorical and utterly resistant to the substitutional strategies that would exchange it.

2. Sound types which are members of a phoneme class; the individual sounds which compose a phoneme (such variation is sub-phonemic); a class of phones such that all are members of the same phoneme; they may occur in the same phonetic environment, or in different positions, with non-distinctive differences among them.

1986

Language Writing: from Productive to Libidinal Economy

Barthes, in his masterly reading of Balzac's *Sarrasine*, distinguishes two fundamental types of texts: the readerly (*lisible*) and the writerly (*scriptable*). The readerly is the classic text, grounded in a transmission theory of communication and in an ideology of exchange, the human condition of whose reader Barthes sums up in the following way:

> Our literature is characterized by the pitiless divorce which the literary institution maintains between the producer of the text and its user, between its owner and its customer, between its author and its reader. This reader is thereby plunged into a kind of idleness — he is intransitive; he is, in short, *serious*: instead of gaining access to the magic of the signifier, to the pleasure of writing, he is left with no more than the poor freedom either to accept or reject the text: reading is nothing more than a referendum.[1]

The writerly text by contrast is resistant to habitual reading; it is "the novelistic without the novel, poetry without the poem . . . production without product"[2] making the reader no longer a consumer but a producer of the text. The writerly proposes the *unreadable* as the ideological site of a departure from consumption to production, presenting the domain of its own interior, interacting elements (Barthes' "magic of the signifiers") as the networks and circuits of an ultimately intractible and untotalized meaning.

What I would like to question in this approach to the unreadable is Barthes' and subsequent writers' tacit identification of

This paper was first presented as part of The Festival of Canadian Poetry, organized by Robert Bertholf and Robert Creeley, State University of New York at Buffalo in October 1980.
1. Roland Barthes, *S/Z*, tr. Richard Miller (New York: Hill and Wang, 1974) p. 4.
2. Ibid. p. 5.

production, creativity and *value* that attains the status of an ideological occlusion. Or to phrase it differently: what alternative approaches are open to the opaque text other than semantic production?

I

SEMANTIC PRODUCTION AND THE ISSUE OF
THE UNREADABLE TEXT

I refer to Language Writing as an heterogenous body of writerly texts that made its appearance throughout the seventies and early eighties in the magazines *Hills, Roof, This, Tottel's;* the small presses of *Tuumba, Burning Deck, Sun & Moon,* and whose major theoretical articulations have appeared in *Open Letter, Alcheringa* and *L=A=N=G=U=A=G=E.* This list is not exhaustive and neither is the following one of significant practitioners: Bruce Andrews, Charles Bernstein, Clark Coolidge, Robert Grenier, Lyn Hejinian, Jackson Mac Low, Bob Perelman, Stephen Rodefer, Peter Seaton, Ron Silliman, Barrett Watten and Diane Ward. A certain definitional miasma has arisen that has argued for a consistent *school* or *movement* in this body of work, but such imputed consistency is contradicted by the facts themselves. My own attempt here is to release a few flies into the ointment by outlining three major notions that relate significantly to the historical and epistemological situation of Language Writing and to take account of the major critical implications that issue from the "theoretical wound" of any appeal to defetishization by way of a return to semantic productivity. In the paper's second part, two alternative economies to the utilitarian value of semantic production are proposed: libidinal and general economies. There will be no argument along the lines of an excluded middle and the three economies are presented in mutually non-privileged situations.

Writing emerges as a profound dialectic of its occasion, one which is both personal and historical. I will take as a premise that writing must emerge inside the problematics of the concept of writing itself (which today in the light of Deleuze, Kristeva, Lacan and Derrida are enormous), that the purpose of a certain writing should be to raise these problems, that writing's contemporaneity is always an historical problem and that the problem of history itself is, to a large extent, the problem of ideological inscription.

There are at least three major structural-epistemological shifts of great significance that we should measure against their historical ideological antecedents; they are not intended to project a set theory of Language Writing but are nevertheless important to an understanding of the complex context that forms the ground for any new scriptural practice.

I. FROM WORD TO SIGN

In Language Writing it is the sign rather than the word that is the critical unit of inscription. This shift of writing *from a verbal to a semiological context* was certainly anticipated as early as the *Course* of Saussure where he describes the linguistic sign as a binary, oppositive relation that involves two functional elements: a discharging signifier and a discharged signified.[3] The signifying act (from which all linguistic meaning arises) comprises a passage from the sounds and formal graphic shapes that make up the signifier over to what those shapes represent (or discharge) in the form of a mental or acoustic image. Implicit in Saussure's theory of the sign is the notion of meaning presenting itself as a *diacritical dependency* on the oppositions of one signifier to another, which marks a fundamental break with the earlier atomistic theory of meaning that the classic notion of the word as a container supports. Saussure breaks with the belief that linguistic identity is substantial; he shows that language comprises only differences without positive terms and linguistic identity takes the form of such formal relational differences within the total system.[4]

3. The roots of western semiotics can be traced back through Saussure to the Stoics. There are no complete texts on the subject, however, and any notion of Stoic language theory must be gleaned from the scattered fragments and quotations surviving in such anti-Stoic works as the Pyrrhonistic tracts of Sextus Empiricus. From Sextus, we learn of frequent references to a *signifier* and a *signified*, but reference to the *sign* itself is lacking. Early Greek writing on language theory (in both the Stoics and in Aristotle) illustrate the symptoms of confused argumentation through an inadequate separation of the logic of the sign from theories of both rhetoric and logic. For a concise summary of the development of semiotics from the Stoics, through Aristotle to St. Augustine, see Tzvetan Todorov, *Theories of the Symbol*, tr. Catherine Porter (Ithaca: Cornell University Press, 1982).

4. Whilst Saussure's *Course in General Linguistics* stands as probably the key document in the turning point of Sign Theory it should be pointed out that Saussure himself did not write the book. The *Course*, as we have it, was compiled in 1916 — three years after his death — from his students' notes taken down during his lectures

A writing grounded on this notion of the sign takes the form of a negative articulation along an axis of absence and betweeness and upon which meanings are effected through differential relations and more by what words *don't* say than by what they do.

2. FROM WRITING AS META-SIGN TO WRITING AS WRITING

From the dawning of a consciousness about their opposition, writing and speech have been hierarchized with writing condemned to a secondary position as a debased system of silent markers. Lying behind phonetic ideology's devaluation of writing is the dream of a union of form and meaning in some kind of suppressed, but recuperable, plenitude. Plato in the *Phaedrus* and Aristotle in the *Peri Hermeneton* both treat writing as the sign of a sign.[5] Speech, being closer to the breath and body of the subject is thereby seen as closer to an authentic presence and is granted a fundamental anteriority to the written mark. Writing, at best, is an untrustworthy representation of a representation. Speech is the living and the living is the originary of all value. This phonetic-pneumatic myth of a breath governed, anterior authenticity has been protected at the expense of the written through western thought from Plato to Nietzsche; it is significantly virulent in Charles Olson and the aesthetics of presence that grew up around his notions of projective verse. In his *Letter to Elaine Feinstein*, Olson comes remarkably close to

at the *Ecole practique des hautes études* in Paris. Saussure's "actual" beliefs, like many of Wittgenstein's and the entirety of Socrates', are quite literally hearsay. There is a revealing, interrupted passage (Ms. fr. 3957/2) in the collection of Saussure's papers at the Public and University Library of Geneva which reads:

> absolutely incomprehensible if I were not forced to confess that I suffer from a morbid horror of the pen, and that this work is for me an experience of sheer torture.

5. For a full discussion of the Platonic attack on writing see Jacques Derrida, "Plato's Pharmacy" in *Dissemination*, tr. Barbara Johnson (University of Chicago Press, 1981). Derrida argues that Plato's condemnation of writing involves a covert appeal to a double sense of writing: the one physical, the other metaphorical. The well-known passage in the *Phaedrus* where King Thamus responds to Theuth's proffered gift writing is appended here for convenience:

> The fact is that this invention [writing] will produce forgetfulness in the souls of those who have learned it because they will not need to exercise their memories, being able to rely on what is written, using the stimulus of external marks that are alien to themselves rather than, from within, their own unaided powers to call things to mind. So it's not a remedy for memory, but for reminding that you have discovered.

the anti-representational, anti-referential position that Language Writing grounds itself within: the attack on the completed thought, the dead-spot of description and the centripetal, self-annihilating push of language chained by reference to reality all promise a sense of writing based on textual immanence. But in many places come the appeals to primaries, origins, returns and anti-miasmic backtrackings that betray this link to phonetic ideology:

> Verse now, 1950, if it is to go ahead, if it is to be of *essential* use, must, I take it, catch up and put into itself certain laws and possibilities of the breath, of the breathing of the man who writes as well as of his listenings.[6]
>
> Because breath allows *all* the speech-force of language back in (speech is the "solid" of verse, is the secret of a poem's energy), because now, a poem has, by speech, solidity, everything in it can now be treated as solids, objects, things . . . [7]

This is reminiscent of Plato's attack on writing in the *Phaedrus* as a dead and rigid knowledge learned by heart, promoting of a repetition without knowing. The link is clear and can be easily verified in parallel readings of the *Cratylus, Phaedrus* and Olson's *Human Universe*. In his essay on Projective Verse (which arose out of the contemporary issues of prosody circa 1950) we can detect this underlying ideological seam that permits Olson to argue for a specific value in verse without questioning the problematics of a value *per se*. His criticism of closed poetics actually reduces to a criticism of a closed interior and moves by a line of argument that derives its ammunition from a long tradition of western metaphysics. And the ideological operation is not too covert: breath, by providing "solidity", "thing-ness" is closer to a presence and must therefore be fixed anterior to writing, whilst writing has the status of a repressive exterior that constrains the authentic structure of breath. In the double appeal of breath and syllable, Olson attempts to externalize a closed interior. The typewriter (as Olson defends it) ironically rescues writing from its historical villain's role by pushing writing further away from its traditionally tight, symplegmatic involvement with speech, giving it the formal (and ideological)

6. Charles Olson, "Projective Verse" in *The Human Universe and Other Essays*, ed. Donald Allen (New York: Grove Press, 1967) p. 51.
7. Ibid. p. 56.

distance of a *notation* as distinct from a supplement.

Writing, however, is neither a fixed, repressive exterior nor a meta-sign; it is, as Derrida and others have convincingly argued, a fundamental trace structure and as such is *always* present in speech *as speech's necessary condition*. (Derrida announces this structure by various terms — the supplement, the hinge, the *differance*, the *pharmakon* — as the most general structure of semantic economy). Sign production (the discharge-discharged dynamic of the signifier-signified) operates as a delay that also differentiates. It is the nature of the linguistic sign to be neither itself nor any other thing (Saussure fails to point out this violently contradictory logic of signification which is, nevertheless, implicit within his own diacritical formulation of the sign). The signifier — because it is always standing for a signified — can never be itself; whilst the signified — in always being stood for — is constantly withheld and likewise never present. This is what Derrida terms *differance* (difference *and* deferral) which cannot be fixed in space and time but constitutes the pre-logical basis of all sign production:

> We provisionally give the name *differance* to this *sameness* which is not *identical:* by the silent writing of its *a*, it has the desired advantage of referring to differing, *both* as spacing/temporalizing and as the movement that structures every dissociation . . . *Differance* is neither a *word* nor a *concept*.[8]

Implicit in *differance* is the fact that sound can certainly be heard in language but likewise *can never be present inside it.*[9]

3. FROM POEM TO TEXT

Text here is not simply a lexical preference but marks a shift in the conception of scriptive work from a fixed object of analysis or conception, to an open, methodological field for semantic production. Language today no longer poses problems of meaning but practical issues of use; the relevant question being not "what does this piece of writing mean"? (as if meaning

---

8. Jacques Derrida, "Differance" in *Speech and Phenomena*, tr. David B. Allison (Evanston: Northwestern University Press, 1973) p. 129-30.
9. What is at issue is not a triumphant return to writing of its appropriated rights, nor a reversal of the valuational poles in the binary opposition of speech/writing. Rather it is the issue of re-situating writing *within an expanded notion of itself.*

was somehow a represented essence in a sign the activity of reading substantially extracts) but "how does this writing work"? There is a radical shift in Language Writing from the poem as object, to the text as a methodological field that implies also the issue of a sociological detachment of the writer from his historical role and ideological identity of author. Language Writing resists reduction to a monological message, offering instead an organized surface of signifiers whose signifieds are undetermined. There is a primacy lent to readership as a productive engagement with a text in order to generate local pockets of meaning as semantic eruptions or events that do not accumulate into aggregated masses. The texts, whilst written, demand writers to produce *from* them, for what the texts deliberately lack are *authors*: the traditional literary fiction of a central, detached but recoverable source of origin. Vicki Mistacco has suggested the term "ludism" for this type of writing:

> 'Ludism' may be simply defined as the open play of signification, as the free and productive interaction of forms, of signifiers and signifieds, without regard for an original or ultimate meaning. In literature, ludism signifies textual play; the text is viewed as a game affording both author and reader the possibility of producing endless meanings and relationships.[10]

Language, in the following text, reveals itself as a primary, nonintentional scriptive play, incapable of being foreclosed or exceeded and offering itself as a highly volatile circulation of signifiers.

> my high
> mallorca
> tailored
> sitten (s)ought sunk
> ogled a blond
> (pilaf)
> ( )unched
> th... b...rb...n th...mb...l...n...
> mAgiC
> "moon" and "stars" and lentil
> agaze[11]

10. Precise source not located.
11. Charles Bernstein, *Disfrutes* (Peter Ganick, 1980).

There are obvious iconic constraints: why the justified left-hand margin? why the symmetrical elisions? And equally there are resonating alter-texts: do the parentheses suggest a reading of Husserlian bracketing? are the words hung in quotations textual complications or textural echoes? does the eighth line suggest a move towards completion (plenitude) or decomposition (absence)? What is the semiotic suggestion in the eruptive capitalizations in line nine? Do these suggest an intentional presence or semantic freeplay? What is important to grasp here is the characteristic *excess* of this text. In a way it cannot be spoken about but only participated within and a criticism would comprise the documentation of its reading as an extended writing. It might be argued that texts like the above have no concern with communication (or at least with the dominant theory of communication that sees it as a transmission from producer to receiver along a semiotic axis of production-consumption, giver-recipient) but rather with establishing a politicized effervescence within the code in which signs can never settle into messages from "authors" and intentional language can hold no power. At this point semantics would seem to get returned to the order of production and use value as part of the historical step towards the re-politicization of language as an open field of truly human engagements.

What Language Writing is proposing is a shift for writing away from literature and the readable, towards the dialectical domain of its own interiorities as primarily an interacting surface of signifiers in the course of which a sociological shift in the nature of readership must be proposed. For the texts of Andrews, Bernstein, Coolidge, Watten cannot be consumed but only produced. There is an operation in excess of Barthes' unreada-ability, however, for beyond the appeal to semantic production is a certain revelation and critique of the ideological contamina-tion operative upon the very order of sign production. The issue, of course, is political, but it is not an issue of extra-linguistic concerns to be discussed by means of language, but one of detecting the hidden operation of those repressive mechanisms that language and the socio-economic base actually share. In Language Writing this critique has so far taken the form of exposing through their political analogies two major fetishisms operating in language: grammar and the referent.

GRAMMAR, STATE AND CAPITAL

Grammatical effects obtain not only in language but in state operation also. Deleuze and Guattari describe the State as "the transcendent law that governs fragments" — a description that applies equally to grammatical as to political control. As a transcendent law, grammar acts as a mechanism that regulates the free circulation of meaning, organizing the fragmentary and local into compound, totalized wholes. Through grammatical constraint then, meanings coalesce into meaning. Denied independent and undetermined discharge through a surface play, the controlled parts are thrust into an aggregated phrase that projects meaning as a destination or culmination to a gaze. Like capital (its economic counterpart) grammar extends a law of value to new objects by a process of totalization, reducing the free play of the fragments to the status of delimited, organizing parts within an intended larger whole. Signifiers appear and are then subordinately organized into these larger units whose culmination is a meaning which is then invested in a further aggregation. Grammar's law is a combinatory, totalizing logic that excludes at all costs any fragmentary life. It is clear that grammar effects a meaning whose form is that of *a surplus value generated by an aggregated group of working parts for immediate investment into an extending chain of meaning*. The concern of grammar homologizes the capitalistic concern for accumulation, profit and investment in a future goal. Language Writing, in contrast, emerges more as an expenditure of meanings in the forms of isolated active parts and for the sake of the present moment which the aggregative, accumulative disposition of the grammatical text seeks to shun. (We must return shortly to this point and see how Language Writing conceived as semantic production is not entirely free of this "grammatical" concern).

REFERENCE, REPRESENTATION AND COMMODITY FETISHISM

Fetishism is a mechanism of occlusion that displaces and eclipses the true nature of commodities as the products of human labour and interaction, detaching them magically from their productive bases and presenting them as self-perpetuating "things" that take their place within social circulation as an exchange value. The referential fetish in language is inseparable from the representational theory of the sign. Proposed as intentional, as always "about" some extra-linguistic thing, language must always refer beyond itself to a corresponding reality. The linguistic task is not to draw in and centre a productive activity within itself, but to fulfill a deictic function that points beyond itself to an exterior goal. The referential fetish thrives on the myth of *transparent signification*, on words as innocent, unproblematic sign-posts to a monological message or intention; it wants a message as a product to be consumed with as little attention as possible drawn to the words' dialectical engagements. Reference reaches its most fetishized form in the readable best-seller, the world of rapid and simple linguistic movement in which language reduces to the status of perfect fenestration: a clear window of words to carry a reader effectively along a story line.

I have argued that Language Writing involves a shift away from literary concerns and back to the ground of semantic production; it chooses a context of productive play for a re-politicization of the word as a scene for common human engagement; it similarly exposes the fetishization of the linguistic sign by ideological constraint that brings the linguistic order disturbingly close to that of the political order. Central to both this shift and exposé is the felt need to extend writing beyond a simple relation to consciousness towards a dialectical relation with production. This is seen as a primordial political act that detaches the reader from language as a communicative subject in order to re-attach her as an agent of production. Behind this is an implicit operation of judgement: a commitment to the primacy of utilarian values and a commitment that will be examined in this paper's second part.

II

FROM SEMANTIC PRODUCTIVITY TO LIBIDINAL INTENSITY AND GENERAL ECONOMY

Work corresponds to the care of tomorrow, pleasure to that of the present moment. Work is useful and satisfactory, pleasure useless, leaving a feeling of unsatisfaction. These considerations put economy at the basis of morality and at the basis of poetry.[12]

If Language Writing successfully detaches Language from the historical purpose of summarizing global meaning replacing the goal of totality with the free polydynamic drive of parts, it nevertheless falls short in addressing the full implications of this break and seems especially to fail in taking full account of the impact of the human subject with the thresholds of linguistic meaning. It is at the critical locus of productive desire that this writing opens itself up to an alternative "libidinal" economy which operates across the precarious boundaries of the symbolic and the biological and has its basis in intensities. François Fourquet describes the libidinal complex as a complex not of representations "but of intensive forces, active only in the realm of power in the most material, the most 'political' sense of the word . . . The libido is force, pure power . . . the libido does not have an image. It is not representable".[13] Libidinal intensities are oppositionally related to the fixity of the written; they are decoding drives that seep through and among texts, jamming codes and pulverizing language chains; they are liberative of the energy trapped inside linguistic structures. Libidinal circuits, however, are intractable, intensely permeative and impossible to locate as specific, operational factors; they derive from the pre-linguistic (infantile) drives of both the writing and reading subjects. It is at that pivotal point, where language is simultaneously composed and dissolved, made and unmade, consumed and regurgitated, that language connects with the unconscious and its drives.

Barthes:
THERE EXISTS FUNDAMENTALLY IN WRITING A
"CIRCUMSTANCE" FOREIGN TO LANGUAGE.

Kristeva:
COMMUNICATION DOES NOT EQUAL WRITING.

Bataille:
IN A SENSE POETRY IS ALWAYS THE OPPOSITE OF POETRY.

---

12. Georges Bataille, *Literature and Evil*, tr. Alastair Hamilton (London: Calder & Boyars, 1973) p. 36.
13. François Fourquet, "Libidinal Nietzsche" in Semiotext(e), III, 1, 1978, p. 71-4.

Libidinal drives are propelled by an instinctual, non-semantic force and push rhythmically *through* language. Semantic shifts and devices also allow these drives to situate as violent imprints, or to push through as ruptures, in the linguistic order, unsettling it and its support mechanisms: logical sequence and the unitary writing and reading subject. Controlled inside this libidinal economy, meaning presents itself as a membrane through which instinctual drives force passage or have that passage denied. The major premise in libidinal economy is that language is possessed of a double disposition: one towards naming, logicalizing, predicating; the other towards an assertion of pre-linguistic gestures (what Kristeva has termed the semiotic order) that push through but remain unattached to symbolic meaning.[14]

What is being suggested is a writing through language towards that constituent of language that exceeds the linguistic is inherent in many of Language Writing's texts. This is a short section from *LEGEND:*

```
whch nugkinj      .
          without sJuxYY senshl   .
                        "sensual"
          though he meant it
                    for ray for is for si heh hahpeh uvd r fah
                              breaks at the point
                                             .

is beh aht.
          baht at
                        (the moors at ilkley.  june.  nineteen or
                              sixty three)
                                             .

si gidrid.  impOg   a rising or simply the
          Qwerty.15
                                             .
```

Typography here is in alliance with a pre-linguistic drive and forms a tactile investment within the symbolic-grammatical order; it is a kind of eroticism performed upon the body of the

14. A detailed treatment of this double disposition can be found in Julia Kristeva, *Desire in Language*, tr. T. Gora, A. Jardine & L.S. Roudiez (New York: Columbia University Press, 1980) and *Revolution in Poetic Language*, tr. Margaret Waller (New York: Columbia University Press, 1984).
15. Bruce Andrews, Charles Bernstein, Ray DiPalma, Steve McCaffery, Ron Silliman, *LEGEND* (New York: L=A=N=G=U=A=G=E/Segue, 1980).

syntagm. Capitalization has neither grammatical nor anagramic intent but is a pure register of eruption at the meeting of the linguistic sign with the pre-linguistic drive. In contest are two systems or linguistic dispositions: a limiting, organizing system which pushes the independent letter as a component towards word and phrase (which are themselves the components in the production of meaning) and the other a disorganizing disposition driving the letter into clusters that register closer to the order of a pre-linguistic "thing" (similar to the function of the letter in the unconscious as Lacan has demonstrated) experienced as marks or gestures rather than semantic exchange objects. The sign here is decidedly ambivalent, a pressure point produced by the confluence of conflictual drives; detached from all notions of knowledge, meaning and truth they suggest themselves as modalities of purposeless flow. If meaning can be considered as the surplus value of signification, then the forces of libido can be thought of as the surplus value of meaning itself.

Libido is NOT utilitarian; it is not a producer but flows and spills and breaks in an unmeditated outlay of blind power. Libido is politics beyond politics and the texts that it saturates are barely texts. Similarly libido cannot be a theme or a representation; it can only be the register of intensities despite linguistic constraint and can only seek detachment in discharge. Libido is a pure, intransitive desire whose dynamic is suggested in the very nature of the linguistic sign. For the signifier too can be described as an essential desire and drive to discharge which, like libido, threatens an existence on that level where language is closest to being a body without a head, a vast, undifferentiated torso of inscription, a scarred, incised surface over which the flows can move as intensities along formless, non-productive paths.

What needs to be insisted upon is Language Writing's unavoidable proximity to these non-productive values. I have outlined it's connexion with libidinal intensity and now want to suggest its proximity to sovereign value. The concept of sovereignty is not well documented; it first clearly enters a philosophical arena with Hegel's *Phenomenology* and surfaces radically in much of Nietzsche's writings; it can be traced through the writings of De Sade, Lautréamont, Baudelaire, Ebenezer Jones (a lamentably neglected Victorian), Genet, Blake, Emily Bronte and Kafka; it has been the subject of extended study by Georges Bataille (in his *Eroticism* and *Literature and Evil*) and received considerable attention from Sartre and André Breton. The latter speaks of sovereignty as that point "where life and death, the real and the imaginary, past and future, the communicable and the incommunicable, the high and the low are no longer perceived in contradiction to one another". Bataille describes it as that "power to rise indifferent to death, above the laws which ensure the maintenance of life". Sovereignty "is the object which eludes us all, which nobody has seized and which nobody can seize for this reason: we cannot possess it, like an object, but we are doomed to seek it. A certain utility always alienates the proposed sovereignty". The sovereign gesture is hence a gesture (without true responsibility) beyond use value. Seeking to detach energy expenditure from utility it finds best operation in an economy of *unproductive consumption* — an economy that Bataille has termed *General Economy:*

> The general economy, in the first place, makes apparent that excesses of energy are produced, and that by definition, these excesses cannot be utilized. The excessive energy can only be lost without the slightest aim, consequently without meaning.[16]

Bataille further distinguishes a sovereign from a regular communication:

> Communication, in my sense of the word, is never stronger than when communication, in the weak sense, in the sense of profane language or, as Sartre says, of prose which makes us and others appear penetrable, fails and becomes the equivalent of darkness.[17]

Sovereign communication, like Language Writing, rejects the model of communication as a transmission-reception by two individual, reflective consciousnesses. But whereas Language Writing evolves along an historical continuum and accepts this break with conventional communication as a chance to return language to a defetishized arena of production, sovereignty enters the non-utilizable arena of mutual impenetrability. Here, the communicative act involves the destruction of the com-

---

16. Georges Bataille, *L'experience intérieure* (Paris: Gallimard, 1943) p. 233.
17. *Literature and Evil*, p. 170.

munication model: a simultaneous (and frequently momentary) cancellation of both reader and writer as isolated beings in a communication that rises above, and indeed obliterates, the beings who communicate.

Language Writing should be encountered at the bifurcation of these two orders of value: productive utility on the one hand, and sovereignty on the other. In a text such as the following do we counter the work and produce a reading or proceed further into the *textual experience* of the unreadable?

> Bers phone the the.
> Give showed mail ing.
> The on won so.
> Ly fetch wonders note.
> It's a gim, a de.
> On the know, the on, the don't.
> Back how's is backs.
> To one it, it irons.
> Ops a ed, a are any this.
>   Don.
>
> Trucks one.[18]

What becomes critical in language texts like the above is this double disposition that simultaneously petitions active productive engagement and a negative refusal to engage and as a consequence, a fundamental relativization of values. It is when texts are experienced as multiple peaks of ambivalence (as both wastes and potentials, inscriptions and deletions, productive encounters and nonproductive consumptions) that a sovereign immobility may result: from the inability to choose and the impossibility to either pursue a writing or experience a deletion. If what Language Writing proposes is a radical change in semiotic competence, then the writing itself admits of an ability to move beyond all reading procedures towards a new relationship to meaning itself: a relation of sovereignty. If semantic productivity sees a complete freedom in relating to texts, one would be forced to ask why freedom here *must* be constrained by a need to produce. The challenge to readership would appear to be the challenge of developing capacities to experience the problema-

---

18. Clark Coolidge, "These" in *Space* (New York: Harper & Row, 1970) p. 89.

ticity of the problem itself, to experience the unavoidable
inability to decide and to regulate all pressures to rush immediately into solutionary strategies. It should be possible
within these texts to institute a double rhythm of reading:
utilitarian-productive and non-utilitarian resistant and to allow
their interaction and mutual relativization *inside a dialectical
economy.*

1980

Writing Degree Xerox: Some Notes Towards a Reading of Richard Truhlar's *Priapus Arched*

Priapus Arched is first and foremost the elimination of speech.[1] A silent text in which the voice — traditionally taken to be the origin of speech and which writing in its function as a secondary operation, attempts to figure — is gesturally removed. This leaves writing in a drift towards a self-effacement through a gestural violence perpetrated on the written mark. Created out of a matrix of literacy it petitions a post-literateness as the necessary condition of its being experienced. The work, in fact, demands that its reading be an anti-reading, and it is this anti-nomial stance that permits the work its radical break from the philosophemic forces ("truth", "transparency", the utilitarian engendering of value, "telos") that would prohibit *Priapus*

 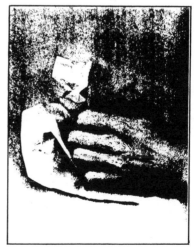

1. *Priapus Arched*, by Richard Truhlar (Toronto: Kontakte Editions, Series 1, No. 1, 1976).

Arched at the outset from staging itself as a theatre of deletions. Demoting the emphasis upon an operative "truth relation" (that the text be "truly" this thing) it enters into a gestural disputation of the contradictory intensities and circulations that constitute a textual effect.

Truhlar's project is less scriptive than violently tactile: the recording of a physical attack upon the semic substance of its language. Through the exploitation of xerography (as a para-textual assault upon a text) Truhlar is able to frame the logo-centricity of his manuscript material within an "aberrant use" of mechanical duplication as a gesture upon the text, a sadistic lamination, a reproduction of the termination of a reproduction: the physical destruction of the work itself. Moreover, it is the work's constant threat to site the problematicity of textual presence with the climactic conclusion that writing, as we incontravertibly experience it, need not exist. In the xerographic arrestment of tactility, not only is syntax displaced, but a violence is perpetrated against the philosophic rule of spacing, i.e. the very gaps of language.

Priapus Arched enacts a further violence: a meta-structural implosion of the page. Page, as the support surface of written communication, is put in opposition to itself, contests the fabric of its own uni-graphicality and demonstrates a radically contradictory nature. It is in the extent of this auto-stigmatism that page relates to its identity as *difference* not *conflict*.[2] Through a chain of such contradictions *Priapus Arched* questions its basis in existence, the (im)possibility of being there, the inability to present itself as a material unit let alone convey a message. In this scene of cancellations and expungencies language, text and page contest existence in a continuously indeterminate system of interventions. The work that this "is" situates in its own paradoxical liminality: an already fractured threshold.

Both the verbal sign and the photographic assault upon the sign interweave to force the reader into witnessing a catastrophe of both object and perception. Initiating a shift across the registers of reproduction, from writing to a gesture *as* writing, Truhlar invests an emotional release not in words, but inside a

---

2. " 'Let difference surreptitiously replace conflict'. Difference is not what makes or sweetens conflict: it is achieved over and above conflict, it is *beyond and alongside* conflict. Conflict is nothing but the moral state of difference". Roland Barthes, *The Pleasure of the Text*, tr. Richard Miller (New York: Hill and Wang, 1975).

non-verbal action upon them. The text is a mutilated trace, the
reproduction of a physical gesture laid across the form and
substance of its language. It is highly relevant that Truhlar
chooses the manuscript version of a text rather than a "final"
printed, commodital form for mutilation. Initiating a deforma-
tion at this intermedial point, we see how a textual *product*
never really exists. As manuscript the text still occupies a space
of human labour within the matrix of an ever possible revision.
This premature exposure leaves the text in a transitional state,
subjected to a violence divulged in the material substance of the
language and directed against its significatory status. *Priapus
Arched* is located then, on a threshold of language and reproduction (both are affiliate systems of representation and fraterni-
ties of mimesis) where it interrogates the very existence of the
placement. Poised both interior and exterior to the thing it is
and is not, the work demonstrates its nature as a trace structure.

Barthes has gone far in describing the kind of textual world
that *Priapus Arched* inhabits:

> How can a text, which consists of language, be outside language? . . .
> by a general labour of extenuation. First the text liquidates all meta-
> language, whereby it is a text: no voice (Science, Cause, Institution)
> is *behind* what it is saying. Next, the text destroys utterly, *to the
> point of contradiction*, its own discursive categories, its sociological
> reference . . . Lastly, the text can, if it wants, attack the canonical
> structure of the language itself . . . lexicon (exuberant neologisms,
> portmanteau words, transliteration), syntax (no more logical cell, no
> more sentence). It is a matter of effecting, by transmutation (and no
> longer only by transformation) a new philosophic state of the language
> substance . . . outside origin and outside communication.[3]

A collection of effacements: of author, text and page, with
each registered in the mechanism of a reproduction that mimes
the inscription of an end to the legible? It is this more than
anything that is guarantor of the work's contemporaneous
relevance. The print of a hand, the trace of a gesture are all that
remain of the writing. Nor do these endure with the semantic
force of an ideogram but with the nihilistic power of a refusal
that lies conceptually beyond transgression. This is essential, for
there is a tendency to assign *Priapus Arched* to the status of a
negative value (no text, no readability, no message) thereby

3. Roland Barthes, loc. cit. p. 30.

keeping it within a conceptual sphere of binarity as the negative component within a system of two terms (readability/non-readability, communication/non-communication). But *Priapus Arched* is beyond such conceptual closure; it situates as readability's *heterological* object, an expulsed interior whose contaminatory presence indicates the impossibility of the application of a coupled, evaluated opposition. As such, *Priapus Arched* falls outside the scope of Aristotelian categorization. Language, as an instrument of lucidity and communication has disappeared into the mechanism of reproduction. And with this a certain philosophic hold over writing. We might cite Benjamin at this point on the status of the object in a condition of reproducibility:

> . . . the technique of reproduction detaches the reproduced object from the domain of tradition. By making many reproductions it substitutes a plurality of copies for a unique existence. And in permitting the reproduction to meet the beholder or listener in his own particular situation, it reactivates the object reproduced.[4]

The liquidation of a fetish of historical placement (i.e. the precious "moment" when Truhlar's manuscript is destroyed) entails also the destruction of the authority of the manuscript as a privileged possession and incurrs the dissemination of its end in a curious phenomenological decentralization. *Priapus Arched* in fact detaches from a personated historicity to find its place within the inscription of a larger history forged outside the "aura" of the subject and the object. The contextual disintegration that housed the valorized relation of an author to his text gives way to an expanded context of societal suture; one too, that Benjamin has noted:

> To pry an object from its shell, to destroy its aura, is the mark of a perception whose "sense of the universal equality of things" has increased to such a degree that it extracts it even from a unique object by means of reproduction.[5]

What *Priapus Arched* destroys is an endemic sociological space. For with the loss of writing inside the reproduced recording of

---

4. Walter Benjamin, "The Work of Art in the Age of Mechanical Reproduction" in *Illuminations*, tr. Harry Zohn (New York: Schocken, 1969) p. 221.
5. Loc. cit. p. 223.

that loss is instituted a radically altered relationship of authority to reader. Where the former is removed from an ownership based on substantive duration, the latter gains pluralization and is removed from a "cult" relation to a unique text.

Perhaps *Priapus Arched* goes further to expose the fetishized economy that underlies and undermines all reading, which would propose itself as an activity whose privileged duration matches the time of the written signs. But such a reading would exonerate and repeat what has been discredited and removed. More powerful is the emergence of a context of non-linguistic forces that push reading aside and return the text to a social scene of spectacle: a public execution. The final gesture of *Priapus Arched* towards a radical expenditure and waste points to the calculated uselessness of this work. Placed outside of reading and hence value it lies beyond any makeshift utilitarian horizon; it occupies the centre of a cultural degradation, a ruthless and uncompromising instantaneity beyond the grasp of a contemplative subject.

The term which might best describe the methodology of *Priapus Arched* is *bricolage*. Bricolage is a dialogue with "the materials and means of execution" (Claude Levi-Strauss). The elements which the *bricoleur* collects and uses are "whatever happens to be on hand". They are preconstrained "like the constitutive units of myth, the possible combinations of which are restricted by the fact that they are drawn from the language where they already possess a sense which sets a limit on their freedom of maneuver". The *bricoleur* is the collector of and constructor out of oddments: the miscellaneous shards of codes and objects. Derrida, among many, has pointed out the structural weakness in this praxis:

> The only weakness of *bricolage* . . . is a total inability to justify itself in its own discourse. The already-there-ness of instruments and of concepts cannot be undone or reinvented.[6]

Truhlar, as *bricoleur*, borrows a text in order to destroy its textuality, but in so doing attests to the necessary dependence of that destruction upon a residual reserve or preservation. The fortuitousness of the *bricoleur's* components are at the same

6. Jacques Derrida, *Of Grammatology*, tr. G.C. Spivak (Baltimore: Johns Hopkins University Press, 1974) p. 138.

time his most necessary and unavoidable materials, leaving the work detached from any meta-linguistic support or critique and floating in the amorphousness of its own non-definition. Structurally speaking, the text frames a further text moved *back* into the intermediate stage of manuscript. This element of distancing and the concommitant emphasis on the work's physical rather than semantic *ideal* properties, constitutes the pre-contstraints of the materials. *Priapus Arched* is thus an extremely complex *writing of the victim*. Because of his initial preference for manuscript, Truhlar denies himself from the out-set the possibility of an unmediated intention. The words in *Priapus Arched* cannot be used but merely acted upon through a gestural meta-language that stages the violence of the *bricoleur* against the structural dependencies of his activity.

For the *bricoleur* there is and must always be, a presence anterior to origin. Since there is nothing new there can be no beginning, simply the reassembling of an antecedent presence that is perpetually postponed. But the destruction of the page can only take place upon the supportive continuity of the page itself. Traditional categories are not destroyed but expanded to accommodate their historic contradictions. Through his access to technological reproduction Truhlar has transformed this page into the monstrosity of a 'pataphysical recording surface; a blank judicial sphere, an ambiguous gap inside an overwhelming sacrificial economy. Thereby *Priapus Arched* conveys at least this one extreme suggestion: that there is ultimately no linguistic object, only a radically unsettled linguistic function and its even more precarious abandonment.

1978

(Immanent)
(Critique)

It should even then have still appeared
where this is. Notby me   ans of an a-
ppropriation but as a sampl e question
-ing which space this was. If one choo
sesto elimina   te suspicion or suspen
d (not by a thread but in aliquid) a
certain break implicit in the sign. Th
-en what mar   ksar e   thes e?

We have displaced them to an
end and we have bracketed them
both. There is the case (left
open in a legal sense a discourse
but also at a station) Of a vaGue
-neSS of false patronymies. The

signant's ring inside the tele-
phone re-named-for-speech. Tel
-estics as a basis for attenuated
woofs. A langscape ? Perhaps.
But why wiTHin the protocol of
RuLe. Against what sense does
language brush and could be read
as . . . . Logic

's tacit chunks. Behind the turn
are still . . . . th
ese marks . . . . &
they too are a language. T
he relief of theory turning
cool set down against the b
ook's code pushing back a f
alse void in a clinamen. "

The shadow of address insid
e her dress   w   a   s
t   u   r   ne   D   ”

w
(r)
i
(t)
(i)
n
g

this willingness of white to be
the bankrupt ground for metaphor
a trope in pitch to writing's
neutral wing (i.e. an army of a
flank the farthest section of)
a hospital . . . .

We should adjust this in (w)edg and consider it t sentence through a tissu ill announcing in its wa e know by now each parag repeating in the nouns i s described as originato erent bar that circumscr tire machine that this b in the full range that t

ils" give rise to "sewin side the double moment o there is thus to be trip + a portrait + a zoograp

body of the writer it sh med abysses might interp marker's (arms) the fold ers downward to the wris nvoke and double outward hrust as though about to dge or boundary before t pivot (the variant of th ier (the noun neck caugh the sign invested with n

word is voice the twenty inge.

wardly towards a certain he slide(e) of a single e not as a sneeze but st y a similar detonation w raph prevents the knife t commandeers the slashe ry discrediting the diff ibes the play of this en etweeness should adjust his hinge announces.

"Sa gs" (folds not seeds) in f each reader's entrance licity in effect a mouth hic operation.

From the ould be clear how two na ose a graft or fold the ing of a glove (the fing t) the fold that marks i s in an ordered series t cancel out the leading e he fractured multiples a e paragraph) and chandel t inside a cryptic light o colour)

the eighteenth second paragraph still h

So it will be ju
ribed inside (a consta
literalist species a l
l space (the movement
ateral play that's ali
discredited and the su
cross a form of patria
ate machine (tongue +
= the beyond) which is

a shattered shaft and
the phallus (as we sh
emerge a fold in spac
bsence) premature in i
disguised inside the p
bent moment (it falls
he splice from splinte
is a stratified format
ked by wrenching to th
rustean scene a fabric
n rhythmus yes but als
to the eight decentere
once more in an absolu
yfish" in the aureole
escends to signify the
from a human scorch. E
(chapter) and enclosin
auris hence auricular)
on of a human face wit
inattention near paren
ts elytrons. Now, HOW
f différance?

st a reverie intact insc
nt inwarding towards) a
amination upon a littora
of the hinge through a l
en to metaphor) the bar
rface fold transparent a
rchy but towards a celib
the sign of a design too
trajectory.

Or perhaps
no exclusive allusion to
all see this constantly
e into a later form of a
ts belatedness the code
aradigm impressed to one
to matter here to hold t
ring into what elsewhere
ion) keeping reading lin
e choreography as a proc
which the metre makes (i
o as a distance measured
d morphic frames) we are
te coincidence with "cra
(the halo) where a sun d
solar power is emanating
xtended around the head
g in itself the ears (an
We note the compositi
h attributes of gold and
theses none other than i
AM I TO SPEAK OF the *f* o
f difference?

1983

The Elsewhere
of Meaning

This will not be an exhaustive treatment of a fascinating, important and comparatively unknown Quebecois writer. The historical problem of articulating the work of Claude Gauvreau and Quebec's Automatiste Movement to the European surrealism of André Breton is an issue both vital and too expansive for this essay.[1] I will use Gauvreau, detached from his historical context, as a representative pre-text for a widely implicative writing: the automatic text.[2] A representative writer and a representative text. *Jappements à la Lune* was Claude Gauvreau's

1. The socio-political context in which Gauvreau's writing appeared is vital to an assessment and understanding of the full scope of his work. Through the war years and 'forties French-Canadian writing *speaks* as an oppressed, colonial effect, whose cultural possibilities were strictly determined by political conservatism and a powerful Catholic church. The Asbestos Strike of 1949 served to polarize the socio-cultural space with writers, artists and a united intellectual youth on one end, and a reactionary front of clerico-political conservatism plus agrarian interests on the other. It was into this atmosphere that *Réfus global* appeared on August 9, 1948: the collective manifesto of the *Automatistes* and to which document Claude Gauvreau was a signatory. The following description (by Paul-Emile Borduas) of Quebec's deplorable situation should be kept in mind through the intentionally narrow range of the present article. Its references to colonial oppression and European intellectual dominance (through an instrumental memory) are important factors in any assessment of the Automatistes' break with transatlantic surrealism and Breton's "colonization of the unconscious":
   "A colony trapped and abandoned as long ago as 1760 beneath unscalable walls of fear . . . A little people, huddled to the skirts of a priesthood viewed as sole trustee of faith . . . A little people, grown from a Jansenist colony . . . Heirs of a mechanical papacy, invulnerable to redress, great masters of obscurantism, their institutes of learning still hold sway through an exploiting use of memory, static reason, and paralysing intention. A little people . . . spellbound by the annihilating prestige of remembered European masterpieces, and disdainful of the authentic creations of its own oppressed." Paul-Emile Borduas, *Writings 1942-1958*, tr. F-M. Gagnon & D. Young (Halifax: Nova Scotia College of Art, 1978) p. 45. For more details of the Automatiste Movement and examples of their writings, see the special issue of *La Barre du Jour*, 17-20, Jan.-Aug. 1969.
2. Automaticity is the key concept of Surrealism. In the 1924 Manifesto Breton defines Surrealism as "n. Psychic automatism in its pure state, by which one proposes to express — verbally, by means of the written words, or in any other manner — the

last book consisting of eight short poems composed between 6 October 1968 and 25 March 1970. Two days of writing with a year and a half hiatus that fills the last eight pages of Gauvreau's mammoth fifteen hundred page *Oeuvres Créatrices Complètes*. Poem number six reads in its entirety:

> nrôm atila atiglagla glô émect tufachiraglau égondz-apanoir tufirupiplè-
> thatgouloumeurector ezdannz ezdoucrémouacptteu pif-legoulem ôz
> nionfan nimarulta apiviavovioc tutul latranerre dèg wobz choutss
> striglanima uculpt treflagamon [3]

There is discernible a production motivated not by utility and exchange (which the dominant presence of meaning and communication would inject into the signifying scene) but by an unmediated inscription of the materiality of the letter. Immediately apparent is the poem's refusal to satisfy any habitual expectancies of meaning. It is not a system of signs for comprehension but a complex of pro-productive paths through seemingly indifferent and intransitive letter productions. A motivation, if traceable at all, might be desire projected as a pure phonic expenditure.[4] Yet the *Jappements* are decidedly *not* sound poems; they are texts to be understood primarily as a writing, a differential organization and dissemination of sound under the specific conditions of *inscription* and within an extended theory of the image. The ultimate fate of these poems must be given over to a grammatological and not a performative judgement.

actual functioning of thought, in the absence of any control exercised by reason, exempt from any aesthetic or moral concern". *Manifestoes of Surrealism*, tr. Richard Seaver & Helen Lane (Ann Arbor: University of Michigan Press, 1969) p. 26. The pioneering work in automatic writing can be credited to Pierre Janet, Leon Solomons and Gertrude Stein. Janet published his *Psychological Automatism* in 1889 in which he recommends that patients be equipped with writing materials and that the pen be allowed to "wander automatically on the page, even as the doctor penetrates the mind". While attending Johns Hopkins University in pursuit of a degree in medicine, Gertrude Stein carried out a series of experiments with Leon M. Solomons in motor automatism. The results were published in the *Psychological Review*, September 1896 and May 1898. The experiments covered both automatic writing and automatic reading.
3. All quotations from *Jappements à la Lune* are taken from the *Oeuvres Créatrices Complètes* (Ottawa: Editions Parti Pris, 1977).
4. Desire figures large in Gauvreau's theoretical writings. In *Lettre à un Fantome* he writes "the only path to follow is shown us by DESIRE. The fact that any child can make an authentic masterpiece makes me think that *desire* can be born in anybody. But as long as this *desire* is not *permitted*, as long as it does not frantically claw at the surface, in total honesty and with total risk, nothing can point to a new road". Quoted in "Les Automatistes", *La Barre du Jour*, 17-20, Jan.-Aug. 1969, p. 344.

It is from the standpoint of a theory of the image, its Surreal appropriation and Gauvreau's modification, that we will proceed to examine the *Jappements*. The Surrealist sense of image, as canonized by Reverdy, involves the linking of discrepant realities:

> The image is a pure creation of the mind. It cannot be born of a comparison, but arises from the bringing together of two more or less distant realities. The more distant and exact the relationships of the two realities thus brought into contact, the stronger will be the image, the more emotive power and poetic reality it will have.[5]

Reverdy's definition is itself a development from the earlier seed description of Lautréamont's: "Beautiful as the chance encounter on a dissection table of a sewing machine and an umbrella". Max Ernst similarly provides a structure of image based on linkage:

> The joining of two apparently unjoinable realities on a plane which in appearance is unsuitable to them.[6]

It is worth noting that this surreal image is already constituted *beyond* the signifier in the arena of the real. Its language must utilize an unquestioned representational function of the sign, productive of a pictorial, figurative scene. The Surrealists' appeal to dream sources and the unconscious thus included a preservation of a recognizable, referential constituent, relying on juxtapositional and contiguous operations to create the image.

5. Pierre Reverdy, quoted in Michel Carrouges, *André Breton and the Basic Concepts of Surrealism*, tr. Maura Prendergast (University of Alabama Press, 1974) p. 96. Breton himself describes the mechanism of the image as an interstitial combustion or event effected in the space between two terms: "In my opinion, it is erroneous to claim that 'the mind has grasped the relationship' of two realities in the presence of each other. First of all, it has seized nothing consciously. It is, as it were, from the fortuitous juxtaposition of the two terms that a particular light has sprung, the light of the image, to which we are infinitely sensitive. The value of the image depends upon the beauty of the spark obtained; it is, consequently, a function of the difference of potential between the two conductors. When the difference exists only slightly, as in a comparison, the spark is lacking . . . And just as the length of the spark increases to the extent that it occurs in rarified gases, the Surrealist atmosphere created by automatic writing . . . is especially conducive to the production of the most beautiful images. . . . Everything is valid when it comes to obtaining the desired suddenness from certain associations." Quoted in Michael Benedikt, *The Poetry of Surrealism An Anthology* (Boston: Little, Brown and Co., 1974) p. xxi. For an interesting critique of Breton's method of argument, (especially its resort to analogy and, more especially, its appeal to photological metaphor) see Jacques Derrida, "White Mythology: Metaphor in the Text of Philosophy" in *MARGINS of Philosophy*, tr. Alan Bass (Chicago: University of Chicago Press, 1982).
6. Michel Carrouges, loc. cit. p. 97.

It is clear from Gauvreau's own writings that the *automatiste* embraces a much larger area than the Reverdian image. Gauvreau, in fact, distinguishes four essential types of poetic image: rhythmic, reflective, transformational and explorational. The rhythmic image (*image rhythmique*) is basic to sonorous constitution and includes the sono-rhythmic disruptions of the verbal order. The reflective image (*image mémorante*) includes a general simile and the comparison/correspondence between like elements. The transformational image (*image transfigurante*) includes the majority of surrealist imagery and is produced through the extreme straining of the reflective image-disposition so as to effect an actual transformation of the elements. In the explorational image (*image exploréenne*) a total transformation of the elements occurs to a degree such that they are no longer recognizable. It is this last type of image that Gauvreau practises in the *Jappements*, moving towards a new textual morphology, uncompromisingly non-figurative and articulated within the phonetic combinations of sound clusters.

Considered at this extreme point in the history of the Image it is hardly possible to treat the *Jappements* as pure phonetic outlays. It would appear, that as instances of the *image exploréenne*, the poems' materiality derives from a *scrambling* of signifiers, a decomposition of their letter elements and a reconstitution in extreme, unfamiliar groupings, so that a passage out of the material experience is forestalled.[7] Whereas the orthodox surrealist image permits a reader to transfer onto a reference, the transference in the *Jappements* can only bear on its material and arrangement. The *Jappements* induce a deliberate crisis in the writing's semantic system.

7. Several linguists (including Jakobson and Mukarovsky) have argued for an habitual human tendency to convert all phonetic into phonemic material. Presented with an unintelligible utterance — like one of the *Jappements* or Hugo Ball's Dadaist "poetry without words" — an auditor would immediately "transphonologize" it into a context readily assimilable to her individual linguistic habits. Such an argument would appear to essentialize a psychological disposition to recovery and construction, which the current writer does not accept. Yet this transphonologizing disposition does pose a challenge to the more extreme readings of Gauvreau (through a Nietzschean negativity for instance) that would credit to Gauvreau some kind of ultimate, logoclastic force. What is of interest is Gauvreau's own ambivalence towards the logoclastic project, both destroying the word by the letter (in a kind of insane psycho-drama of the metonym) and recollecting the alien sequence of sounds and graphic compounds into an under-language that gestures towards discrete meaning and differentiation. Ultimately we are left with a sense of the *Jappements* as written in "another language", like the trans-rational *zaum* compositions of Khlebnikov, or Stefan George's private language "inaccessible to the profane multitude" into which he reputedly translated

It would be difficult to uphold the total absence of meaning from this procedure. Gauvreau throughout, remains attached to a notion of image and thereby maintains a stubborn, if tenuous, link to representation. A profound ambivalence is spelled out in this single area of a strained representation. On the one hand Gauvreau is alert to the possibilities of a non-semantic text, a liberation of letters from the word and the staged loss of instrumental reason in the sacrifice of a binding semantic order. In this part aspect, Gauvreau's writing *is* a material surface to which there is no assignable limit by either intention-expression, or interpretation. On the other hand, Gauvreau remains connected to an expressionist mandate: the expression of a "surreal" field which lies external to the text and as a consequence takes his place within the tradition of dualistic thinking (conscious/unconscious, internal/external).

ghédérassann omniomnemm wâkkulé orod ècmon zdhal irchpt laugouzou-
    gldefterrpanuclémenpénucleptadussel ferf folfoufaulô farmurerr a
    clô dzorr[8]

There exists here, a profound disjunction between meaning and the phoneme, a radical incompatibility that nonetheless binds the sound, through the phonemic outlay, to an order of meaning. Within the spacing of the letters (it is the spacing that makes this amalgam of letters a writing) is a differential operation that maintains the traces of a semantic "law". The erosion of meaning is active but never results in an entire demolition. It is as if an order of communication has been abandoned to be interiorized and to exist now, not between a sender and receiver, but between the phonematic elements themselves.

The passage from the phonetic to the phonemic is never fully

Book I of the *Odyssey*. As such they may be considered as perverse attenuations of transmission, still petitioning a communication. For the complex problems and discussion of the possibility of private language see Wittgenstein's *Philosophical Investigations*, tr. G.E.M. Anscombe (New York: Macmillan, 1953) and *The Private Language Argument*, ed. O.R. Jones (London: St. Martin's Press, 1971). Curiously enough, one of the first arguments for all language as essentially private comes from the great English empiricist John Locke who states that "words, in their primary or immediate signification, stand for nothing but the ideas in the mind of him that uses them, however imperfectly soever or carelessly these ideas are collected from the things which they are supposed to represent. . . . That then which words are the marks of are the ideas of the speaker: nor can anyone apply them as marks, immediately to anything else but the ideas which he himself hath . . ." *Essay Concerning Human Understanding*, III. ii.2, 11th ed. (London, 1735).
8. *Jappements à la Lune*, poem 8.

determinable in the *Jappements* and it is doubtful that a "pure" phoneticity, a sovereign materiality of sound is ever realized.[9] There is always the gesture towards familiar phonic patterns. The letter groupings often seem to serve as graphic *indications* not entirely contained within the category "meaning" but constantly suggesting it as a juxtaposed elsewhere. As such graphic indicational phenomena, the *Jappements* petition the semantic as a structural proximity that is never entirely reached. By preserving the *semblance* of words (i.e. a disposition, through intelligible spacing, to significance) the writing remains attached to the spectre of a semanticism. With phoneticism unchallenged and phonemicism constantly beckoning, the theme of voice persists, harbouring — as it has always done — the privileged category of the subject.[10]

So Gauvreau's demolition of the pictorial image is a qualified success. Interestingly Gauvreau does not resort to a painterly method that would have allowed him to avoid the ambivalent implications of spacing. His tactical assault is not, for instance, palimpsestic; it does not layer language and obliterate the signifier by a smothering, vertical materiality.[11] Nor does he choose the gestural route of the personal script that would lead to an *illegible* writing (as in the case of Max Ernst, Henri Michaux, Réquichot, Paul Klee and the "hypergraphy" of Maurice Lemaitre).

9. A purely acoustic approach to the poem had been developed early in the century by Saran and Sievers in Germany and by Verrier in France. All three were attacked by the Russian Formalists (viz. Eikenbaum, Jakobson and Tynjanov). Sievers' notorious proposition that all verse theorists should adopt the attitude of a foreigner who listens to a text without understanding the language of the writing, was condemned by the Formalists as being impossible (see footnote 7). Sievers, Saran and Verrier no doubt would have been sympathetic to the *Jappements* as a species of *poésie pure*. And Gauvreau of *their* approach?

10. The *Jappements* would seem to involve the constitution of a "spontaneous" subject, counter-disposed to the subject of instrumental, rationalist discourse. Spontaneity itself would demand that the subject be split between a conscious and unconscious base. The extremity of Gauvreau's push towards the non-semantic does not accomodate a free-play between these terms, but rather demands the theoretical bracketing or putting out of play of the conscious.

11. Through the tactic of the overprint difference itself is obliterated and writing smothered in its own surplus. Ironically perhaps, Gauvreau's own direction does not take him into the painterly practices of the Automatistes (Riopelle, Leduc, Borduas or Claude's own brother Pierre) where a layering of the painterly surface is intrinsic to their demolition of the figural. Gauvreau does not explore such visual techniques to "dis-figurate" his writing but experiments with the bruitist inventions of the Dadaist sound poets. His notion of image, whilst non-figurative, is decidedly phonetic and lettristic. Gauvreau thus avoids the immense potential that concrete poetry offered both Automatiste theory and practice. For further discussion on palimpsest and overprint see *Bill Bissett: A Writing Outside Writing* in the present collection.

beûlokdokbloughezoum achia chichenéchiné chachouann gduppt étréofla-
glontz amu mimaulomaromurméftéjauglionair-aretel lingz ling-z liop
apoutréflobgipct gougouz gou ératra telfombrati iéthol argeltz nautel
pouvouran [12]

There are several moments in this poem that suggest something other than a pure, indifferent outlay. A persistent visual
logic can be sensed in the poem's spatio-temporal unwinding.
Hyphenation registers ideogrammatically in the phonic cluster-
ings and carries a strongly analytic or compounding power. In
line two the juxtaposition of "lingz/ling-z" results in a micro-
relation between identical letters. The reoccuring accents
(graves, acutes, circumflex) moreover, frame the poem defini-
tively as francophonic. Gauvreau in addition preserves the
system of phonetic oppositions that produce a communicable
"value": ("lok/dok", "mi/mau").

Likewise Gauvreau does not opt for staging the meaningless
within meaning (as in journalism, for instance, or the formulaic
narrative repetitions of the TV soaps) where the semantic
system implodes to a dead point, or to a totally empty exchange. Meaning is neither demolished nor imploded, but
disembodied and re-situated outside the text as a spectral
ordering. Whilst clearly demonstrating that letters can have a
density other than their inscription in known writing, the
Jappements suggest a possible semantic beneath their acoustic
surface; a persistence of meaning in its own absence, banished
to be reinscribed as the otherness of the phonic order. We are
in the presence then of two competing systems: a propulsive,
instinctual, non-semantic force that pushes rhythmically — and
through the agency of the letter — *through* language. And a
spectral economy, a recovered and remotivated "memory" of
meaning, situating as a trace or imprint on the non-semantic
flow and pointing constantly to its own possibility to be present.
By legitimating (or "de-repressing") automaticity and spontaneity in the explorational image, Gauvreau reverses the terms of a
bi-polar relation. It is now the traditionally dominant force of
grammar, syntax and meaning that are repressed beneath the
level of a featured anarchism. What remains unchallenged is the
bi-polar relation itself.

12. *Jappements à la Lune*, poem 7.

The rule of meaning which survives the departure of mean-
ing(s) is the underlying implication of the *Jappements*. Meaning
has become the dead space of its absence and shows that lack to
be the predicate of its continued existence. We will not attempt
to induce this hysteric economy into the solution of the dialectic
but simply state a space beyond *automatism* and its dream of a
recovered, spontaneous body, where — to paraphrase St.
Augustine — meaning reveals itself to be "a sound which is
made by no language"[13] and where insinuates the ultimate joke
of the Sign: a cynical absence whose abstract power as a value
we have not escaped in our journeys through the *Jappements*.[14]

1986

13. As well as the History of Surrealism, to which Gauvreau can be related, there is
also the genealogy of the imaginary text. From Aristophanes' non-semantic parodies
of philosophic discourse in *The Clouds*, through the 'pataphysical "Ecto-Cretan"
language invented by R. Murray Schafer, the field is rich in personally invented
languages. Thomas More has been credited as the pioneer inventor of imaginary
languages. More attached a specimen of Utopian verse to the first edition (1516) of
his book *Utopia*. Better known than More's are the specimens of linguistic invention
in Book II, Chapter 9 of Rabelais' *Gargantua and Pantagruel*. In this chapter Panurge
speaks in numerous real and imaginary languages including *language lanternois* ("Prug
frest frins sorgmand strocht druhds"), *language des Antipodes* ("Al barildim gotfano
dech min brin") and a language of Utopia ("Agonou dont oussys vou denaguez
algarou"). In both Rabelais' and More's examples there is a detectable morphology
and syntax that authenticates them beyond writing as a language. Rabelais' word and
sound choice is determined partly by analogy with a variety of existing languages
which seems to be the method in part of both Hugo Ball and Gauvreau. The construction of More's language has been elucidated by Émile Pons in his masterly
article "Les Langues imaginaires dans le voyage utopique: un précurseur, Thomas
Morus" in *Revue de littérature comparée* 10, 1930: 592-603 to which the dedicated
reader is referred. An analysis, comparable to Pons', is always possible on Gauvreau's
texts but so far has not been forthcoming.
14. This final judgement is a judgement on the *Jappements* alone. In earlier texts
Gauvreau created powerful, interactive economies of meaning and non-meaning. The
following is an example from *Les Boucliers Megalomanes* composed 1965-67:

Stahlfeûré
ozbli stubadauklé vneû ochtepe fri max maulon
Les diabéjizes croxcafublixtent les rums de la punia frey
Folfi
cozcodcré clubte cloftbe criniau
Les végétaux aux arsives précieuses cadoumouflent les jeans aux
     romblères macmiafes
Doj dé zé blé bazdu frita

Lyric's Larynx

It is sound more so than meaning binds
the body to language.

As well as composition there is outlay.

Sound and rhythm pose
the elsewhere of meaning.

Death drive: an asserted differential
negativity: i.e.
the phoneme.

The body at all times houses the
linguistic and pre-linguistic.

"the frontiers of the cultural and
biological are not fixed".

Capitalism begins when you
open the Dictionary.

Archiv für gesamte Phonetik, III, 1939
links errors in pronunciation due
to dental abnormalities less
to the dental disorders than to
impairments of
hearing.

"what you take to be a shattering
of language

is really a shattering of
the body".

Greek: phonos = murder
Greek: phonē = a sound

The historical rhythm of the body
is not to be found exclusively
in a Marxian model of dialectical
materiality, nor in a species
of Spenglerian patterns, but within

the poly-logical infractions and
dissections of what politically is
specified as madness
and poetic language.

The unconscious is not "a world"
which sound poetry describes.
It is rather the absence
of a reference that points to the
unconscious as an
absent agent, never to be described
but gesturally felt in

the sonorous intensities and
rhythmic cuttings of the pieces.

Sound carries the anteriorities
of language.

Language is "the figuration
of a world redeeming itself".

1630. Publication in France of
Aglossostomographie containing the
description of a tongueless mouth
which speaks.

When we eliminate the word do we remove the chance
of a dialectic between meaning

and music?

Sound's inevitable movement
is from a biological to a social order.

"Krrrrlqui vashto'oimph hnph xxxr lllllk
pattoosty".

Sound as substance is also
the sign of substance.

1781. Christoph Hellwag in *De formatione
loquelae* poses the question:

if we owe
our faculty of
speech to our
articulatory organs, how
was it possible

for the serpent,
which lacks these
organs, to talk
with Eve?

Aristotelian form is a goal
arrived at as a postponed reward
by way of a completion. As such,
it is complicit with classical notions
of reference.

Circa 1930 Wilhelm Reich declares form
to be *frozen energy*, opening a path
to a new conception of form as
the aggregate of departures not
arrivals.

Desire is not
a transitive verb.

When considering a non-semantic

poetry, it will be
energy that constitutes
the essence of communicated
data.

Group soundings. The poem as
community. "Living syntax", "multiple
meaning", "multiple body".

1718. Jussien's treatise
On the Girl with No Tongue published,
providing empirical proof of
the dispensability of the tongue
to the pronunciation
of all linguals.

Saussurean linguistics posited
a system of language from which
the agency of
the subject was
excluded. The sound poem (or
a text-sound writing) re-inserts
the primary agency of the subject
as an instinctual
body-before-self.

Conspicuous consumption i.e.
good for one performance. Does
this expose an improvisatory
fetish?

Sound poetry is much
more than simply returning
language to its
material base. It

registers the convergence
of symbolic order with genetic
code and has potentially both
a biological and social
programme.

Beyond the single voice is
also beyond Philosophy's great
Moment.

1912. Lev V. Scerba,
to account for
the phenomenon of
interior, silent speech,
proposes a relationship
of emitted sound
to a corresponding
"acoustic image". Sound
is thus interiorized
for the first
time in history
and separated from
a necessary
motor-auditory mechanism.

Network: co-ordinates i.e.
meaning. Eros. Subject.
Other.

Against the order of
word, meaning, nomination
and syntax (i.e. against the
socio-cultural system of communication)

place the gestural body, attaching
itself to sound and rhythm
as autonomous discharges (expenditures)
outside the utilitarian
production of meaning.

Sound Poetry is performance
in its radical triple aspect:
1) a *sacralized* disposition by which
history enters the *written* body.
2) the condition of writing *after* the book.
3) the poetry of a community without distance.

1879. Baudouin de Courtenay now
launches the new discipline
of *psychophonetics*
to investigate the psychological determinants
of human sound.

As well as the "performance" of
a subject of outlay, sound poetry
is also available as a collective symbol of
the social revolt against meaning.

Deprive language of its mandate to mean
and language is deprived of its
most exchangeable element.

1870. University of St. Petersburg.
Baudouin de Courtenay, in his Inaugural
Lecture, introduces the concept of
the phoneme, launching a new discipline
"etymological phonetics" to analyse
relations between

a sound's motor-acoustic properties
and its lexical-grammatical
value.

"When literature seeks
to break its
linguistic mould and
become ideolect, when
it seeks untranslateability,
we have entered
a new world
of feeling".[1]

1978

1. Despite the sound poem's conventional genealogy through Dada and Futurism,
there is an alternative line of connection to what Kristeva terms the subject-in-
process. This line would stress not the connections to the discourse of art, but to
the Freudian and Lacanian implications in current semiology.

"The theory of meaning now stands at a cross-roads: either it will remain an attempt at formalizing meaning systems by increasing sophistication of the logico-mathematical tools which enable it to formulate models on the basis of a conception (already rather dated) of meaning as the act of a *transcendental ego*, cut off from its body, its unconscious, and also its history; or else it will attune itself to the theory of the speaking subject as a divided subject (conscious/unconscious) and go on to attempt to specify the types of operations characteristic of the two sides of this split: thereby exposing them, that is to say, on the one hand, to bio-physical processes (themselves already an inescapable part of signifying processes: what Freud labelled 'drives'), and, on the other hand, to social constraints (family structures, modes of production, etc.)". Julia Kristeva, cited in Umberto Eco. *A Theory of Semiotics*, (Bloomington: Indiana University Press, 1976) p. 317.

Within this context of a "trans-semiotics", the sound poem could be considered as the textual embodiment and performed manifestation of these subjective determinations of utterance.

The ~~Line~~ of Prose

In the entirety of its history prose has never petitioned the line as a sign of a value. Rather it has countered poetry and its lines of prosody, symmetricality and purposeful, significant endings with an utterly apathetic disposition towards its terminals. Yet while breaking down the binding, evaluated linearity (i.e. the *law*) of the poetic line, prose does so within the time of the line itself. The prose line does not exist as a motivated, positive phenomenon. Prose periodizes its significations within the unit of the sentence and the larger unit of the paragraph, which organize closures of a thetic, expository and narrative order.

We have come to think of this inertia, this non-appearance of the value of the line, not as an aspect of the critique of value (and hence a powerful, contemporary force of negation) but as the product of historic rationalist forces (specifically the classic sense of language as a neutral ground). Yet the refusal to engage in valorization might serve a deconstructive "end" and unmask the metaphysical strain in poetry which demands a self-evident presence, a parousial meaning and significance invoked inside the romantic dream of a recovery, through the written mark, of a speaking body without writing. It might further place prose outside — not counter to — the scope of ideology, as a heterological gesture that would open up the question of ideology's paradoxical dependence on a type of coercion that itself relies upon a generated response for its power and that is threatened with impotence in the face of a passive, unresponsive gaze. In this respect at least, the inertial disposition of the prose line might be construed as a negating, non-productive force that mirrors accurately a corresponding disposition of society in the face of a plethora of meaning. As such too, it would duplicate the temporality of the masses.

The system of productive sign economy, its constant proffering of uses, values, differences and purposes, would be thrown back on itself. The prose *line* would be experienced as a loss without retention. Constantly escaping and withdrawing behind the manufacture and transportation of its utilities, it would declare itself of the order of a *general* economy: one of inevitable excess, irreversible loss and unreserved expenditure (in opposition to the restricted economy of accumulation, investment and profit). The line of prose would thereby be closer to a sacrificial economy (and all its implications) than to Capital and would intone its own eschatology as one of the several that inhabit writing.

1985

Strata and Strategy: 'Pataphysics in the Poetry of Christopher Dewdney

In a review of Dewdney's *A Palaeozoic Geology of London Ontario*[1] William Gairdner makes his own guess at the book's intentions:

> The book . . . seems to wish to impress upon us the notion that rocks, geological periods, and fossil forms have some sort of meaningful relation to ourselves, and our souls.[2]

Condemning the poems as "too intellectual" and the prose as "too suspect", Gairdner typifies that kind of reader-critic committed to a passive sense of his own role in any textual engagement, seeing the position of reader to be receptor relative to source, from which originates some kind of ideal or pathetic transference. The notion of reading that Gairdner supports is clearly a notion of recipience and consumption and not a co-production of the text. Whilst Gairdner's response to the book is not in every sense erroneous, it is on the fundamental level of Dewdney's work entirely irrelevant, assuming as it does a theory of language that is patently not one shared with the poet. Gairdner's demand for a more emotional poetry presupposes a language in which the word functions as an innocuous transparency, as a clear, neutral vehicle of message; it is a sense of language that has been seriously questioned since the time of Mallarmé, in whose work language appears ambivalent and suspect, the poems themselves being often of an intensely metalinguistic concern. When Gairdner makes the above observation he raises an issue of fundamental concern to the theoretical ability of a language to communicate adequately

1. The Coach House Press, Toronto 1973.
2. *Open Letter*, 2.9, Fall 1974, p. 102.

a reality outside itself. For the "notion" of rocks, geological periods and fossil forms is a *notion* intrinsically embedded in the nature of language, as too is the sense of discernment between individual rocks, strata and fossil forms, all of which involve a taxonomic differentiation dependent on the classifying functions of language.[3] If these metalinguistic ramifications eluded Mr. Gairdner, luckily they did not Dewdney himself, whose two main books to date[4] embody some of the most significant explorations of the parameters of the linguistic sign to have appeared in this country. Condemning Dewdney's prose as "too suspect" belies the short-sightedness of Gairdner's reading, for it is precisely the "suspect-ness" — not only of Dewdney's own prose but of language itself in its classical guise — that seems the work's central concern.

In another review of the same book, Barry Alpert comes much closer to the core of Dewdney's techniques:

> Dewdney's poems incorporate an apparent grounding in geology not strictly as a means for digging deeper into the literal place where the poet was born and still lives but also as a methodology for identifying and dealing with the fossilized remains and living structures of the language he inherited at birth.[5]

Whilst Alpert's co-opting of the poems to a poetics of place is subtle and specious, the methodological point is well taken and it is to an exploration of the "apparentness" of the geological grounding and to the full nature of the methodology that the rest of this essay will be devoted.

3. Taxonomy analyzes wholes into parts. Individual things are first isolated, analyzed and then recombined in a spatial relationship of hierarchy, so the complicit link with phoneticism should be obvious. M.M. Slaughter has remarked that "there is evidence to indicate that decontextualization and taxonomic analysis develop with the onset of written and/or printed language and with increasing literacy, where words become physical, visible objects". M.M. Slaughter, *Universal Languages and Scientific Taxonomy in the Seventeenth Century* (Cambridge University Press, 1982) p. 9. This trajectory of taxonomy back to a picto-phonetic notion of language is not without interest or relevance to Dewdney's 'pataphysical intervention into the scene of science.
4. i.e. *A Palaeozoic Geology of London Ontario* 1973 and *Fovea Centralis* (Toronto: Coach House Press, 1975). An earlier work, *Golder's Green* 1971, was not available to me at the time of writing. Printed by Dewdney himself in an edition of 200 copies, it predates both the other books and introduces the 'pataphysical terminology which develops into the all-inclusive structure and model of *A Palaeozoic Geology*. At the moment of adding this footnote (1986) Mr Dewdney has gone entirely carboniferous.
5. Barry Alpert, "Written on the Wind (of Lake Ontario)" in *Open Letter* 3.2, Fall 1975.

1

Dewdney's work is part of a long vector of thinking going back through Alfred Jarry and Swift to Rabelais; a vector which stresses a universal convertibility through the instruments of language. It is a sense which, applied as a principle in Dewdney's work, is investigated neither laterally nor quantitively, but vertically and structurally by means of an intellectual framework or 'pataphysical model from which the principle can be examined in function under a controlled situation. I mention 'pataphysics as that term comes closest to describing Dewdney's methodology. Jarry (who is credited with the invention of 'pataphysics) defines it as "the science of imaginary solutions, which symbolically attributes the properties of objects, described by their virtuality, to their lineaments." It is by nature an expressly pseudo-science which provides a solution to a non-existent problem. Dewdney offers his "imaginary solution" to the pseudo-problem of poetic form itself. The problem is "pseudo" as the problem of poetic form is intra-problematic with the issue of linguistic structure. That the problem is a pseudo-problem in no way nullifies the pursuit of a solution, for the pursuit in itself will evince the problematic nature of both "problem" and "solution" as the terms are shaped and defined through the suspect processes of language.

A persistent thread through Dewdney's books is a double exposure (as both pretence and virtue alike) of any scientific outlook articulated through its discourse. What forms is a structural ambiguity designed to unhinge the critical faculty and to relocate it within the tensors of the model:

I stand perhaps in the tiny grace of your features
semblance correct within an anaesthesia
everlasting the love you spoke of.
No one methodology lupine within contexts
your hand is real, and lips
congealed upon contact with . . .

which, as example, is taken from *Fovea Centralis* but equally illustrates a more general strategy of metalanguage, a counter-communication designed to articulate a blind faith to the illusory correspondence between words and their "things". What becomes established is a high degree of linguistic opacity revealed in the concrete facade of the utterance, and a suspect personism of the initial "I" that carries its discourse as a coherent pathology. The tone, in fact, is aphasiac in a poem that enunciates the pathological nature of an asymmetrical relationship of meaning to speech, of intention to effect. (Wernicke's aphasia, we might note in passing, is characterized by a rapid and coherent grammatical speech but is entirely devoid of content). The significant point here is the pathological implications of the poetic form: that a resort to counter-communication can emerge from the pathogenics of language. Dewdney's work is a highly successful evasion of experience that underscores the hiatus between word and thing. Constructed is an analogical framework of great complexity with a method (the operating 'pataphysics) based largely upon a posited similarity in features between language and geology and intended to function *translatively* as a modifying instrument upon the data of experience.[6]

Central to this translative method is the key notion of fossil which forms the analogical catalyst and bridge between geological and linguistic zones.[7]

> Devoid of perception the
> blind form of the fossil
> exists post-factum.
> Its movement planetary, tectonic
> The flesh of these words
> disintegrates.
> (as the words must be placed together
> in light of theiyr skeletons)
> Or rather the motion ascribed to
> becomes a vehicle (for Paraclete.)

The model articulated supports a deeper (linguistic) model in

---

6. Analogy can provide fruitful models for textual innovation but it should be borne in mind that such models are *continuous*. For analogy is dialectical in its structure and supposes a continuity from one term or group to another by symmetrical or proportional means. Analogy produces a fission or joining of terms rather than a fissure and as such would appear to be counter to dissemination.

7. "The bridge is not *an* analogy. Recourse to analogy, the concept and effect of analogy are or make *the* bridge itself. . . The analogy of the abyss and the bridge over the abyss is an analogy to say that there ought to be an analogy between two absolutely heterogeneous worlds, a third to pass over the abyss, to cicatrize the chasm and to think the gap. In short a *symbol*. The bridge is a symbol". Jacques Derrida, "Parergon" 43, quoted in G.L. Ulmer, *Applied Grammatology* (Baltimore: Johns Hopkins University Press, 1985) p. 104.

such a way that the passage overlaps in content and carries two simultaneous threads of meaning. The shift in content from fossil to word merely refocusses at a different point on the surface of this overlap between the two co-existing models.

The ontology of fossil charts a tension held between vertical and horizontal axes. Fossil, being located within both the vertical structure of a land form and the horizontal structure of a time continuum, is a hinge and density of tension with grip on geological strata and evolutionary continuum; a rivet through geography and history. As a memory store (the fossil's post-factum existence) it balances the time continuum, whilst as a phenomenon of strata it is a (momentary) surface of a visible terrain. Dewdney's fossil, moreover, is not object but space formed by the withdrawal of the object; it is ellipse in strata whose extrapolation is the linguistic sign in its state of non-signification. To see word as fossil is to see a signifier detached from a signified, and in Dewdney's work, it is the expressed state of a problematic model. In the poem quoted Dewdney brings word and fossil into symbiosis: as word is the vehicle of fossil in the text, so fossil describes the signifying state itself. Just as fossils verbalize so words fossilize, both are "blind forms" whose existence is after the fact.[8] Fossil and word are the equivalent centres of an absence, language like land-mass is an articulated surface (stratum) just as uttered word is a surfaced articulation (fossil-fold). Fossil relates to stratum as "parole" relates to "langue", as syntagm to paradigm, and as a specific reading of a text to the text itself. Strata becomes the possibility of fossil as fossil becomes a realization of that potentiality in strata.

It is through these two aspects of the geological model that Dewdney carries out his meta-linguistic explorations, the task being facilitated by the fact that both strata and fossil have all the implications of the linguistic sign. Indeed, adopting Saussure's famous formula of the Sign — S/s: Signifier over signified, we can see fossil as a variation on this equation:

---

8. This notion of "absence" will bear comparison with the notion of *differance* in the work of Jacques Derrida. Derrida views writing as "trace" or deferral — a quality inevitable within the spatial existence of differentiated and differentiatable verbal signs.

S/ . . . .
                    .
          .(s)
              with the signified "withdrawn"

leaving the Signifier detached and with its power of signification
short-circuited. At this point the ".(s)" acquires a kinetic motivation graphing the entropic spiral of an inwardly directional
discourse. Letter becomes self-directional, equation becomes
score.

Further linguistic implications attain on the larger level of
the grammar, where fossil operates as a linguistic insertion into
a geological fact providing an answer to a question never asked.
It is from this precessional answering that palaeontology formulates its questions by a system of back-formation. The fossil is a
"sentence" that answers a non-existent question and hence is by
nature 'pataphysical. As a sentence or sign construct fossil also
violates the non-specificity of strata; it is an animal intrusion
into, and reorganization of, a mineral context in the similar way
that grammar organizes a specificity forced out of the un-
bounded potentiality of language before any individual instantiation.

The image of the fossil derives from a geological model that
mirrors the further systems of lexis and grammar. The two
images of fossil and strata are 'pataphysical spatializers that
serve to distance language and place it under observation.
There is implicit in this approach a need to transform the
diachronic flow of the speech act into the synchronic form of
a 'pataphysical structure: the fossil epitomizes this transformation and is for Dewdney the paradigm of diachronic/synchronic
conversion.

It is the chosen model of 'pataphysics that is instrumental in
Dewdney's large scale sense of evolving structure. In *A Palaeozoic Geology*, for instance, there is a total cohesiveness to the
book's structure that betokens an attention to the interrelating
strategy of parts. It is not simply a collection of discrete poems
but an evolving exposure to a configurative field. Above the
simple movement of word and poem, is a larger multi-directional
and transformational motion measurable above the local events
of the syntax in the functional property of the model. It is a
movement in which metaphor and model, dynamic conversion

and steady state, unstable readjustments in perceptual focus
and stable cognitive grasp, achieve synthesis. Schematically this
structure balances the lateral and longitudinal experiences. The
section "Log Entries", for instance, promotes the footnote to
a complete structural technique, rendering any reading relational in a vertical descent from the "experience" of a text,
down to its corresponding "explanation". The sections "Litho-
logy of the Memory Table" and "Memory Table" themselves
(by contrast) inaugurate the book's lateral support with a
correspondence established "across" textual zones. In other
words, the total structure of the book projects the geometrical
properties of fossil (horizontal continuum through time i.e. the
palaeontological "line", and vertical descent into strata i.e. the
geological "plummet").

In Dewdney's hands, fossil takes the form of metaphor
extended into model functioning as a replacement for the
data of experience. It is on this point too — the capacity for
substitution — that the properties of fossil and linguistic sign
coincide. Both are instruments, in C.S. Peirce's words, that
replace "a someone with a something". One of the great
rewards of Dewdney's books is to trace beneath the 'pataphysical dimensions of the geological model (i.e. Mr. Gairdner's
"suspect prose") the function and topology of the linguistic
sign itself.

2

The mind is a cavity in which
sensitive plates, exposed to
unimaginable radiations
dance over blind flowers.

There is a cold hexagonal fire
in the insect's eye.
                    (Dewdney)

       what if
    i go crazy
    racing
              running thru th fields flames pourin outuv
    my crazy hed my arms turning to watr liquid melt
    in flesh yu got to turn around now well thats

who it is early songs yu may have a choice
   do yu have any
             (Bill Bissett)

The "I" persona provides the semic activity in any poem with a cellular integrity. Topologically, the "I" marks, in linguistic form, a bioenergetic placement of action at the boundary of the skin. It is the ability of a poet like Bissett to make words hover, as events, at this physical margin. Punctuation is reduced to a minimum and line length works, almost electro-cardiographically, as measure of the human pulse in language. There is a marked absence in Dewdney of this sense of language pressing at the margins of cellularity, in its place is a stress upon neural circuitry through an intellectual model. Bissett's language is decidedly bioenergetic and the dialectic of syntagm and paradigm is dramatized in extremely physical terms. Speech issues bardic from this cellular, yet constantly threatened, integrity as a consequence of which the poem carries a maximum of linguistic hyperaction and emotional resonance, terminating with a severance of speech at a physical boundary. By contrast, Dewdney's language has no absolute human issue but merges and interconnects with quasi scientific and 'pataphysical circuitries: "The mind is a cavity in which/ sensitive plates, exposed to/ unimaginable radiation/ dance over blind flowers". Voice itself is annihilated in model with the structure of the speech-act stabilized eidetically in a pseudo-intellectual structure around which the problematics of meaning and the position of a subject of knowledge are allowed to circulate and exhibit themselves. Dewdney presents experience as "absent", "withdrawn", converted into 'pataphysical complexities and ultimately entropic, with parallel anatomy to fossil (. . . the mind is a cavity . . .) where experience retreats into the counter-factual. We may compare too, the orthographic peculiarities. Bissett's personal modifications in spelling act mantically as "coefficients of weirdness" (Malinowski's term) and register the urgent biological current beneath the speech-act. In Dewdney, where orthographic variants are virtually limited to the one spelling of "theiyr", the effect is ideogrammic ("they" and "their" become inseparable ideas) with the concomitant sense of the stubborn resistance of the word itself to any kind of grammatical evolution. "Theiyr" stands in

the text as fossil stands in strata, fixed in form and diachron-
ically untouchable. It is, quite literally, the fossil concept
projected onto the orthographic face of language.

3

The technique of the migratory model has its effect on image
too. Throughout one senses image falling between taxonomy
and vortex as:

> Unborn concretions
> rolling in theiyr oiled memory jackets
> beneath the
> vibrating mask of the lake

where image "classifies" the linguistic energy present in the
formative flow, at the same time stressing the energetic drive
beneath the classifying act. The effect is something like exposing the neurochemistry of intellection-in-process, whilst the
strategy seems obvious: to clothe fictively a *genuine* movement
in order to isolate that movement for observational purposes.
Image in its straddling of class and vortex becomes an efficient
distancing device:

> Unborn concretions
> rolling in theiyr oiled memory jackets

where nothing is fixable in the "real" extra-linguistic world,
but shows a capability of being experienced as a kinetics of
syntax itself — the "roll" of the signifier in its verbal jacket.

"Log Entries" is possibly Dewdney's most complex single
piece to date challenging the reader to experience the text as
particle and feedback. The piece comprises prose passages,
extremely fragmented, un-hinged from context and drifting as
verbal particles across the top surface of each page. Page itself
must function as the ocular instrument for observing this
incessant linguistic flow, whose points of origin and of destination are equally obscured. Below each prose fragment and
placed in obvious iconic disjunction are corresponding poems
"of explanation". The structure bears comparison to Jack
Spicer's "The Heads of the Town up to the Aether", which
similarly distributes a meaning through vertical placement of
separate texts. In the light of the established geological model,

"Log Entries" takes on a particular quality as a zone of per-
ceptibility placed before the reader. The prose registers eidetic
as a section of strata in discourse, with the text's explanatory
"beneath" working geologically as "set in" the page. It holds
the same thrust of reference and solution as does the fossil, and
to explain the prose as fossil would be to explain the stratum
that encloses it.

An added complexity in "Log Entries" comes from the
accompanying illustrations which are not merely decorative
additions but function as significant inter-textual instruments
central to the evolving concept of fossil in the book and the
expanding dialectical implications of the linguistic sign. Picture
relates agonistically to word, competing with it for the property
of fossil — suggesting evidence of "a war for metaphor and sign"
and waged between word and picture. In this present case the
Saussurean formula is modified from "signifier over signified"
to "signifier versus signified", for the presence of illustration
(for instance in the poem "Coelacanth") administers a counter
thrust to the referential push of the word, presenting a "counter-
image" to the image that emerges in the verbal text. As word,
through its fossil analogy, is seen as a signifier detached from a
signified, so illustration as a non-verbal "concrete" picture is
seen as the signified detached from a signifier. There is a path
through reference from the word to its evocation, but the
picture is a pathless, immediate and non-verbal presence. The
dialectical pressure that arises (between word and picture)
articulates the breadth of Dewdney's metalinguistic explorations and centres upon fossil as "illustrative" as much as
"verbally descriptive" of the language strata.

Less oppositionally, illustration extrapolates the missing
element in the ontology of the sign as it emerges and develops
through the book. It can be understood as what is removed
when the verbal sign "withdraws" and at the same time as that
which "enters" the former locus of the sign to smother all
resultant absence. As the sign's missing term, illustration offers
the elements for a reconstitution, allowing a grasp of an
evolutionary 'pataphysic, an imaginary solution to the imperfections of the sign.

In the structure and sequence of *A Palaeozoic Geology of
London, Ontario* (which derive largely from developed implications of the imported 'pataphysical model — geology) Dewdney

lays out a schema for linguistic evolution — from word, conceived problematically as a signifying "absence", through "illustration" as the missing element (the absent term), to "Forgeries": the final section of the book which completes this evolution. In "Forgeries" we get beyond the semiotic paradox of the word-fossil-image complex into a clearer, non-analytic sense of language as communal event or game. The poems read as scores projected for happenings, in the main, outside of speech; they are the final transference of the poem from meta-linguistic analysis to blue-print for human action:

> One person leaves the room while the others
> Select two words that sound alike when spoken.
> 'How about you, Joan, have you ever had a teapot,
> one you can't eat, I mean?

This activity of syntax — the roll of unborn concretions — projects onto the social level of ludic interaction at which point speech simultaneously gains an innocence and its Wittgensteinian complexities. It is language released from schema and model and relocated in the human syntax of group participation. "Forgeries", although apparently obtrusive and disconnected from what has gone before, in fact completes the book's broadest theme: the evolution of structure and context from analogy through testing and contrast to a superstructure in game. Structure initially derives exogamously from an imported, alien, yet analogous model: geology; it is then tested, its complexities revealed (word-fossil-picture-strata) until, in "Forgeries", the book enters game and the freedom to *invent* one's own rule structures. With this in mind, to enter "Forgeries" is to reach a rite of passage to a new relationship to structure.

Much of the success of *A Palaeozoic Geology* derives from the structural cohesiveness of the whole book. In *Fovea Centralis*, where the 'pataphysics is realized more on the level of a shifting vocabulary than on a synchronic structure, this cohesiveness is lacking. There, the 'pataphysical model acts as the dramatized term in a dialectic, played off (in the form of technological speech and style) against a more recognizably traditional vocabulary of sentiment whose shortcomings rest in the stylistic inability to rise above the level of lateral displacement:

Immersed &
inside the areola of summer darkness
we fused in the natural grace of our moving.
(our knowledge terrible & flickering
in retinal heat-lightning on the horizon &
over our phospheme faces)

Yet the level never shifts into simple, metaphoric substitutions. A strong, dialogic interplay between different discourses holds the language to an opaque, referentially unfilling body of signification.

4

"Forgeries" on a semantic level confirms Gairdner's evaluation of Dewdney's prose as suspect. What Gairdner fails to do, however, is move beyond a shallow accusation of aesthetic inadmissibility. Indeed, what the book's title suggests is a search beyond suspicion into the realm of blatant counter-factuality. The etymology of "forgery" is complex, having connexions with the folk latin *faurga*: a workshop and O.F. *forge*. An important cognate is the latin *fabrica*: a workshop, from the latin *fabri*: a workman. To forge is to fabricate and both are to make; Greek "make" is *poesis*, from which derives "poetry" completing the etymological link of the poem with the lie. Poetry is forgery, the production of the counter-factual, as Hermes the god of poets doubles as the god of thieves and liars. *Mendacium est enuntiado cum voluntate falsum enuntiadi* is St. Augustine's definition of the lie as "the willful utterance of an articulate falsehood", a definition which comes as close as anything to the root nature of 'pataphysics. It is a mendacious presence that characterizes both *A Palaeozoic Geology* and *Fovea Centralis* where Dewdney brings out the creative potential of the lie to support the bond between a technical display of the energies of writing and the emergent tissue of a fiction. It is a presence structured on the proposition, implicit in St. Augustine, that falsity is an integral achievement of discourse. The whole tone of

Facing you in my head, the stars of
dawn you saw last in the meccano warehouse
photographing your obsession and its natural generation

from a disjointed season.

recalls the sequential dialogues of mutual deception engaged in
by Odysseus and Athena in Book 13 of *The Odyssey* — discourses of reciprocal untruths that carry no moralistic overtones
but the simple feeling of lies existing to display the verbal craft
behind them. Perhaps both Dewdney and Homer would have
agreed that lies occur merely so we may "speak them". Dewdney's most articulate statement of this art of the untruth occurs
towards the end of *Fovea Centralis* in "from A Handbook of
Remote Control":

> The remote control personality constructs a
> meticulous lie around another being. Particle
> by particle the solid reality that composed the
> allegorical ground he stood on is replaced by
> fantasies and lies. (fossilization)

Fossilization is the act of metaphor magnified to a global
strategy, a tactic of replacement applicable to the realities
surrounding other beings. This verbal vitality resident within
mis-statement takes on special implications in the light of
Dewdney's 'pataphysics. For what it opens is the polysemous
nature of discourse, which becomes a stratum holding
striations and multi-directional cracks ("lithographies") that
graph a particular geometry of consciousness alert to the
dangers and opacities of language, the guilt of the anarchic
word and the semantic intractability ("remote control") of
the lexeme.

Dewdney's language does not command assent but rather
offers participation on the level of doubt, suspicion and
accusation. His work serves to mobilize an intellectual stance
against the surface of the verbal sign, suggesting that we dig
deeper into the etymological strata for the key term: fossil
from *fodere*: to dig as towards the latent truth and/or the
latent lie. The tone of this mendacity within the 'pataphysics
instigates a confrontation with the linguistic form that carries
it. It is this sense of language, rejected as vehicular instrument
and critically challenged as suspect environment, that is the
major implication of both books. Beyond mendacity,
however, is the vitality of articulation which carries its own
positive implications: that all events are capable of alteration,

that a lie attacks language at its weakest fabricative point:
reality itself. Swift saw the lie as constituting the essential
difference between a man and a horse, Dewdney shows it as the
chief agent of anti-matter, as the shaper of new forms at the
margins of reality, chiselling away at the mass of "that which
is" to release the fragments of "what are not" and which
equally well "can be". "from A Handbook of Remote Control"
is 'pataphysical hyperbole in the grandest Swiftian manner, a
dextrous overstatement of the notion that language has its
worth more in the capacity to mis-inform (and hence create)
than in the ability to inform and consolidate what's already
there. Information, the honest statement of the facts, is the
path into the entropic state of fossil. As lie, however, language
is a weapon at the service of a guerrilla epistemology and is,
in the words of George Steiner, "the main instrument of man's
refusal to accept the world as it is".

1975

Writing as a General
Economy

I've chosen to approach writing and the written text as an
economy rather than a structure. The latter tends to promote
essence as relational, which has the clear advantage of avoiding
all closed notions of the poem as "a well-wrought urn" but
suffers from a presupposed stasis, a bracketed immobility among
the parts under observation and specification. As an alternative
to structure, economy is concerned with the distribution and
circulation of the numerous forces and intensities that saturate
a text. A textual economy would concern itself not with the
order of forms and sites but with the order-disorder of circulations and distributions. A writing by way of economy will
consequently tend to loosen the hold of structure and mark its
limits in economy's own movement.

Specifically, I want to focus on writing as a general economy
and start by presenting Georges Bataille's concise definition
of it:

> The general economy, in the first place, makes apparent that excesses
> of energy are produced, and that by definition, these excesses can-
> not be utilized. The excessive energy can only be lost without the
> slightest aim, consequently without meaning.

The application of this definition extends far beyond scriptive
practice and would include all non-utilitarian activities of excess,
unavoidable waste and non-productive consumption in which
one might specify orgasm,[1] sacrifice, meditation, The Last

First presented to the Department of Social and Political Theory, York University,
Toronto, November 1984 and in revised forms at the Poetry Project, St. Mark's,
New York, January 1985 and New Langton Arts, San Francisco, January 1986.
1. Incest, for example, could only exist within the operation of a restricted language.
As Lyotard describes it "only in words can the mother be conceived as a mistress; in

Supper,[2] and dreams.[3] It would connect too with the theories
in Barthes' later writings regarding a certain hedonism in reading
and a shift in emphasis from a utilitarian understanding (including a readerly production of meaning) towards a pleasure or
"jouissance" of texts.[4] Apart from a brief look at potlatch,
however, I will limit the discussion to writing and approach the
subject from two directions. The first will be descriptive and try
to indicate the unavoidable presence of general economic operations as an aspect of language's fundamental constitution. In a
second part I will consider general economy as a model for
writing, hinting towards an extremely tentative "poetics of the
general" that might serve a praxis of challenge to conceptual
dominants of traditional writing such as transmission theory of
communication, the continuous subject, the valorization of
representational and referential procedures etc. and try to show
how a strategy of the general economy can help loosen the
philosophical hold that utility, as an unquestionable value, has
maintained historically over the notion of writing.

    We will oppose this economy to restricted economy whose

orgasm, she is no longer the mother, no longer anything". Outside of interested
meaning, in the system of general economy, libido would not be of the order of a
transgression (a crossing of boundaries that simultaneously annuls and preserves the
partitionality) but of a liquidator of social definition and categories.
2. The Last Supper, as a problematic moment in diachronic Christology, has been
dealt with by Hegel in his early theological writings; it is the issue of the predication
of transubstantiation upon an alimentary model. In the conversion of Christ's body
and blood into bread and wine (and bear in mind the eucharist is not a simple metaphoric substitution) there is an intrinsic contamination of two codes. Christ becomes
bread and wine, yet the attendant implications of the subsequentiality (digestion,
absorption and elimination) are carefully avoided by the early Fathers, who ignore
the repercussions of Communion as a general economic action.
3. Dreams, it would seem, occupy a liminal, indeterminate position between a
production and an involuntary expenditure. This indeterminacy is reflected in
Freud's own hesitation in affirming the dream as either an absolute communication
(and hence capable of being submitted to interpretation) or a conflictual, intra-
psychic "spillage". Freud hence draws the distinction between the dream *per se*
(which is of the order of an involuntary outlay and eludes intentionality) and the
dream *text* which is open to interpretation. It was Freud's inability to incorporate
all elements of the dream text into the productive sphere that led also to his positing
of certain *hieroglyphic determinatives* or meaningless elements, whose function is "to
establish the meaning of some other elements". (S. Freud, *Standard Edition*, Vol.
XIII p. 177). Finally, to take note of Freud's theory of neurosis, it would seem that
the latter is located inside a restrictive economy. Freud sees as inevitable, the
transition from the primary process, which is understood as a direct discharge or
expenditure, to the secondary process that postpones this discharge and channels it
off into *investment*. This passage from primary to secondary processes, according to
Freud, constitutes a necessary condition for the formation of neurosis.
4. The French word *jouissance* is notoriously untranslatable (itself a case of
unavoidable loss) but signifies both "bliss" (as a state of pleasure) and "ejaculation"
(the precise moment and intensity of the coming).

operation is based upon valorized notions of restraint, conservation, investment, profit, accumulation and cautious proceduralities in risk taking. Both these economies need to be distinguished from political economy which articulates the bourgeois theory of production and from Rousseau's use of the term "general economy" in his *Discourse on Political Economy* of 1758 where *general* and *political* are bracketed together and contrasted with *private* and *particular* economies i.e. the economies of an individual household or family. I want to make clear that I'm *not* proposing "general" as an alternative economy to "restricted". One cannot replace the other because their relationship is not one of mutual exclusion. In most cases we will find general economy as a suppressed or ignored presence within the scene of writing that tends to emerge by way of rupture within the restricted, putting into question the conceptual controls that produce a writing of use value with its privileging of meaning as a necessary production and evaluated destination. Often we will detect a rupture made and instantly appropriated by the restrictive. The meaningless, for example, will be ascribed a meaning; loss will be rendered profitable by its being assigned a value. In effect, what will be dealt with is a complex interaction of two constrastive, but not exclusive economies, within the single operation of writing. Restricted economy, which is the economy of Capital, Reason, Philosophy and History, will always strive to govern writing, to force its appearance through an order of constraints. The general economy would forfeit this government, conserve nothing and, whilst not prohibiting meaning's appearance, would only sanction its profitless emergence in a general expenditure; hence, it would be entirely indifferent to results and concerned only with self-dispersal. A general economy can never be counter-valuational nor offer an alternative "value" to Value for it is precisely the operation of value that it explicitly disavows. It follows also that the general economy can never offer a full critique of value but only risk its loss, accompany it to its limit and in the slide of value and meaning throw both into question. It will engender neither uses nor exchanges but eruptions without purpose within structures of restraint as that economy which shatters the accumulation of meaning.

To turn to the promised descriptive project and look at the

presence of general economy in language's fundamental constitution: speech and writing "originate" as material substances in
the act of incising graphic marks upon a substance, in the physical
act of gesticulating (sign language for instance) and in the
expulsion of certain sounds through the buccal cavity. In all
three cases there is an uncontestable graphic, phonic or gestural
materiality that is a necessary condition of, yet insubsumable
to, the ideality of meaning. A profit, in this way, shows itself to
be predicated upon a loss, for the physical act of speaking or
writing must withdraw so that what has been said or written can
appear meaningful.[5] Meaning this way is staged as the telos and
destination of the de-materialization of writing. The sound and
rhythmic components of language can never be reduced to the
operation of language per se. Hjelmslev is one of several contemporary linguists who distinguish language as a system from
its material support in sound and ink. The phonē (i.e. any
objective speech sound considered as a physical event regardless
of how it fits into a pattern of meaning) is just such a threshold.
As its material support, sound and ink are separable from the
signifying process, but at the same time the process is unsup-
portable without it. In light of this one could consider language's
materiality as meaning's heterological object, as that area
inevitably involved within the semantic apparatus that meaning
casts out and rejects. Language fractures at this radical point of
support, severing the system per se from a plurality of speech
and writing effects. It is because of this general economy of
materiality that writing can function as an entirely referential
project, pointing out beyond itself to an adequated zone of
non-linguistic "reality". When writing situates in a reference to
a field of objects it relates to something other than itself becom-
ing projective and a carrier of meaning. So writing's initially

5. Greimas, for one, speaks of the radical *bi-isotopic* nature of language. For Greimas,
the two isotopies are "enunciation" and "statement" (*enoncé*). The latter's subject is
determined retroactively, hence, a production of restricted economy, whilst the
subject of enunciation "enacts" itself in real time through the production of linked
and temporally deferred utterances. The letter is pure contiguity and pre-symbolic.
Indeed, Lacan has gone so far as to claim that the time of enunciation is a "thing"
and as a thing, exists outside the *structured* time of symbolizing discourse. We might
compare Greimas' notion of the posterior statementalization of enunciation with the
recently developed notions of digital and analog codes. Through this latter availability, the statement would be comprehensible as a co-optation of a digital (i.e.
discontinuous or paratactic) by an analog (or continuous) code. The affiliations
(real or imaginary) between these satellitic couplings (digital-analog, paratactic-
hypotactic, enunciation-statement, restricted-general) is too large and complex an
issue to be dealt with adequately in this footnote.

general economy is immediately recouperated as a restrictive operation by which writing does not lose a world of objects but appropriates and retains this in itself as an homogenized territory of meaning, ideality and sign.

As well as this expenditure of materiality from language, the field of objects must also de-materialize, drawing away into nomination and denotation (the targets for deixis) in order to be present *inside* language as a referent. Two instantly appropriated general economies then, are immediately invested back into ideation. Under this restrictive action language never presents itself as a breached system involving two intersecting economies of both waste and retention. The language of instrumental reference will always repress this breach and downplay the constitutional presence of a material exhaustion.

METAPHOR

I want to consider metaphor as a second example of a general economic operation. Clearly metaphor is not a simple designation but a substitutional device that carries a noun or nominal phrase (as a virtual designator) elsewhere *towards* another term. I am stressing the word *towards* because the problematics of the transit inform the very nature of the figure. We will examine this point shortly. Metaphor, in fact, attacks the notion of absolute meaning. At least one aspect of the metaphoric operation involves the institution of an identity between dissimilar things, an annexation of *otherness* and the suppression of difference, and if this aspect comprised the entire action of metaphoricity, then it would stand as a unilateral operation of equivalence that *prima facia* would sanction exchange. But this reduction of difference to identity is never an absolute moment in metaphor; there is always another constitution that threatens presence, an operation of metaphor not as trope but as locus for the contestation of difference. In effect, there is always the threat of substitution going astray in the substitutional passage, of the movement elsewhere towards the appropriation of the otherness collapsing and actually engendering a heterogeneity. Curiously enough it was Hobbes in *Leviathan* (1651) who first sensed the errant nature of metaphor. There Hobbes confined the figure to the realm of sedition. Approaching metaphor's more political and philosophical implications, he noted the radical ambivalence of metaphor, its striation of both truth and falsehood that commits it to general economy. Metaphor is seditious precisely because it loses that which it purports to retain, replacing the unequivocal relation of the word to truth with skew, breach and uncertainty. In a simple metaphor such as "the talons of the law", there is a loss of clear, incontestable reference to bird and a similar loss of abstraction in the term "law". Rather than effecting an indisputable substitution (which would presuppose the transcendental principle of equivalence that institutes the exchangist economy) the semantic mechanism is rendered nomadic, meaning wanders from one term to another and any relationship through substitution and equivalence can only be asserted within the framing and staging of a certain loss.

We would examine further this constitutional ambivalence with a consideration of metaphor's binary *other* in the great structuralist drama: metonymy, and argue that metaphor, as a substitutional figure, requires a necessary passage through metonymy (its other term). Any purported resemblance between two terms (such as metaphor necessitates) must be predicated upon a contiguous scene, a pre-figurational, pre-rhetorical placement of terms in a scene allowing the spatio-cognitive assertion of resemblance. Now this is a metonymic predication. Jakobson, of course, in the footsteps of both Freud and Saussure, established metaphor (the axis of selection) and metonymy (the axis of combination) as a coupled opposition which subsequently became the diametrical matrix of all structuralism. But metaphor shows itself to be much more than a discrete figure, indeed it reveals itself to be radically contaminated by metonymy, unavoidably ambivalent in its functional relationship to both substitution and equivalence. Terms such as "mother tongue", "table leg" and "watch face" seem structured on this contaminated sense, an indecision between metaphor and metonymy, marking a hesitation between substitution and contiguity.

We can see metaphor as a figure of economy rather than structure, predicated upon a certain scarcity (i.e. the lack of a univocal designator of an object or target term) that distributes its indeterminacies among the significatory scenes it helps to establish, offering displacement as a *potential* disposition but fixing a residual potentiality between the two terms. What seems incontrovertible in this "improper" displacement of metaphor is the loss of both heterogeneity and identity. The move towards the annexation of the difference occurs as much because two things are *not* the same as because of any similarity between them. The movement to resemblance effects an escape of difference, yet there is always an irreducible, unmasterable remnant in the figure that is neither resemblance nor difference but the indeterminacy of both. Metaphor then, would inhabit the two domains of exchange and residue as well as being inscriptional of both profit and loss.

THE PARAGRAM

> A text is paragrammatic, writes Leon S. Roudiez, "in the sense that its organization of words (and their denotations), grammar, and syntax is challenged by the infinite possibilities provided by letters or phonemes combining to form networks of significance not access-ible through conventional reading habits . . ."[6]

The percolation of language through the paragram contaminates the notion of an ideal, unitary meaning and thereby counters the supposition that words can "fix" or stabilize in closure. Paragrammatic wordplay manufactures a crisis within semantic economy, for whilst engendering meanings, the paragram also turns unitary meaning against itself. If we understand meaning in its classical adequation to truth and knowledge, then para-grammaticized meaning becomes a secretion, an escape or expenditure from semantic's ideal structure into the dissemina-tory material of the signifier.

The paragrammatic path is one determined by the local indications of a word's own spatio-phonic connotations that produce a centrifuge in which the verbal centre is itself scattered. Paragrams are the flow-producing agents in a text's syntactic economy inscribing themselves among that other economy whose notion of word (as a fixed, double articulation of signifier/ signified) upholds the functional distributions of a presentation.

6. Quoted in Julia Kristeva, *Revolution in Poetic Language*, tr. Margaret Waller (New York: Columbia University Press, 1984) p. 256. Sections of this discussion of the Paragram occur in a slightly altered form in *The Martyrology as Paragram* in this present work. Both discussions were written in ignorance of Kristeva's own article *Pour une semiologié des paragrammes* (in *Tel Quel*, Spring 1967) to which the reader is encouraged to refer. Both Kristeva's and my investigations seem to have been inspired by a common source in Saussure.

The paragram, moreover, is a fundamental disposition in all combinatory systems of writing and contributes to phoneticism's trans-phenomenal character. Paragrams (including anagrams) are what Nicholas Abraham terms *figures of antisemantics*;[7] they constitute that aspect of language which *escapes* all discourse and which commits writing unavoidably to a general economy and to the trans-phenomenal paradox of *an unpresentability that serves as a necessary condition of writing's capacity to present*. All of this suggesting a constitutional non-presence in meaning itself.

Ferdinand de Saussure's most controversial and least understood work is his extensive research into late Latin Saturnian verse. Saussure compiled 139 notebooks on paragrammatic and anagrammatic embeds in Saturnian verse, Homer, Virgil, Seneca, Horace, Angelo Politian and the Vedic Hymns. What Saussure found in all these works was the persistence of a recurrent group of phonemes that combined to form echoes of important words. In the *De Rerum Natura* of Lucretius, for instance, Saussure detected extended and multiple anagrams of the name APHRODITE. Implicit in this research is the curiously non-phenomenal status of the paragram. For whilst assignable to a certain order of production, value and meaning, the paragram did not derive necessarily from an intentionality or conscious rhetoricity and seemed an inevitable consequence of writing's alphabetic, combinatory nature. Seen this way as emerging from the multiple ruptures that alphabetic components bring to virtuality, meaning becomes partly the production of a general economy, a persistent excess, non-intentionality and expenditure without reserve through writing's component letters. Through a very specific project, Saussure seemingly hit upon the vertiginous nature of textuality, seeing in this paragrammatic persistence an inevitable indeterminacy within all writing.

This unavoidable presence of words within words contests the notion of writing as a creativity, proposing instead the notion of an indeterminate, extra-intentional, differential production. The paragram should not be seen necessarily as a latent content or hidden intention, but as a sub-productive sliding and slipping of meaning between the forces and intensities distributed through the text's syntactic economy. Paragrams

7. Nicholas Abraham, "The Shell and the Kernel", tr. Nicholas Rand, *Diacritics 9*, 1979.

ensure that there will always be a superfluity of signifiers and a degree of waste and unrecouperability of meaning. Understood as a trans-phenomenal element of language, not an intention of the subject, paragrams open up a general economy on the level of signs and meanings.

Saussure himself remained puzzled by his discoveries. In 1908 he is found writing to Leopold Gautier "I make no secret of the fact that I myself am perplexed − about the most important point: that is, how one should judge the reality or phantasmagoria of the whole question".[8] In other words, does this persistence of anagrams indicate a conscious creation or could it be simply a retrospective "creation" evoked and projected by a reader? Saussure's dilemma on this point is symptomatic of a need to attach a value to trans-phenomenality and thereby evade the issues of a general economy. For if we admit that the paragram can be both fortuitous and intentional, a conscious creation *and* a trans-phenomenal infra-production, then we must further admit to the infinite resourcefulness of language itself to produce aimlessly and fulfill in effect all the features Bataille assigns to a general economy: unmasterable excess, inevitable expenditure and a thoroughly non-productive outlay.

Such features of general economic operation as I've outlined do not destroy the order of meaning, but complicate and unsettle its constitution and operation. They *should* destroy, through their presentation of constitutive contaminants (loss in

---

8. One of history's finest paragrammatic moments occurs in August 1610 when Galileo sends Kepler a note containing the cryptogram:
SMAISMRMILMEPOETALEUMIBUNENUGTTAURIAS.

Recognizing it as an anagram, Kepler translated it into five Latin words − *'salve umbistineum geminatum martia proles'* (Greetings, burning twins, descendents of Mars) − which he understood to mean that Galileo has observed that Mars has two moons. Galileo, however, actually meant the message to read, *'altissimum planetam tergiminum observavi'* (I have discovered that the highest of the planets (Saturn) has two moons). The interest of the paragrammatic mistranslation is that the sense intended is referentially wrong (with his primitive telescope Galileo mistook Saturn's rings for moons), while the interpreted sense is referentially correct. Mars does have two moons, although they were not observed until 1877.
Quoted in Gregory L. Ulmer, *Applied Grammatology* (Baltimore: Johns Hopkins University Press, 1985) p. 151-2.

Galileo's anagram is fine evidence of the aleatory presence within the combinatory phonetics of western writing, a presence which always threatens an excess of meaning over intention, thereby guaranteeing a certain semantic loss.

presence, metonymy in metaphor etc.) any essentialist notions of meaning and the operation of a subject within such unicities. Perhaps too, through the reader's own macro-structural applications of general economy, we might be warned of the socio-political implications of a yoking-of-passage, elusiveness and de-centralizing tendencies to the projects of self-interest, law and truth.

At this point, however, I want to move on to the second part I promised and consider general economy's application as a speculative model of writing in which the socio-political and phenomenological implications, outlined and hinted at, might enter into a sign practice. I will begin with Hegel whom Derrida describes as *the first philosopher of the Book*. Hegel offers a *prima facia* inspiring theory on the nature of transgression and the task he describes as "the labour of the negative" that involves "looking death in the face" as a confrontation with the meaningless. In *The Phenomenology* Hegel writes of this "labour" as the mind's basic work of theoretical appropriation:

> . . . the life of the mind is not one that shuns death, and keeps clear of destruction; it endures death and in death maintains its being . . . It is this mighty power . . . only by looking the negative in the face, and dwelling with it. This dwelling beside it is the magic power that converts the negative into being.

One would initially suppose Hegel sympathetic to the general economy. Closer scrutiny of the whole section however, exposes Hegel to severe critique and *The Phenomenology of the Mind* has not escaped the attention of Kojeve, Bataille nor Derrida. The section I want to dwell on is the section dealing with the independence/dependence of self-consciousness, where Hegel presents his famous and highly contentious master-slave dialectic that constitutes a keystone in his thinking on the nature of servitude and the subordination of one self to another. This dialectic is immense in its repercussions and, among other things, it is vital to an understanding of Hegelian semiology and is still a lasting critique on Roman Jakobson and transmission theory of communication.[9]

Hegel posits two modes of consciousness: the Master which is

9. For a brief critique of this theory see my article "And Who Remembers Bobby Sands?" in the present collection.

a pure self-consciousness whose existence is in and for itself and is a thoroughly independent mode; and the Slave, whose essence is to exist for another. In the dialectic of the master-slave, the master is self-conscious of his command of the slave (who is himself a consciousness defined by his dependence on the performance of work for the master). Hegel draws from this relation the conclusion that the self-consciousness of the master is not a pure mode but one defined by — and dependent upon — the slave's own dependence on him. The master hence is subordinated to the worker's servitude, whilst the slave in his turn enjoys the privilege of being his master's truth.

On close scrutiny, Hegel's dialectic of mastery shows itself to be precisely, though not obviously, a dialectic of prohibition and an example of restricted economic practice. Crucial in Hegel's argument is the inviolable, irreducible status of self-consciousness itself. Transgression and the negative in the Hegelian system do not risk the loss of subject. In the relation, subject and object, master and slave, mutually determine each other but do so across the partition that the preservation of self-consciousness (as a conserved category) erects and maintains. It is this prohibition: against the forfeit of self-consciousness and thereby a risking of the subject's own loss, that allows Hegelianism its basis for the possibility of knowledge and theoretical appropriation. It is this barrier, understood as the unquestioned boundary between subject and object, which totalizes the subject as a self-reflexivity and assures for it the homogenization of nature through knowledge. Hegelian negativity shows itself to be, in Derrida's words "the reassuring *other* surface of the positive"; in it, death, the break-down or dissemination of the conscious subject and the loss of meaning are risked only to the point of a final, possible recouperation.

A similarly restrictive operation is found at work in Hegel's concept of *aufhebung* (a notoriously untranslatable word but usually rendered in English as either transcendence or sublimation). What the term describes is a double movement of both negation and conservation in which each successive step in the mind's theoretical appropriation of the object-field is *lifted up, interiorized and preserved* on a higher level. This is clearly not the negativity of general economy (which would be aimless and without meaning) but the action of a subject within restricted economy where nothing is wasted and profit is squeezed out of every negative labour.[10]

In this light, it might be interesting to compare instances of current writing to a "Hegelian project". What is striking in Ron Silliman's *Ketjak*, for instance, is the work's double orientation towards, on the one hand, a textual production through a "random" economy or a free-play of signification (the sentences that comprise the work functioning as autonomous units that resist the syllogistic integration of traditional discursive prose and thetic discourse), and on the other hand an accumulative, preservational movement, committed to the non-contamination of a transcendental "procedure" that seems precisely modelled on the Hegelian *aufhebung* and permits the structure to fore-ground itself as a first order attention. For in *Ketjak* certain phrases transcend a particular context and are raised to the order of a new paragraph. Procedurality in this way functions as both the occasion for, and the limitation of, sign difference. Silliman's adoption of an atemporal "formula" for progressive textual integration comes close to the application of a tran-scendental rule that functions as an ideal pre-determination of sequence settling temporality inside the writing whilst itself remaining atemporal. This Hegelian aspect applies to most instances of procedural writing: the systematic-chance texts of Jackson Mac Low, the "snowflake" forms of Dick Higgins, John Cage's mesostics (which can be read as "recoveries" of the paragram from a trans-phenomenal disposition in writing) and Brion Gysin's permutations.[11] This is not, of course, to con-demn the texts which in many cases represent the most vital and important works of contemporary writing.

---

10. The restrictive goal of Hegelian negativity is evident from this passage in *The Encyclopoedia*: "Our goal [in theoretical activity] is rather to grasp nature, to understand it and to make it our own, so that it won't be for us something strange and beyond" (note to entry 246). Negativity is a strategic continuity of the subject through successive operations that allows the accomodation of all objects as an internalized reserve. The integration of the *aufhebung* is close to Benveniste's notion of linguistic meaning. In Chapter Ten of his *Problems in General Linguistics*, Ben-veniste defines the meaning of a linguistic unit as "its capacity to integrate a unit of a higher level". *Problems in General Linguistics*, tr. M.E. Meek (Coral Gables: University of Miami Press, 1971) p. 107. Against both Hegel and Benveniste we will cite the following conjecture of Lucretius in *De Rerum Natura*: "if everything is so transformed as to overstep its own limits this means the immediate death of what was before".
11. Chance generated writing is further restrictive in still being tied to a notion of *reward*. Despite the inevitability of loss an indeterminate profit is involved. Chance, like money, links to a notion of *fortune*.

General economy proposes a different mode of negativity and transgression in which the struggle for mastery and the transcendental petitioning are abandoned. As we noted, in Hegel's dialectic of lordship, transgression is compelled to enact itself across a permanent barrier that separates the two terms and which remains impervious and inviolable to any appropriation. Transgression consequently occurs as an eruption on one or the other sides of the barrier. General economy however, treats the barrier between terms NOT as a shared boundary but as an actual target for dissolution, whose removal then allows the abolition of both terms as separate identities. This is the type of transgression that Bataille terms "the sovereign moment": an operation entirely devoid of self-interest and whose direction is towards break-down and discharge rather than accumulation and integration. Bataille describes sovereignty as "the power to rise indifferent to death, above the laws which ensure the maintenance of life"; it is "the object that deludes us all, which nobody has seized and which nobody can seize for this reason: we cannot possess it, like an object, but we are doomed to seek it. A certain utility always alienates the proposed sovereignty".[12]   Breton himself spoke of sovereignty as that point "where life and death, the real and the imaginary, past and future, the communicable and the incommunicable, the high and the low are no longer perceived in contradiction to one another".[13]

A writing based on general economy would strive towards a similar dissolution of categories and boundaries and utterly refuse a line of mastery. Already then, it becomes highly problematic whether or not a *conscious* strategy of sovereignty can ever be possible. Renouncing mastery, it can never find a place within a project of knowledge and there are doubts as to whether a general economic writing could actually be sustained beyond a fleeting instant, registering its effects as anything more than a momentary rupture. What a writing of this kind

12.   Sovereignty would thus appear to be of an intransitive nature and would hence stand comparison with recent "desire" theories (Lacan, Deleuze & Guattari) and with proposals for a basis of writing in a non-transitive project. On the latter see especially Roland Barthes "To Write: An Intransitive Verb?" in *The Structuralist Controversy* ed. R. Macksey and E. Donato (Baltimore: Johns Hopkins University Press, 1972) p. 134-156.
13.   Once again, however, we trace in Breton a slide back into restricted economy: the abolition of the terms is seen as a recovery of non-contradiction and the loss thereby rendered profitable.

would require is a whole number of losses and the absolute degree of risk taking. It would need to adopt the Hegelian stance of looking negativity in the face but would require going beyond that stance and risking totally the subject-object relationship.[14] Proposed would be a writing that transgresses the prohibition of the semantic operation and risks the loss of meaning. This would not constitute an utter rejection of meaning, for rejection would only resituate meaning (through a kind of negative bracketing) as a separated but still relational term. Rather the loss of meaning would occur within meaning itself in a deployment without use, without aim and without a will to referential or propositional lordship. A return to the material base of language would be necessary as a method of losing meaning; holding on to graphicism and sonorities at the very point where ideation struggles to effect their withdrawal. An obvious example of this general re-materialization of language is the sound poem, what the Dadaist Hugo Ball called "poetry without words". Sound poetry has a long history through Silesian baroque theories, Dadaism, both Russian and Italian Futurism, the Lettriste movement of the 1940s up to its recent manifestations in the work of Bob Cobbing, Jean-Paul Curtay, the Four Horsemen, Bernard Heidsieck and many others. The sound poem can never be reduced to its textual "equivalent" or notation; it is essentially performative and implicates the subject not as a speaking subject, but as a phonic, pneumatic outlay. In contrast to Projective Verse that seeks a re-incorporation of breath inside the textual economy as part of an extended tradition of representation (viz. the representation of the body in language and process) sound poetry is a poetry of complete expenditure in which nothing is recoverable and useable as "meaning". Involved is a decomposition of both an operative subject and the historical constraints of a semantic order. Sound poetry shatters meaning at the point where language commits

14.   In the strategy of general writing both subject and language get returned to their materiality in permitting meaning to slide. We might say that the subject "forgets" her writing as belonging to a project of meaning, whilst writing itself annihilates the subject expressing himself through it. The subject's continuity is no longer guaranteed through language (unlike the subject in restricted writing). The moment of meaninglessness, of course, can never occur inside language, but the movement towards it can. The reader likewise would enter the writing as a textual subject to whom reading (in Paul De Man's words) "is dramatized not as an emotive reaction to what language does, but as an emotive reaction to the impossibility of knowing what it might be up to".

its move to idealization; it sustains the materiality and material effects of the phonematic structures whilst avoiding their traditional semantic purpose. As a poetry of purely phonic out-lay, the sound poem also puts the subject into process, exploding the unitary contours of consciousness and propelling textual experience into a festive economy.

Another example is this excerpt from a text of Charles Bernstein's. Less grounded in a notion of a performative subject and developing economic implications through its totality of writing effects, it still provides a good example of re-materializa-tion and the accompanying interaction of general and restricted economic tendencies:

> Ig ak abberflappi. mogh & hmog ick pug eh nche ebag ot eb v joram lMbrp nly ti asw evn ditcr ot heh ghtr rties. ey Ancded lla tghn heh ugrf het keyon. hnny iKerw. in VazoOn uv spAz ah's ee 'ook up an ays yr bitder guLpIng sum u pulLs. ig jis see kHe nig MiSSy heh d sogA chHooPp & abhor ih cN gt eGuLfer ee mattripg.[15]

Capitalization here serves no grammatical purpose but is simply a fortuitous registering of eruption at the meeting of the linguis-tic sign with its un-incorporatable materiality. In contestation are both general and restricted economies: a regulating, conser-vational disposition that limits and organizes the independent letters, pushing them towards the word as a component in the articulated production and accumulation of meaning, and the other disposition which drives the letters into non-semantic material ensembles that yield no profit. Meaning re-attaches itself through homonymic agents and associational effects ("inVazoOn uv spAz" suggesting in this way "invasion of space"). Yet the interaction of both dispositions detaches the letter groups from all certainty of meaning. These groups offer themselves as festive expenditures, sacrificial modalities of waste.

The next example is an early poem of Rochelle Owens: *Groshl Monkeys Horses* which similarly situates a reader in an unavoidable proximity to non-productive elements with no possibility to master the language through an accumulated comprehension:

---

15. Charles Bernstein, *Poetic Justice* (Baltimore: Pod Books, 1979) p. 25.

Pius 12 (Nahautl) pippin.
Common Bot. Stop talkin!
(Peep) Earliest (Mastic tree)
Wrestled christ chinese
Kunklebone (Mees) Any
Groshl Monkeys Horses
Abt. 25 miles up (full moon)
Zauschneria hanj-
Ing
Forth 70 obs. (Honigcumb)
Suck respect and english
Man huggah-homo-greek
Names and heb. hypop.
Jambey zhak-me-no caucus me-
Yawcus mother MOTHER
HYStrix ANNA BI-BI
BI[16]

There is a non-utilitarian, hedonistic pleasure derivable from the
non-productive consumption of this text. The text has numerous
points of indeterminacy (for example is "Comon Bot." a
sentence or an abbreviation? Is "Kunklebone" a typographic
error? Or further, what would constitute an "error" in a text
like this?) all of which call attention to the material relationship
of the poem's parts.[17]

As an example of the eruption of a more momentary general
economy, I've chosen a short poem of Wordsworth's — one of
the Lucy Poems:

> She dwelt among the untrodden ways
>   Beside the springs of Dove,
> A maid whom there were none to praise,
>   And very few to love.
>
>
> A violet by a mossy stone
>   Half-hidden from the eye!
> Fair as a star, when only one

16.   Rochelle Owens in *Yugen* 6, 1960, p. 25.
17.   Samuel Beckett's prose economies require an entirely separate treatment. At
this point, however, we might take note of his work *Fizzles* (ca. 1960 but not translated until 1973) whose original French title *Foirades* means "shit" or "diarrhea" and
solicits appreciation of the works as expenditures. The constant passage of words in
these pieces through metonymic relations and juxtapositions (the techniques of
anaphora and parataxis are frequent) certainly suggests an alimentary model for the
writing.

Is shining in the sky.

She lived unknown, and few could know
    When Lucy ceased to be;
But she is in her grave, and oh,
    The difference to me!

Cleanth Brooks, in a reading typical of the New Criticism, explains the poem as structured by an ironic tension that treats the images in the second stanza as equivalent.[18] On close scrutiny of the poem however, it seems difficult to uphold a unity of tension by a mode of irony. Brooks forces essentially heterogenous elements to confirm to his own presuppositions of what a poem should be. Brooks initiates the following question: "Which is Lucy really like — the violet or the star?" and goes on to answer she is a violet to the world and a star to her lover. Brooks creates the classic double bind; he excludes the third possibility that Lucy is like neither and effaces the fact that the grammatical data in the three stanzas do not support a reading of the images having a common referent. It is certainly permissable to treat the opening shifter "she" as referring to the "maid" of line 3, yet there is a rupture between stanza one and two that introduces an undecidability. Do we treat the "violet" as a metaphoric device substituting for both the maid and the pronoun of stanza one? or does it introduce a fresh referent? There is a semantic wandering across the gap of the stanzas, the substitution (if it is a substitution) goes astray and heterogeneity threatens the poem's unity of subject. Line 7 adds a further indeterminacy. Does the stellar simile refer to the violet in the same stanza, or to the maid of stanza one? In the final stanza the proper name enters as designator, but significantly enters at the precise moment death is announced, entering the poem to mark immediately its own erasure. In a poem predominantly of a restricted economy (the symmetrical balance of line and stanza and use of rhyme scheme all suggest an exchangist economy of signifier and signified) these compound indeterminacies erupt and cause the poem's referential certainties to slide. In the penultimate line, moreover, something quite catastrophic happens to the entire semantic order. The abrupt

18. Cleanth Brooks, "Irony as a Principle of Structure" in *Literary Opinion in America* ed. M.D. Zabel (New York: Harper & Row, 1962) p. 735.

ending of the line with the gestural cry "oh" injects a sovereign implication that momentarily abolishes both meaning and subject; it is the one point in the poem where the material body inscribes a subject, not as a continuity or a self-consciousness, but as a pure operation of outlay. In the gestural cry, and in a manner similar to laughter, the speaking subject is utterly decommissioned and language, as a semantic, restrictive economy, is put in question. Are we in or out of meaning at that point in the poem? There is a risk taking, a sliding away from communication and exchange towards expenditure in what Bataille would call the poem's *heterological moment* of total expulsion, a suspension of meaning within the scriptive parergonics of meaning, an eruption of silence within sound forcing the text to confess its own precarious status as signification.

The local passage from meaning to meaning is traditionally conceived as an accumulation or integration within a larger meaning and instituted upon the productive basis of a value. In the following example meaning cites itself within a purposeless continuum. The Lucy poem reaches sovereignty as a momentary rupture within the fabric of the meaningful which however, in its elusiveness, risks meaninglessness to the full, whereas this text contests discursive difference and articulation (a motion within restricted economy) by grounding signification in a continuum, not of presence, but of expenditure:

> The night Carson knocked the owl over. I'll go out on a temperature mountain. Cent calls by the way. Vista cardboard. Subgum forks. The Seven Caves. The tribute to the aluminum cylinder. Packed to line up the sights. They buried the openings among the blocks to be carted away. Ball courts. Dogs should have licence plates. Front and back. A plastic thermometer. Stalactite plunged in cement. Fossil tubes. Animate gossamer rides on amber beer. Gothic Avenue is dusty. Selected AM radio stations. Cod portions. Vermillion.[19]

Meaning here slides away from a directed purpose into a perpetual overturning of signs that never coalesce into an exchangeable identity. The refusal to integrate and raise to a higher compound level of meaning releases contiguity from the institution of hierarchy. Writing here attains the level of a waste in Barthes' insightful notion of that term as a proof of "the

19. Clark Coolidge, *Smithsonian Depositions* (New York: Vehicle Editions, 1980) p. 22.

passage of the matter it contains".[20]

In conclusion let me compare general economy with gift economy of the kind enacted in the Haidan potlatch ceremonies or the Kula ring, which Marcel Mauss and Bronislaw Malinowski have detailed[21] and to which I'll appeal in a concluding examination of the following proposition: TO WASTE IS TO LIVE THE EXPERIENCE OF WEALTH.

We can contrast gift economy to barter, a pre-Capitalist exchange that bears striking similarities to the semantic exchange within the dominant conception of translation. Barter rests on the protection of a third, transcendental term, a copula of equivalence which sets up the exchange as an action directed towards equilibrium. Worth (like the notion of a "third" equilibrated meaning between the source and target texts of translation) is inserted as a universal third term against the scale of which the sets of bartered terms float until a point of stasis or equivalence is reached.

In gift exchange, however, the object is exhausted, consumed in the very staging.[22] The status of equivalence is removed along with any structurally necessitated reciprocality. In the potlatch, commodities have an alimentary status and wealth is literally expelled. Consumption is understood as a movement and hence a certain momentum replaces equilibrium as the controlling notion of the exchange. In this way, potlatch can be seen as structureless, or at least as avoiding the closed binary correlation of a giver and receiver in which consumption can only occur across the partition preserved through a condition of puchase and ownership. Potlatch does not demand a presupposition of reciprocity. A receiver is not obliged to return.[23]

20. Roland Barthes, *The Grain of the Voice*, tr. Linda Coverdale (New York: Hill and Wang, 1985) p. 273.
21. See especially Marcel Mauss, *The Gift: Forms and Functions of Exchange in Archaic Societies* tr. I. Cunnison (New York: Norton, 1967).
22. There are certain gesture signs that suggest a similar exhaustion in their staging. Pointing, the opening of arms, embraces, handshakes, relate as much to a system of expenditure as a semiotics of transmission.
23. There are limits to which this analogy can be taken. Potlatch, we must not forget, is an agonistic act designed to elicit *a return with interest in the form of further loss*. Consequently, a fundamental exchangism is preserved to operate as the *raison d'etre* of the potlatch. As an example of symbolic exchange, it nonetheless illustrates an important transaction that is not based on preservation (beyond the preservation of the exchange itself as continued loss). The exchange, though present, is immediate and instantly subordinated to a termination.

Potlatch establishes status and position (i.e. social value and hence a "meaning") not from commodity possession, but from the rate and momentum of its disposal. In Kwakiutl communities televisions are thrown into the sea, precious objects broken and their parts distributed in order to catalyse the circulation. The commodity ("meaning") is always kept in movement and gains enrichment as it passes hand to hand. There is no association of wealth with investment and accumulation[24] but the implication of a status that accrues to such people *who would actually dispose of wealth*. Gift objects are frequently pluralized[25] through a kind of inverse metonymy in which the whole exists in order to generate its parts. The objects are broken and their parts scattered to increase the momentum of the giving. Accumulation is unthinkable in potlatch beyond its provisional power to permit an *immediate* distribution.

The application of this economic model to writing practice should be obvious, and though falling short of a perfect general economy, potlatch does offer an interesting analog system. The immediate tendency is to stress the homology between the "wealth" of potlatch and writing's "meaning", so that the intense exchange within the textual experience which would register as semantic loss, would not gain the status of a content (hence a transferable "transmission" to a reader) but would manifest as a loss-exchange among the signs themselves. To envisage such a

24. The notion of inevitable expenditure and outlay is a commonplace of 17th century Baroque eschatology. Among the numerous possible examples I will cite Jeremy Taylor from his *Rule and Exercises of Holy Dying*, a popular *artes moriendi* from 1651:

> . . . while we think a thought we die; and the clock strikes and reckons on our portion of eternity; we from our words with the breath of our nostrils we have the less to live upon for every word we speak.

This is not Charles Olson's concept of breath as a charged energy transfer, but the profound coupling of cognition and the subject's ontology with an economy of death.
25. Pre-capitalist economy furnishes an interesting case of quasi-potlatch. Although exceptions exist, it is in general true to say that surplus value was born only with Capitalism. The Middle Ages were characterized by a type of *economic man* whose pattern of wealth was that of a vast accumulation during life, a subsequent renunciation, and a final, indiscriminate dispersal close to death. Philanthropy was born of this condition of a dramatic distribution of wealth that coincided with the moment of death. The French historian Philippe Ariès argues a profound ambivalence in the pre-capitalist man between a love of wealth as worldly possessions and an ultimate (postponed) belief (the dominant theological belief of the Middle Ages) that all material wealth was unsightly in the eyes of God and must be renounced in order to redeem the soul. Jacques Heers regards this belief and its consequent effecting of enormous distributions of donations to churches and benevolent institutions, as the major cause of the economic collapse of the 14th century nobility. For the spiritual

text would be to envisage a linguistic space in which meanings splinter into moving fields of plurality, establishing differentials able to resist a totalization into recoverable integrations that would lead to a summatable "Meaning". This plurality, moreover, must be irreducible and must demonstrate the intransitive drive towards de-centrality, the fact of a limitless loss and the status of writing as a scriptive gesture of infinity within the finitude wherein all spatio-temporal activities must exist. As such it could never rest at a holistic proposal but only stress the infinite play of parts within the significatory activity called writing. [26]

1985

pressure to discharge wealth indiscriminately, together with the pre-industrial nature of that wealth (jewels, land, horses, precious objects) made the concept of investment (and thereby the production of surplus value) all but impossible.

There is, too, the interesting example of Adam Smith. In his *Theory of Moral Sentiments* (1759) Smith argues that surplus income is meaningless to the recipient. The wealthy landlord (Smith's argument runs) can hardly consume more than the poorest peasant and accordingly must distribute his surplus wealth to his retinue and servants. This is a forced expenditure (or seen that way) and suggests strongly Smith's recognition of an operating general economy within the "industry of mankind" and the wealth of nations. It should be borne in mind, however, that Smith's argument is part of a complex attempt to justify the proposition that the apparent inequality of human incomes and the restricted control of wealth is in actuality productive of an equal distribution throughout the entire social spectrum (by virtue of this persistently forced expenditure).

26. It would be impossible to conclude without mentioning Saussure who posits (among several binary combinations) the relationship of *langue* (i.e. the set of linguistic rules, structures and possibilities that exist apart from the local particularities of usage) and *parole* (the local and particular applications drawn from the sets of *langue*). Saussure's is an important and in many contexts a useful distinction. Subjected, however, to the critique from general economy and gift exchange, it would be halted at one strategic point: where *parole* instantiates *langue* and registers not as an enrichment through continued circulation (leading as it would to a sedimentary theory of language) but as an invested instantiation of a parent term.

Mac Low's
Asymmetries

We can trace in Jackson Mac Low's work the putting into play of a kind of writing machine that opens up scriptive practice to an infinite semiosis through the infra-textual and combinatory nature of words. We can see also the effects of a radical detachment of writing from its traditional involvement with unitary meanings. There is a re-alignment in his texts of the significatory space with a kind of theatre of linguistic event which is predicated upon semantic provisionality and dispensability. What Mac Low orchestrates are two radically divergent orders of meaning. One, a conventionally articulated meaning that describes itself through a linear order, i.e. a syntactic chain of discrete, detectable units. The other, a saturated, cryptonymic meaning, essentially trans-phenomenal, hidden as a latent signification within other word chains, errant, evasive and beyond an immediately legible appropriation. This second meaning is released through a particular reading-writing procedure, one that disengages language from representation and writing from an intentionalist imperative.

The work is most impressive in its consistent emergence out of a set of austere principles that emphasize the traditionally negative or counter-values in writing: grammatical transgression (even suspension), the elimination of a conscious intention, the removal of the writer as a subject "responsible" for the texts it "writes", diminished reference and the absence of the subject from the productive aspect of meaning. Mac Low himself has drawn comparison between his own chance operations and a certain use of chance in Zen Buddhism:

> Yes the Zen Buddhist motive for use of chance (&c) means was to be able to generate series of "dharmas" (phenomena/events, e.g.,

sounds, words, colored shapes) relatively "uncontaminated" by the composer's "ego" (taste, constitutional predelictions, opinions, current or chronic emotions).[1]

Clearly, Mac Low's project of negativity is not a Hegelian one. For where the latter would uphold a purpose of mastery and appropriation, Mac Low's would renunciate control and shift determination into the mechanics of the systematic-chance procedure that occasions the emergence of the writing. In a work such as *Stanzas for Iris Lezak*,[2] the systematic exclusion of the subject permits a degree of semantic indeterminacy that is unobtainable in conventional (i.e. authorially directed) composition. The freeing up of the textual space to establish itself as a random economy, denying the writer a personal intervention into the scene of meaning, permits a quality of verbal combinations (clashes, junctures, intersections, incompatibilities) that could not be arrived at through the controlled ordering of an intentional agent. Word order is supplanted by word distribution, and the chance juxtapositions create texts that escape the finality of logical value:

> Burroughs until regularly. Rest of under grab he since
> used next to in legend.
> Realized existed give under *Lunch*, you
> remains eating Stein the
> orgone flights
> until 1955-56 down existed rigorous
> garden room. Another brewed.
> Have emotional
> sheet it night catch eating
>
> unhappy. Sit endless drink
> 1953, each.[3]

This is typical of Mac Low's programmatic substitution of a patterned production for the augmentive ordering of grammatical meaning. The result is a complex recombination of verbal particles, coming together in a new context and emerging as hybrid codes. For instance, one could trace a chronological

1. "Museletter" in *The L=A=N=G=U=A=G=E Book*, ed. Bruce Andrews & Charles Bernstein (Carbondale: Southern Illinois University Press, 1984) p. 26.
2. *Stanzas for Iris Lezak* (Barton: Something Else Press, 1971).
3. Ibid. p. 340.

code (in the recurrence of historic dates), a nominal code (the presence of proper names), an actiant code (the positionality and effect of the occurrence of verbs that register variously as commands or narrations) and a descriptive code. All of these weave together in a way that relativizes the minimal grammatic government of the words and reduces to a minimum any hierarchical organization.

There is evident also an encounter between two adversarial drives: a logic (receding in most texts) that orders a linear development of meaning along the grammatical lines of a subject-verb-object, and a para-logical drive within the rule determinants of the letter patterns, that settles meaning as highly local and de-centralized "events".

Among the many things that Mac Low's writing contests is the traditional notion of writing as an originary production and in this offers expanded possibilities for the writer as a *subject beyond expression*. Here is Mac Low's own description of the systematic-chance method used to generate the asymmetries:

> The "Asymmetry" method produces poems that are, in a sense, "self-generating." Beginning with the first or a chance-designated subsequent word in a source text, the first line of such a poem spells out this word: the second line spells out the second word of the first line; the third line, the third word, & so on.[4]

What is striking in this description is the way that textual production is grounded in the problematics of repetition. The asymmetries, in fact, approximate a *translational* procedure, an activity between texts and one that endorses language as both a sedimentary and a cryptic system. Through chance operations verbal arrangements are manifested that were present — but resisted appearance — in their source texts. The asymmetries, in this way, are a highly selective reading of an existent writing. They may be compared also to collage, which too develops a re-cycling and citational capacity. Mac Low's insight (and in this he is remarkably similar to Wittgenstein) is that to shift a word from one set of surroundings necessarily provokes a change of verbal function in response to variations in the new context. This is a radical departure from the use of

4. Ibid. p. 409.

quotation in Pound, Olson or Ronald Johnson, for Mac Low's writings are singular in not so much staging as destroying the difference of the discursive forms they annex.

Mac Low then, utilizes a prior text and opens up (through the implementation of a rule of procedure) the disposition to difference and combinatorial "otherness" within the source words. It must be admitted that the use of systematic-chance procedures in part reduces the contingent manifestations to a subsidiary aspect of the rule's operation. Through all the "accidence" released, the rule itself remains inviolable and transcendentally fixed. Yet equally the rule becomes the occasion for these contingencies to emerge. There is a certain impasse of contradictory forces, both a fission and a fusion. The asymmetry is, at the same time, both a mode of production and a mode of deletion, both a force of distribution and containment. The relativizing play and the resulting ambivalence (between contingency and indeterminacy on the one hand and of rule, determination and inevitability on the other) are thus crucial to the full dynamics of these texts.

Important too, is the linking of a reading to a writing in which the latter serves to elucidate what is already there but concealed in the normal syntactic deployment of the combinants. The asymmetry, as a stanzaic-acrostic form, is also the context of a reading that is re-doubled through a writing. The texts themselves are revealed to be secretions from a prior text that become available to reading only when passed back through a further act of writing. Mac Low's poems thus appear as *a suppressed tendency* within another text (and thereby of the nature of an *essential alterity*). This single inducement moreover points to an economic disposition of the entire textual system. We might call this *the disposition to the paragram* i.e. to the infinitesimal combinations of letters and phonemes that always escape conventional reading habits. The asymmetries *can* be considered as formulations from a rule-governed mode of production, yet we would not wish to reduce the significance of the seriality of the signification (the textual "events" as they are generated) to a mere instance of a law. Like the mesostics of John Cage, the asymmetries bind a group of words and letters to an axiomatic axis (the acrostic), whilst at the same time liberating those words from the binding, grammatical form of the prior text. It is as if the words insist their own right to pursue a different necessity. The asymmetry method drives the source text inside — and thus beyond — an aspect of itself to elevate a different formation. It is because of this radical interaction, between a source writing and its own suppressed paragrammatic interiorities, that Mac Low's "secondary" written-readings gain what Bakhtin terms a dialogic character. The texts further show that there can be no true separation of language from its products; that any writing that avails itself of an alphabetical combinatory system is problematized and contaminated at source by its own proliferational tendencies.

Beyond any local appreciation of these poems are the intertextual implications that the entire systematic-chance method of composition carries and which dilate the chance technique into a methodological force propelling the poem beyond its object form into a gesture of excess. Mac Low has chosen as the compositional base of the asymmetry the locus of writing's *productional contradictions*,[5] where meaning is both produced and lost, through and beyond the control of an ordering subject. As Mac Low himself reminds us, the asymmetries are essentially self-generative language events that elude all productive finality. Constituting also a semantic margin where the system of meaning overflows the limits prescribed by a self-identical and intentional subject, they thereby invalidate any purposeful boundaries that would struggle to determine where meaning in writing begins and where meaning ends.

1975

5. There is a striking similarity between the structure of the asymmetries and Marx's analysis in *Das Kapital* of capitalist formation, where the latent contradictions within capital accumulation (surplus value and wage labour) push the system beyond itself into another mode of production. To treat the asymmetries as built-in critiques of their own sign-production, in which the paragrammatic disposition within the source texts push beyond themselves into another sign economy, is not only legitimate but *crucial* to a full appreciation of Mac Low's work as a critique of language under Capitalism. Let me briefly paraphrase the relevant section from *Das Kapital* to stress this linguistic analogy: the extraction of meaning (surplus value) from a text, necessitates the suppression of polysemy, ambivalence, errant connotation and undecidability (i.e. the semantic-paragrammatic work force) by means of the integrational drives and hierarchical constraints of grammar, in order that meaning does not proliferate beyond a bounded, intentional horizon (i.e. that surplus value is not eroded). It would be dangerous, of course, to push this analogy too far between paragrammatic suppression and the class struggle, yet the parallel critiques offered, through *structural* rather than interpersonal relations, do hint at the relevance of Mac Low's work to Louis Althusser's critique of Marxist humanism.

Index

anti-production, 98
anti-reading, 93
anti-semantic force, 105
antisemantics; figures of, 64
anti-text, 93
Antin, David; on origins of cinema, 82n
Apollinaire, Guillaume: *calligrammes*, 30
Archaeology of the Frivolous, The (J.
  Derrida), quoted, 135n
Archiv für gesamte Phonetik, 178
Ariès, Philippe, 220n
Aristophanes: *Clouds, The*, 177n
Aristotle, 76n, 145n, 162; form derived
  from, 180; his *Peri Hermeneton*, 146;
  writing defined by, 146
Armantraut, Rae, 114
Artaud, Antonin, 91, 130; quoted, 106
asymmetries, 45-47, 224-226; and *Kap-
  ital, Das*, 226n; see also: Mac Low,
  Jackson
Atheneum Fragments, The (F. Schlegel),
  quoted, 59
atopia, 92
aufhebung, 211, 212, 212n
Augustine, St., 129, 145n, 198; on lie,
  quoted, 198; on meaning, quoted, 177
aura, 26
Austin, J.L., 125
automatic writing, 170-171n
automaticity, 170-171n; defined by
  Breton, 170-171n
automatisme, 170-177

Bailey, N., 60
Baillie, Joanna: *Miscellaneous Plays*, 54
Bakhtin, Mikhail M., 59, 115, 226;
  "carnivalization", 75, 115; *Dialogic
  Imagination, The*, quoted, 75; and
  dialogic utterance, 75; *Formal Method
  in Literary Scholarship, The*, 66n; and
  heteroglossia, 75; and *Martyrology,
  The*, 75; *Problems of Dostoevsky's
  Poetics*, quoted, 75
Balibar, Etienne: *For Marx*, 27n
Ball, Hugo, 96n; his "poetry without
  words", 173n, 214
Balzac, Honoré de, 39; *Sarrasine*, 143
Baracks, Barbara, 15n
baroque, 77; eschatology, 220n
Barre du Jour, La, 170n, 171n
Barthes, Roland, 19n, 23n, 111, 121,
  150; quoted, 117, 118, 153; *Elements
  of Semiology*, 113; *Grain of the Voice,
  The*, quoted, 143; on literature's wave-
  lengths, 23n; on pleasure 117, 118;
  Pleasure of the Text, The, quoted, 161;
  Responsibility of Forms, The, 19n;
  S/Z, quoted, 143; "To Write: An In-

Abraham, Nicholas, 64, 208; "Shell and
  the Kernel, The", 64n
abstract audience attention, 15n
A Cappella (B. Andrews), quoted and
  discussed, 23-24
acrophonic writing, 32-33
acrostic, 225; see also: paragram
Addison, Joseph, 30; *Spectator No. 62*,
  quoted 58
Adolphus, J.L.: *Letters to Richard
  Heber*, 54
Aglossostomographie, 179
Alcheringa, 144
allegory, 76n; affinity to pun, 76n;
  "Coleridgean", 76n
allophane; defined, 141
Allophanes (G. Bowering), 131-142;
  fetish in, 137; Freud's dreamwork in,
  140; transformational grammar in, 140
allophone; defined, 142
Alogon (M. Palmer), 48n
Alogon (R. Smithson), 48n
Alpert, Barry; on C. Dewdney, quoted,
  188
alterity, 225
Althusser, Louis, 111, 226n; *For Marx*,
  27n
amplifiers, 83
Anacreon, 30
anagram, 64, 119, 207-209; see also:
  paragram
analogical perception, 85
analogy, 190n
Andrews, Bruce, 15n, 27, 123, 125, 144,
  150; quoted, 110; *A Cappella*, 113;
  quoted and discussed, 23;
  L=A=N=G=U=A=G=E Book, The,
  223n; *Legend*, 113, 115; "Red Hallelujah, The", quoted, 24
Angelo, Politian, 208
anti-language, 93
Anti-Oedipus (G. Deleuze & F. Guattari),
  123; quoted 101n